DEEPER AND DEEPER

Also by Gary Lindberg

THRILLERS
The Shekinah Legacy (A Charlotte Ansari Thriller)
Sons of Zadok (A Charlotte Ansari Thriller)

HISTORICAL FICTION
Ollie's Cloud

DEEPER AND DEEPER

GARY LINDBERG

CALUMET EDITIONS

Minneapolis

**CALUMET
EDITIONS**

Minneapolis

Second Edition December 2022

Cover art and book design by Gary Lindberg

To my father, Russell Lindberg. When I was very young, he taught me the joys of reading, and always loved a good story.

CALUMET
EDITIONS

SECOND EDITION DECEMBER 2022

ISBN – 978-1-939548-09-2

10 9 8 7 6 5 4 3 2 1

Cover art and book design by Gary Lindberg

CHAPTER 1

On a cracked square of asphalt deep in the ruins of a Detroit public playground, nine black gang members flaunted their colors, running and soaring in a half-court game of basketball. Four shirts versus five taller skins. No net, just a bent hoop. Graffiti everywhere—on the scuffed court, the sadly leaning backboard, the crumbling brick wall of a vacant building to the north, and on two old cars and a pick-up missing doors and wheels. It was a good-natured, rough-and-tumble game, lots of pushing and sweating and cussing.

But after an inbound pass all motion suddenly stopped cold. Suspicious eyes slid in their furrowed slots toward a ragged chain link fence as a squad car pulled up, the driver's door opened, and two black shoes stepped onto the gravel. The cop kicked a beer can out of the way. From behind aviator sunglasses he studied the motionless gang for a moment.

The shortest gangbanger started to bounce the basketball nervously.

The first cop walked deliberately along the chain link fence. At the ragged end, he grabbed a fistful of links. His feet stopped at a faded line painted long ago on the asphalt; a border of sorts.

The red-attired gang seemed to clot, the members moving toward each other, awkwardly at first, then more confidently as they all took a step toward the cop. The short guy, Dancer, started bouncing the ball with almost machine-gun rapidity.

The cop began rolling up his blue shirtsleeves, revealing sinewy forearms.

A stout gang member wiped the sweat off his forehead.

Astonishingly, the cop had no utility belt, no gun. He'd left these in the squad car. His left foot crossed over the line, then his right. Two more steps—a direct, wordless confrontation.

The tall guy, called Shap by the others, nodded toward Dancer, who was still frantically pounding the ball on the court. *Put-put-put-put.* Acknowledging the nod, Dancer pulled the ball to his chest and then fired it like a cannonball toward the cop.

The cop caught it and gave a droll smile. He yanked off his sunglasses and slid them into a shirt pocket. Jamie Giles was late-twenties, maybe thirty. His eyes darted from one gang member to another. Surprising them all, he dribbled onto the court, evaded a tangle of arms and hands, stepped to his right, and put up a long three-pointer.

"Nothing but net!" he yelled, grinning. "If there was a net."

A scowling skin took the ball out of bounds.

"Sorry I'm late," Jamie said.

"Down by six," Shap replied. "Let's kick some ass!"

And they did. Joining the shirts—so as not to be totally out of uniform—Jamie plunged into the game. He took an in-bounds pass and lobbed it to Shap across court. Shap deftly dished it back to Jamie cutting to the basket for an easy layup and the expected fist pump.

The skins in-bounded the ball, but Jamie sliced in front of the intended recipient, dribbled back to make a legal shot, and hoisted another long one. Slightly off-angle, the ball careened off the crooked backboard, rattled around the rim, and miraculously dropped in accompanied by a chorus of groans.

"Better to be lucky!" Jamie shouted, high-fiving the other shirts.

He turned toward his partner Rico, who was leaning against the front fender of the squad munching a sandwich and watching with keen amusement. Jamie just caught a glimpse of a rusted-out van rumbling around a far corner of the pot-holed street, but a bone jarring bump by a skin pulled him back into the action of the game.

On court, Shap attempted a long shot but missed badly. Jamie went up for the ball, got his hands on it, but came down empty. And astonished. A skin laughed as he dribbled back to mid-court.

"White guys can't jump, ever'one know that," the skin teased.

Jamie came up to guard him.

The skin with the ball began a kamikaze dash toward the basket. Jamie stepped into the path of the fearless ball handler, taking an elbow to the chest and going down hard.

Just as World War III broke out.

Automatic fire from the van tore into the brick wall behind the basket. Two shirts and a skin jerked and fell down in a bloody spray.

Shap rolled to a bunched-up shirt on the edge of the court, scrambling to locate a handgun hidden inside. He started to fire back, but it was a massacre. Rico was pinned down behind the squad car, and Jamie was sheltered by the bloody body of a fallen skin. Suddenly, Shap and two other gangbangers were riddled by a barrage of bullets.

With a screech of tires, the turf battle was over. The van whizzed past the squad car, spattering a final hot line of lead that made the vehicle look like a game of connect-the-dots.

Undamaged, Jamie raced toward Rico who was reloading.

"I'm going to get the bastards!" Rico growled, racing to the bullet-riddled driver's door. Jamie unlatched the vehicle's shotgun, hopped in and buckled up. The chase was on.

Taking the radio, Jamie called in, "Car 265, need assistance!"

The van squealed around a corner and swerved down an alley, scattering two youngsters doing a dope deal.

Rico saw the dust storm of the van's tires emerging from the alley, but nearly missed the turn, taking down a flimsy wooden fence. Up ahead, the van veered left down a main artery.

As the squad lurched out of the alley, Jamie watched the van fishtail down the street. The gang driver, probably rattled, tried to turn right onto a side street but clipped a telephone pole, crumpling the rear right fender and sending the vehicle jittering across the corner of a gas station. The van scraped the rear end of an old Caddy taking on gas but kept on going.

Suddenly the rear doors of the van flew open and automatic fire assailed the squad. Jamie and Rico ducked, but the bullets were off their mark anyway.

Two squads swerved into the street behind Rico and Jamie.

"Here comes the cavalry," Rico said.

"Yeah, but why couldn't they show up *ahead* of the van?"

The van veered left into a rundown warehouse district. The sudden turn slammed the van's rear doors shut.

Rico had made up some ground and was now just a few car lengths behind the van. Suddenly, holes appeared in the van's rear doors. These guys were shooting blind through the doors!

Rico instinctively steered left, trying to stay out of the direct line of fire. Just then another squad car appeared down the street ahead of the van.

The gang driver did an incredible end-to-end swap, still going forward but looking backward. With an awful whine, the tires spun and the van skidded to a stop, instantly peeling off in a new direction.

Right at Rico and Jamie.

"Shit, Rico—look out!"

Rico and Jamie ducked. A shotgun fired at their squad as it just missed a head-on collision. The squad's windshield shattered and fell out.

Really pissed now, Rico did his own nifty bootlegger's turn just in time to see the van fire on the first of two squads that had been trailing his own vehicle. The blast took out the squad's front left tire and the car spun sideways, taking out the second squad directly behind.

There was only one squad assisting now, and it was following Rico and Jamie.

A bicyclist was coming straight toward the van. Before the inevitable collision, the rider tried to jump the curb, but the bike's angle was poor and it bounced back into the path of the van, which struck its rear wheel. The bicyclist shot up and over the van and landed halfway through the glassless front window of Rico's squad.

The van skidded to the right onto a street that paralleled Fleming Channel, the watery border that separated the United States from Canada. Rico swerved to follow, throwing the bicyclist off the hood. The back-up squad screeched to a stop to lend assistance.

The shot-up squad gained ground on the van. To its left was the channel, and just ahead was a small harbor with about two dozen slips and a handful of boats.

Now about four car-lengths behind the van, Jamie was tempted to give these gangbangers a taste of their own medicine—a shotgun blast to the rear wheels. He pointed the barrel through the blown-out windshield, but the bouncing squad almost guaranteed an errant shot in a populated area.

As he thought about his next move, the van's rear doors flew open again. Jamie heard the shots like a string of firecrackers going off. The rear view mirror shattered. The ricochet smashed into the buckle on Jamie's seat belt, knocking the wind out of him. He turned to check on Rico just as two rounds struck his partner in the head and shoulder. Rico slumped left. The squad swerved toward the harbor.

Several sailors dove for cover as the squad flew off the road, careened over the river walk, soared toward the slips, and belly-flopped into the water. The car sunk quickly as a handful of beer-sodden sailors looked on.

Water filled the interior of the squad through the missing windshield. Jamie frantically tried to unfasten his seat belt, but the smashed buckle was jammed shut. His eyes filled with panic as he tried to wriggle free, but he couldn't do it. Strapped in too tightly.

Someone had dove into the water. The rescuer's futile hands tried to wrench open the seat belt, but without a knife it was impossible. The hands disappeared as the diver surfaced for air.

In desperation, Jamie looked around the flooded squad and saw the shotgun lying between Rico and the driver's door. If he could retrieve it and somehow fire at the webbing or the end bracket, maybe…

He stretched mightily, but his hand came a few inches short of reaching it.

CHAPTER 2

An older man with a beard and fleshy jowls walked silently down a stretch of Bahamas beach leaving sandal prints that would quickly be scuffed over by countless tourists. He wore his favorite cobalt-blue shirt with a white scarf and tan shorts, and chomped an unlit cigar as he walked purposefully toward a pink hotel.

Money was not an issue for him, but he despised mistakes and the hotel had made a doozy. He pulled the hotel bill from his pocket, and the error in it fanned the flames of his indignation again. Mini-bar charges—$135.79. And he had only drunk one small bottle of vodka. *It's the principle of the thing!* Someone screwed up. Maybe he should just buy the goddamn hotel so he could fire those who couldn't do their jobs. He intended to let the manager have a piece of his mind. He wouldn't rest until this annoyance was settled and someone was flogged.

Fired, he meant.

This annoyance consumed him. Yes, he could be a bit obsessive about little things. So what? He could afford to be.

On the beach, the bearded man unlatched the gate to the pink hotel and started an angry march toward the front desk to lodge his complaint. He had worked himself up over it.

———

A tall Bahamian, who had been watching the bearded man from a distance, retreated to the driver's seat of his cab. The cabbie had a full head of gray hair, black skin, and gleaming white eyes. Seated there, he clenched his eyes, then opened them wide and reached into the glove compartment, pulling out a knife. He thumbed the sharp edge, making the blade whine. *Ready!* Hiding the knife beneath his shirt, the cabbie stepped out of his vehicle and headed for the hotel entrance as casually as possible.

Inside he found the bearded man in a heated exchange with the assistant manager, who appeared to acquiesce to the guest's demands. The bearded man thrust his head backwards triumphantly—imperiously, even—before dismissing his inferior with the wave of a hand and striding toward the elevators. The cabbie understood that, for this particular hotel guest, every personal encounter was a battle of wills, a test of power.

An elevator door opened, and the bearded man stepped into the vacant car, pressing a button. The cabbie knew where the man was headed.

Fifth floor. Suite 534.

In a few minutes, the bearded man would have company.

The cabbie heard his heart thumping like a bass drum. He looked around, wondering if anyone else could hear it.

————

Underwater, Jamie's heartbeat was unbelievably loud. For over two minutes he had struggled against the seat belt, lungs burning, and eyes bulging as the urge to breathe finally overcame him.

And then he inhaled.

A small burst of bubbles escaped his lips, and a horrible spasm shook his body as water filled his lungs. He shook and coughed. And then, mercifully, it was over. His eyes were still open, unblinking.

No more heartbeat.

A school of silvery fish swam past the open windshield.

_____

A scuba diver maneuvered through the squad's open windshield, his small tank banging against the roof. He looked at Rico, who was missing part of his head. An inky stain of blood near the wound shimmered and dissipated as the diver's movement disturbed the water.

Jamie was strapped into his seat, vacant eyes staring back at the diver as if to say *What took you so long?* The diver pulled a knife from a sheath strapped to his leg and sliced through the seat belt. Jamie's body immediately started to float upward.

On the shore above, seven cops and two paramedics watched the diver nudge Jamie's lifeless body to the surface. A group of weekend sailors stared as the cops pulled the dripping corpse from the water and the diver went back for Rico.

A paramedic checked the body for vital signs, then started CPR. The first thrust of hands on Jamie's rib cage ejected a plume of water out of his mouth.

After several minutes, the paramedic's female partner stopped him. The woman shook her head and looked up at one of the cops, Conner. "He's gone. How long was he under?"

"Went down about twenty minutes ago."

"Okay, we're gonna take him to Detroit Receiving. The M.E. will make the final eval. Sorry, Conner. Hard to lose one of your own." The woman patted the cop on the shoulder. "You get those guys in the van?"

"Not yet, but we will," Conner said. "If it was up to me, we'd hang 'em on the spot."

_____

The tall Bahamian emerged from an elevator on the fifth floor of the pink hotel and looked left. Suite 534 was about halfway down the corridor. He had been there countless times. This would be his last visit.

It seemed to take a long time to navigate the hallway, and each step prompted a tough question, like *Are you seriously going to do this?* But suddenly he was staring at the door, and he felt the walk hadn't taken nearly long enough.

He pulled a security card out of his pocket, tapped on the door and said, "Housekeeping."

No answer.

He slid the card in and out of the slot. The door made almost no noise as he pushed it open. The bearded man was not in the room, but the cabbie could hear water running in the bathroom. Oh, yes—the cabbie remembered how the bearded man loved to soak in the spa. He loved everything— *anything*—that gave him sensual pleasure.

The cabbie stood there for a moment, not sure what to do next.

He heard the water being shut off, then someone splashing and the sudden whir of spa jets starting to pulsate the water. The bearded man was in the tub.

The cabbie shoved the bathroom door open. It squeaked.

Without looking, the bearded man responded. "Maria? Come in, dear."

Like a shadow, the black Bahamian stepped into the bathroom, moving close to the spa. His right hand clutched the knife, but he knew he wouldn't need it.

The bearded man slowly opened his eyes, looking upward. He tried to scramble out of the tub, but his feet slipped on the ceramic and he fell back. He looked up and saw a knife held threateningly above his face. And then the cabbie's giant hand grasped the man's head like a basketball and forced it down into the water. The bearded man flopped and squirmed like a caught fish in the bottom of a boat, but the Bahamian was too big, too strong. A hand managed to reach up and grab the cabbie's arm, but finally it fell limply back into the water.

——

Jamie's lifeless hand hung off the gurney, which bounced and rattled across the rough planks of the dock. Walking alongside the body, a paramedic lifted the cold hand to tuck it under a sheet, but the hand suddenly moved and grabbed his arm.

Like a dog's jaws, it seized him!

And then Jamie gasped and screamed. He bolted upright, holding his chest.

Shaken, the paramedic jumped, staring at the dead man's impossible grip.

Water oozed from Jamie's nose and throat. He coughed and choked but fiercely held onto the paramedic's arm. Then, with almost superhuman strength, Jamie pulled the paramedic close, stared him in the eye, and just as suddenly collapsed, alive but panting for breath.

The paramedic, who'd been pushing the gurney, instinctively started to check out the suddenly animated corpse. His partner was too stunned to respond.

"Let's get him on oxygen! Now!"

With new urgency, they wheeled the gurney toward the ambulance.

CHAPTER 3

Jamie sees sandals scuffing white sand. A beach, and turquoise water. He looks around at the sunbathers and beautiful sky, and just ahead a picturesque pink hotel glistening in the sunlight. The images blur and fade, replaced by a dim corridor and a hotel room door marked by the numbers 534. The door opens and clothing is thrown onto a dark blue daybed patterned with large flowers. Again the images blur and shift, and he is in a spa. He can feel the warmth of the water around him. The door to the bathroom opens. "Maria?" he says. His voice is old and coarse. He glances at the doorway and...

———

Jamie woke up sweating and shouting, almost scaring a nurse at his bedside out of her uniform.

"I'm sorry," the nurse said. "I was just checking on you. Are you okay?"

Panting and confused, he asked, "Where am I?"

———

Two officers escorted a solemn Kathy Giles through the hospital lobby. They'd picked her up at Hal's, a small bistro where she worked as a waitress. Conner and the other cop had wanted Jamie's wife to have personal support through this crisis; they both had wives, too.

Kathy was a slender, raven-haired woman of twenty-eight who often caught the eyes of male customers she served. Her tips were usually large.

As they got off the elevator on the third floor, a nurse approached. "Is this the wife of the deceased?"

The word *deceased* made Kathy gasp. No one had mentioned that Jamie had died.

"Not deceased, April," Conner said, looking at the nurse's name badge. "He *was* deceased—but he isn't any more. You might try a little tact."

Kathy looked up at Conner. "You didn't say—"

"Well, it's complicated. He was dead, that's what the paramedics said, probably drowned. But then he wasn't. He started moving and then he sat up, so I don't know what to say about that. Except he's alive now, and you're on the way to see him."

Conner shepherded Kathy down a corridor to a room filled with a half-dozen uniformed officers. "All right. Move aside, fellas," he said, "the wife's here. Time to get some coffee, or better yet get back to work. The criminals are taking over the city while you're all up here."

Conner waved his fellow cops out of the room to give Kathy and Jamie some privacy and then closed the door behind him as Kathy walked over to her husband.

"A lot of tubes," she said, then wondered why she had focused on the apparatus that was plugged into him instead of expressing her relief that he was alive.

Jamie nodded, then said, "Hi."

"Hi there. Quite a day, huh?"

Jamie suddenly averted his eyes.

"Really sorry about Rico," Kathy said.

"He was a good guy." Jamie's whisper was lathered with sadness.

"So you drowned, they said. And then came back to life. Pretty amazing. Did you, like, see a light at the end of a tunnel… stuff like that?"

Jamie was still avoiding her gaze. "Don't actually remember anything. Bummer, right?"

Kathy pulled a chair close to the bed and sat. "I feel like such an idiot, really I do. I've been doing a lot of thinking lately… you know, what we talked about. Look—I'm truly sorry about what I said."

Jamie's eyes were red and vulnerable. "It's okay. You need time to figure out what you want."

Kathy stared at Jamie for a long time, her eyes starting to glisten with, well… She couldn't hold back the tears, so she tried to disguise them by moving—standing up, and then crawling onto the bed and putting her arms around her husband. But this just made the tears come faster.

Jamie gave her a little hug.

"Oh God—Jamie…"

Jamie pulled her closer.

"I didn't tell you I wouldn't stay," Kathy said between sniffs. "I've just been so—so confused. And then this… and I started to realize how much you mean to me. If I had lost you, I just don't know…"

"Hey, I've done a lot of thinking too. It was pretty dumb for me to think that I could keep a girl like you happy. You're used to having pretty much whatever you need, or want, and look at me… a cop fighting to make ends meet. Your parents were right about me. No future. I just can't help it that I love you."

Kathy sat up and found a box of tissues. She blew her nose and shook her head. "It doesn't have anything to do with where you came from or what you do or what my parents think. It has to do with me… and…"

oh, God. I'm just such a mess right now. I don't know what I want. I thought it might be time to go after my own dreams, but I'm not sure I even know what they are any more."

"Back to college, that's what you should do," Jamie responded. "Finish your degree. I'm a cop. I can moonlight at any number of places… make decent money. I can help, whether we're together or not. For some reason I've been given a second chance here—maybe this is the reason."

"My God, Jamie, I can't believe I was even thinking about leaving. I'm just so… I'm so sorry—"

She turned to find a doctor officiously standing inside the doorway. "You Mrs. Giles?" The question was flung at her like a challenge. Instantly she disliked this white-coated interrogator.

Kathy straightened up, wiping moisture from her cheek with her fingers. "Yes, Kathy Giles. Is he going to be all right?"

The doctor rudely flipped through several pages on the patient chart. "Interesting case. Apparently you were dead at the scene," he said to Jamie, ignoring Kathy's question.

"We're aware of that," Kathy interjected. "The question is, will he be okay now?"

The doctor turned to dismiss the wifely annoyance. "Mrs. Giles, your husband drowned two hours ago. He was dead for possibly fifteen minutes. Attempts to resuscitate him failed. And then he spontaneously came back to life. We don't know if the paramedics simply failed to detect vital signs, or if he actually died while he was underwater."

A mustached man with an enormous girth entered the room.

The doctor continued speaking as if there had been no interruption. "All we know is that, physically, Mr. Giles appears quite normal now. We're going to do some tests to see if there might have been any brain damage or other psychological effects from the trauma, which wouldn't be surprising. Now if you'd excuse us, we'd like a few minutes alone with your husband. This is Dr. Rayburn from the PD's psychological unit."

Jamie squirmed, then manipulated the bed controls to position himself into a sitting position. "I'd like her to stay. In fact, I insist on it." He timidly glanced at Kathy. "We're a team."

The doctor and the psychologist looked at each other, both uncomfortable with Jamie's decision. Finally, the doctor mustered his much-practiced haughtiness and said, "That's impossible, but we can let her know when we're finished here."

Jamie's face contorted with rage. He stabbed a stiff forefinger toward the doctor and roared, "You may leave now! My wife stays. We'll let *you* know when Dr. Rayburn is finished here."

Kathy recoiled at the abrupt switch in Jamie's temperament. She'd never seen her husband so... so *direct*. But she rather enjoyed seeing the doctor put in his place.

The doctor stood there frozen, his arrogance temporarily dismantled. "Go!" Jamie urged.

The doctor flinched, tried unsuccessfully to gather his composure, and finally turned and strutted away.

"Dr. Rayburn, you have some questions for me," Jamie suggested with a sudden meekness. "I must apologize for the rudeness of the staff here. They think they run the place. Please make yourself comfortable." He gestured to a chair opposite Kathy.

The psychologist had seemed astonished and intrigued by Jamie's sudden shifts in demeanor. He turned to Kathy. "It's not unusual, Mrs. Giles, for someone who has had a traumatic event to experience some significant mood swings. I think the doctor was just trying to spare you some of the discomfort of seeing it for yourself during these early hours of recovery."

"Please speak directly to me," Jamie instructed Dr. Rayburn. "I suppose your job here is to decide if I'm fit to go back to work. Well, I'm feeling great. Except for the grief of losing my partner, of course, and the fact that I can't seem to get a minute alone with my wife. So please—do your thing. Let's get on with it."

Rayburn studied Jamie before speaking. "What do you remember about the event you just went through?"

"Remember? Well, I can recall Rico getting his head blown apart. Hard to forget something like that. And the car veering off the road into the water. I can remember struggling to get out of my seat belt—panic, I guess—and then... waking up here, in this room. A miracle, right?"

"Do you remember speaking to the paramedics, or anyone else, before you got here?"

"You mean after I drowned?"

"That's right."

Jamie glanced at Kathy then back at the psychologist. "Nothing. I was dead, right? Until I got here."

"Well, the verbal report from the paramedics stated that you started moving while you were on a gurney on the way to an ambulance. You don't remember that?"

"Not at all."

"The ambulance driver was an African American woman who assisted in the transfer of your body—of *you*, that is—into the vehicle."

"Don't remember that either."

Rayburn glanced uneasily at Kathy, then turned back to Jamie. "The driver stated that as she leaned over you to attach some monitoring equipment, you grabbed her—*provocatively*, she said—and made a lewd suggestion. Any recollection?"

Kathy shifted in her chair. This didn't sound like Jamie at all.

"None," Jamie replies. His eyes darted nervously to his wife once, twice. *Dammit, it's the truth.* No recollection.

"One more question, Jamie. Who is Maria?"

"Maria?"

"You called the driver Maria. Which is not her name. Who is Maria?"

"I honestly don't know anyone named Maria." Jamie lowered the bed a few inches. "This has really worn me out. Is the driver going to file charges or anything?"

"No, she was pretty understanding, considering what you'd just been through. But it's something we have to investigate, isn't it? I'd say probably some sort of PTSD—an out-of-character stressful response to the trauma of drowning. And losing your partner. I think you'd benefit from a couple weeks off, at least."

"Really, I'm okay now, I am. It would be hard to lose any pay right now, you know what I mean? Things are kinda tight."

"Time off *with* pay is what I'm talking about. You're a hero, son. You'll be the lead story on the news tonight. All in the line of duty. So take the time, rest up, and get back to normal. This kind of thing, it takes a toll."

Jamie nodded.

Rayburn stood and headed for the door. "Mrs. Giles, I'm sorry we had to get into this."

Kathy nodded the psychologist out the door, then leaned over Jamie to give him a kiss on the forehead.

But he turned away. "I don't remember any of that. Why would I behave that way?" He looked up at Kathy with vulnerable eyes, his domineering attitude totally gone now.

"I love my wife," he said.

She knew that he meant it.

But a question lingered: *who, then, was Maria?*

CHAPTER 4

At two in the morning, the night nurse shuffled down the quiet hospital corridor to take vitals, administer medications, and generally check on the status of patients under her watch. Nancy Goodwin hated this shift. At her age—over fifty now—she found the work too routine, had trouble staying awake, and even worse, almost never had interesting things occur to her. She'd never admit it, but sometimes she hoped that a medical emergency would occur. Nothing too serious, of course, just something to interrupt the god-awful boredom.

In room 324, Mrs. Jacobson at first didn't want to take her oral diuretic, but finally gave in to Nancy's gentle coaxing. Mr. Aakin woke up cussing as usual in room 325 when Nancy accidentally bumped his bed. *No change in the patient*, Nancy noted with a smile.

She had never met the new patient in room 326, Jamie Giles, a police officer who had drowned and somehow come back to life.

The door to Mr. Giles' room was open a crack. She entered quietly and a widening slash of light from the corridor illuminated a man sitting upright in his adjustable bed, still as a corpse, eyes open and gleaming. Jamie did not move as Nancy approached, did not turn his head or look in her direction. He seemed to be gazing at some invisible object across the room, though there was nothing but an empty chair against that barren wall.

Nancy's heart suddenly began to pound against her sternum. *What if Mr. Giles had died?* No, an alarm would have alerted her. If he was alive, then, he was remarkably unresponsive to her presence. *A stroke, perhaps!* She cursed herself for having wished for a medical emergency, and then crossed herself, a lapsed Catholic seeking forgiveness and protection.

She rushed over and looked up at the monitors. Jamie's blood pressure and oxygen saturation level were both normal, but his pulse was low—well under 50 bpm. Concerning—unless the patient was meditating. She leaned to get a closer look at the young man's face, to look into his staring eyes.

Her face got within inches of Jamie's, and she placed a caring hand on his forehead. That was when his eyes shifted to look at her. The subtle but unexpected movement made her jump backwards.

"Mr. Giles, are you all right?"

Silence.

"I understand from your chart that you've been through quite a trauma."

In a voice that seemed older than a young man's and more formal than a cop's, Jamie said, "You are not allowed to touch me."

"Mr. Giles, I'm your nurse. It's all right."

Jamie's upright posture made him appear almost regal. "Never touch me, unless I ask." His voice was raspy.

Dry throat, Nancy thought. She found a glass of water with a straw in it and moved it close to Jamie's mouth. The straw tip touched his lip.

With an angry motion, Jamie batted the glass out of her hand, splashing water onto the floor.

"Impertinence!" Jamie snarled. "If I want water, I will ask for it. Get me Nehsira!"

Confused and shaken by the outburst, Nancy backed away. "Neh-sye-ruh," she repeated. "Is that your doctor? I haven't heard of him—or her."

Inexplicably, Jamie grew more enraged. He threw off the bed covers and leaped out of bed to stand imperiously before her, but instead slipped on the spilled water, falling sideways and banging his elbow on the side table. As he pulled himself back into bed, a tremendous torrent of profanity erupted from his throat. Nancy believed it was profanity, but in truth she couldn't understand a word of it. Just a tangled snarl of guttural sounds uttered with curse-like intensity.

Racing from the room, Nancy found the charge nurse, who found an orderly, and together the threesome approached the angry den of the madman. As Nancy switched on the light, Jamie looked up as if jarred awake by the sudden illumination. Nancy noticed that almost instantaneously his anger switched from rage to confusion.

Jamie stared at the hospital staff and blinked. "I think I fell," he said meekly, rubbing his elbow.

"Nancy, clean up the floor, will you?" the charge nurse ordered. Then, with an air of immense authority, she approached Jamie and inspected his elbow.

Nancy waited for the madman to complain about being touched, but Jamie said nothing.

"Please remain in bed, sir, while we mop up the water," the charge nurse said. Then she approached Nancy, who was busy mopping. "He seems calm right now."

"He was asking for a *Dr. Neh-sye-ruh*, or something. Who is that?"

"No physician I know. But then I have trouble with all those foreign names."

———

Later that morning, Kathy was the first one to give hell to the hospital staff for allowing Jamie to get out of bed and slip on a puddle of water. *What kind of place are you running here?* Her wrath had been amplified by three police officials whom Kathy had notified immediately. *After what he's endured, you put him through this?* The hospital absorbed the body blows without launching a defense. How could you tell the wife and the entire police department that their hero was a lunatic? At any rate, the charge nurse could not verify the patient's behavior as described by the attending nurse, so the matter was settled with a heartfelt apology by everyone except Nancy, who was off-duty.

Jamie was discharged the following day. After extensive testing, no physical aftereffects of his drowning had been found.

"It's almost like they were anxious to get rid of you," Kathy told her husband on the way home.

The department had kept insisting that Jamie take a paid month off to make sure there were no undetected emotional issues related to the trauma, but against Kathy's wishes Jamie had argued that down to three weeks. If he could scrape the money together, maybe he and Kathy would take a vacation. Seemed like a good idea to Kathy—after all, she was also an unwitting victim of this strange episode.

Kathy insisted on driving her husband home, which seemed to anger him a little. But if it did, he gave in to her without saying a word. He was probably feeling overprotected. To mask the tension in the car, she plugged in Jamie's iPod and turned on his favorite music, a personal mix of indie-rock. Oddly, he just shook his head and turned it off, switching on the radio and searching through the FM stations, finally landing on the local classical music channel.

Kathy didn't mind. She liked classical music, particularly Liszt and Mozart—her mother had been a music professor at the university—but Jamie had never wanted that kind of highbrow stuff in the house. *It doesn't speak to me*, he would say, preferring the raw music from the streets where he grew up. Music that, unfortunately, made Kathy grit her teeth.

So what was this business in the car? Maybe that drowning incident had knocked some music appreciation into him.

Their cracker box suburban home was small and spare, but it had a backyard fence for the children they planned to have some day, and a finished basement that Jamie had turned into a man-cave with a cheap flat-panel TV and home theater sound system from Costco. Kathy didn't complain about the extravagant purchase because Jamie could listen to his music down there without bothering her too much.

On their first evening home, Kathy prepared a candlelight dinner of Jamie's favorite foods: pot roast, oven-browned potatoes, brown sugar-glazed carrots, salad with French dressing, and apple pie. With the candles lit, she called downstairs for Jamie to join her for dinner. He came up immediately, a look of excitement on his face, and set his iPod and portable speaker unit on the table.

Kathy frowned reflexively. After all she had done to make a romantic welcome-home meal for Jamie, he seemed ready to ruin the mood with his music.

"Smells fantastic, sweetheart," he said. "Pot roast? My favorite."

She knew that.

"I found some really incredible music for dinner."

I doubt it, she thought, preparing for the worst.

He switched on the iPod, thoughtfully adjusting the volume to a modest level. The music caught Kathy off-guard. This was no junky, amateurish indie-rock piece; it was classical music. She recognized it immediately.

Richard Wagner's *Tannhauser*.

Jamie was playing the dramatic overture from the famous opera, closing his eyes and smiling faintly. "Now *this* music really speaks to me. Should we eat?"

His wife had no idea what had gotten into him, but *this* Jamie was an improvement over the other one. The music was a bit dramatic for dinner, but she had no intention of discouraging her husband's newly acquired taste in music.

After dinner, he listened to *Tannhauser* all the way through, cradling Kathy in his arms on the basement sofa as if lost in some other world. Kathy could swear that Jamie at times was mouthing the words as they were sung in German—which was ridiculous, because Jamie only spoke English.

This was Kathy's first time listening to music in the man-cave.

And her last time feeling perfectly safe.

———

Unable to sleep, Jamie quietly climbed out of bed and went to his man-cave, switching on the large-screen TV. So many infomercials during the early morning hours! No live sports. A glut of re-runs.

Shuffling through the channels, he stopped at the Travel Channel. which was showing a program on pleasure cruises. It made him think that maybe he and Kathy could benefit from a short vacation. Just get away from the problems up here in Michigan. Get back to being a couple again.

A maddening flurry of commercials interrupted the show. Jamie impatiently reached for the remote, his thumb searching for the channel button. But before he could switch, an image in one of the TV spots stunned him. He set down the remote, staring at the image of a pink hotel. Not just any pink hotel, but the exact hotel he had seen in his unfinished nightmare. The image provoked memories of sandals on the beach, a hotel room door bearing the number 534, the comforting sensation of hot water in a spa, and the horrifying realization that through the bathroom door was entering...

His heart was racing. He felt dizzy, frightened. Only when the commercial's tagline appeared, did he start to calm down.

The commercial identified the pink hotel. It was real! And it was called the Sheraton British Colonial, and it was in the Bahamas.

CHAPTER 5

Back in bed, Jamie struggled to go to sleep, but after an hour he couldn't stay awake any longer.

Kathy awoke and rolled toward him, wrapped an arm over his chest, and put her head on his shoulder. She could hear his breath, listen to his heartbeat, feel the heat rising from his body. And suddenly she remembered that, for a half hour, he had been dead. He had stopped breathing. His heartbeat had stopped. His body had been cold and lifeless. Yet here he was now, sleeping next to her, exuding heat. Suddenly she wanted to thank God for this miracle—not that she actually believed in God, but she wanted to thank someone. Something. Somewhere. So she tried to remember how to pray, and while she was remembering, it happened.

Jamie started to breathe deeply. At first just a deep breath *in*, and after a long pause a stuttering breath *out*. And then his breathing became erratic as if he were struggling for air. His mouth opened, and he moaned, then gasped.

Kathy sat up wondering if the doctors had failed to identify some horrible consequence of the drowning. She hunched against the head-board suddenly afraid to touch him.

Jamie broke into a sweat, soaking the sheet. His eyes flashed open, wide and white. He began to mutter erratically... a strange, guttural string of syllables… as if speaking to someone, giving commands. But it was all gibberish, and the growing intensity of his garbled speech terrified Kathy. Was he speaking to her? There was no one else in the room.

Suddenly he stood up. Naked, he walked to a chair by the window and sat down.

Kathy tried to disappear into the headboard, but Jamie was quiet now. He sat in the chair without moving a muscle, staring at something—not her, something else. Unblinking. As if in a waking coma.

Kathy gathered the courage to speak. "Jamie?"

No response. Jamie continued to sit in the chair, rigidly—almost *regally*, Kathy thought—eyes fixed straight ahead, Tannenbaum's crescendos wafting over him.

"Jamie—what's going on?"

She tentatively crawled out of bed and slowly walked toward the chair, putting her hand on his shoulder.

He jumped as if shocked by a cattle prod, and then looked around, sucking in his breath, clearly disoriented.

"What—?"

"Jesus, Jamie, you scared me."

"I don't know… how—"

"You were sleepwalking. Don't worry about it," she said, taking him by the hand and leading him back to the bed. "You've been through a lot of trauma, God knows. Just lie back and let me help you relax."

He lay down on his back. Kathy snuggled him in a comforting way and instantly noticed that he was aroused.

"Jamie?" she said, recoiling slightly. The disturbing previous moments had not exactly put her in the mood for sex. But Jamie seemed unmindful of her sudden withdrawal. He rolled toward her, then sinuously crawled on top of her, stroking her back, her legs, her hips, and then began devouring her lips with his mouth. His back arched and quickly he was beyond control, heaving and gasping, painfully pulling Kathy's hair despite her protests.

This had ceased being lovemaking.

Finally freeing a hand, Kathy fiercely slapped Jamie across the face.

Stunned, Jamie rolled off her. He stopped breathing for a moment, then lifted himself up on one elbow, looking down at Kathy's tear-streaked face. "Kathy, what is it?"

"What is it?" Kathy repeated, incredulous. "Are you kidding?"

"What's wrong?"

His question was frighteningly sincere, as if Jamie had just entered the room. As if he hadn't been there.

Kathy didn't know what to do, so she rolled over and ostriched her head beneath a pillow.

"Did I do something?" he asked, tenderly putting a hand on her shoulder, maddeningly oblivious to his own brutality.

Now she was genuinely scared, but still mustered up the courage to yell. "Just shut off the damn music!"

CHAPTER 6

Bright skies and songbirds right out of a Disney cartoon provided the unlikely ornamentation for Rico's somber burial. Over one hundred police attended with Jamie, Rico's partner, in the first rank. Father Patterson from Rico's parish read some scripture, but Jamie was not listening. No words about God's mercy or the healing power of forgiveness or the glorious afterlife that Rico surely was enjoying this very moment could warm the coldness in Jamie's soul or disrupt his growing hunger for justice.

He watched his close friend being lowered in an airtight coffin into a hole in the ground. He heard the muffled sobs of Rico's wife, Susana. He saw Rico's two-year-old son, Hector, looking on with dazed eyes, unaware of the unfair loss he had suffered. He had overheard Susana whisper to Hector that *Daddy is with the angels now.*

Jamie was not so sure about that. For him, there were no angels. He had died, and there were no winged creatures waiting for him on the other side. Instead, there had been just a great void. And a light in the distance wavering as if held by an unsteady hand. He had seen the afterlife and, frankly, it was boring.

Why had he come back? he wondered. For what purpose? Had he returned only to suffer the searing pain of his friend's funeral?

The coffin reached the bottom of the hole. The priest mumbled some Latin words and crossed himself, and in that moment Jamie's epiphany fluttered down upon him like an angel, its plumage nearly asphyxiating him with answers.

In a blinding flash, it had become clear what he was brought back to do. The storm in his brain now could be channeled, the hot flush of his unvented anger could be released like a jet of steam at a worthy target, not at his confused and fragile wife.

Thank you, he said to the merciful angel.

And then he smiled for the first time since he had died.

The official part of the ceremony was over. Kathy left Jamie's side to throw her arms around Rico's widow so they could weep together openly, the way women can. Her place was immediately taken by Jamie's partner-to-be, Hal.

"Really sad day," Hal said. "Makes you kinda think about your own mortality, 'specially on *this* job, know what I mean?"

Jamie nodded.

"When will you get back to work?" Hal went on. "I heard a month or so from now."

"You feeling okay?"

"I'm fine. Be back before then, just some legal and insurance bullshit they're fighting through. If I come back too soon and mess up, or get hurt, they could be blamed for that I guess."

"So I was wondering—if you actually died and all that, maybe Kathy could collect on your life insurance. Probably no rider in there that talks about what happens if you come back to life." Hal gave Jamie a sappy grin. "Maybe you can collect twice."

"You mean die again? No way, man. Not for a while."

"Well, I hope you're back soon. They got me teamed with Sam, which is like a death sentence. Guy has no survival instincts. So hurry back, okay?"

"Do my best."

This guy's an idiot, Jamie thought, dreading the long days ahead cooped up in a squad with Hal's inane patter turning his brain into Jell-O. Suddenly taking a full month off didn't seem like such a terrible idea.

———

She didn't know what Jamie had been doing with his time, but it'd been two days since the funeral. Since then, Kathy hadn't seen her husband for more than a couple of hours outside of bedtime. At least she had enjoyed some *alone* time to soothe her frayed nerves. Nights continued to be tense, though. Every time Jamie got up to go to the bathroom, she feared a repeat performance of his first night home, even though he hadn't roughed her up again. But the sleepwalking was driving her nuts. He still rose from his bed at night and walked stiffly to the chair and then just sat there—eyes open, staring into the room as if seeing something that was veiled from anyone else—for a half hour, sometimes more.

She didn't like entering his man-cave—it seemed like a violation of his privacy—but sometimes it needed cleaning, and this was one of those times. Armed with dust rags, mop, and vacuum cleaner, she entered his space and began picking up dirty cups and plates, stuffing abundant trash into a garbage bag, then uncluttering and wiping down the surfaces. *How can anyone live like this?* she wondered.

On a nightstand, next to the fake-leather recliner, she found a book called *Experiencing Death* by Dr. Alice Mallach. Jamie was a movie and video game guy, not a reader, so she was surprised to find evidence that he was actually reading. A scrap of paper marked his place nearly two-thirds of the way through the paperback.

She sat down in the recliner and turned the book over. The back cover proclaimed:

> Tens of thousands of people have experienced death and dis-
> covered an astonishing world beyond life. These are the vivid ac-

counts of fourteen people who came back from the dead to tell us what they found on the other side. Dr. Alice Mallach is the nation's foremost researcher in death experiences. Using regressive hypnosis and other methods she has assembled these startling and provocative stories "to help us all live without fear of dying and with the certitude that our existence continues beyond death."

Jamie was clearly struggling to deal with his own experience and the jarring consequences. Kathy had seen the signs—his erratic behavior and obsession with his partner's death, his need to be alone. While sitting silently in his space, studying the book passages he had highlighted like a schoolboy, she vowed to be more understanding. She may never fully understand what he experienced, or what pain he may be feeling about the loss of his friend, but she certainly could be more supportive.

She leaned back in the recliner and noticed the TV remote on the seat beside her. This basement den was not so disagreeable. It was inviting, even—if you kept the volume down. She clicked on the TV and switched through a few channels, finding a local news broadcast. *She could get used to this.* Jamie was onto something here. With her feet up and the big screen vividly presenting the world to her in HD, she started to understand the appeal. Maybe she'd been too contemptuous about this cozy place. Not that she'd ever let Jamie know that.

She flipped through a few more pages in Jamie's book, listened inattentively to the local weather and a handful of local commercials—she hated that guy who hollered at you about his new car deals—and started thinking about getting a cup of tea. That would make this little cellar sabbatical just about perfect. As she lowered the footrest and leaned forward to stand up, she noticed that the news had come back on.

"Reporter Colin Ash reports from the scene," the anchor said. The picture cut to a young man standing in a street. Behind him were flashing squad cars and a legion of blue-shirted police officers. Something terrible had happened.

"Thank you, Carla. Just down the street from where I'm standing, about thirty minutes ago, three men were gunned down. My sources tell me that all three were members of a local gang called the Violators. One of the three men was twenty-eight-year-old Tayvon Eason, reportedly the leader of the gang, which is said to have committed numerous acts of violence and controlled most of the illicit drug trafficking in the city. The Violators have also been under investigation for the slaying of police officer Enrico Esperanza just nine days ago. There are no suspects in this multiple murder, which police say has the appearance of a gang-style shoot-out. I have Brian Wilkinson, Chief of the Detroit Police Department, with me. Chief..."

The room temperature plummeted several degrees, or so it seemed. Kathy dropped the remote. She was no longer hearing the news broadcast; she was drowning in the black water of dread. She prayed that her instincts were wrong, that her suspicions would prove false, and she would end up feeling foolish. But her churning gut overcame her mental protests, and she surrendered to the fear that Jamie had turned vigilante and murdered these three men as retribution for Rico's death.

My God, what was happening? Before the drowning, Jamie never would have been capable of such a thing. He was one of the good guys, always complaining about the other cops who took liberties with the rules and sometimes took a little cash on the side. But over the past days she had seen his uncontrollable rage. He had assaulted her sexually—*his own wife*—and then conveniently wiped the atrocity from his memory.

It was true—after he died, Jamie hadn't been himself. And Kathy didn't know who he was.

Suddenly she heard the garage door opening. Jamie was home. How could she face him now, with her heart filled with doubts and accusations?

What if he had just been out with his buddies for a couple of beers? *Innocent before proven guilty.*

The thought didn't calm her gut. She didn't know what to do. How could she confront a man who could be a murderer? How could she trust him?

"Kathy, are you home?"

"Just cleaning up downstairs!" she yelled, hoping her voice didn't betray her fear.

"Coming down, Sweetheart."

She heard his footsteps on the stairs and realized that the TV was still on. The reporter was still summarizing the bloody scene across town.

Jamie will know that *she* knew about the killing.

She stooped, picked up the remote to switch off the TV, but the device slithered out of her hands like an eel and slid under the recliner.

Jamie stepped into the room and immediately glanced at the screen, glared at it for a few seconds without moving, then nodded his head. "Justice served," he said, slumping into the companion recliner that Kathy had never used.

She didn't know how to respond.

"Looks great down here. Sorry I left such a mess—someday maybe I'll learn how to pick up after myself." He pushed the seat back and swung his legs onto the footrest. "That story's all over the news. Heard it on the radio coming home. Don't think anyone feels bad about it though."

Kathy took a deep breath, screwed together some courage, and replied, "Depends."

Jamie squinted and turned to face her. "On what?"

"On who did it. A gang? No problem, let 'em kill each other off."

"Who else?" Jamie demanded.

Kathy couldn't bring herself to say *rogue cops* out loud, or *you, Jamie, maybe it was you.*

"Truth is, I'm the one responsible." Jamie said this so matter-of-factly that Kathy didn't catch his meaning for a few seconds.

But then the chill deepened. She had no words left.

"I've been dreaming for the last week that these bastards would find justice. *Praying* for it, and I'm not a religious man as you know. I've even made a few plans myself for how… well, how justice might be served, since the system seems incapable of doing a damn thing about it."

"What are you saying, Jamie?"

"I'm saying that if one man focuses so intently on one thing as I've been doing, then maybe it's possible the universe might adapt somehow and make that thing happen. So somehow I might have brought about the death of those gangbangers."

"But you didn't shoot them, right?"

Jamie turned to her, his veined eyes exposing the pain inflicted by her careless question. "Don't be fuckin' stupid!" he said. "I'm a cop! *Still* a cop. I arrest people who do stuff like that."

"Sorry." But not really. She tried to assess his reaction, which was drizzled with sincerity—but *too much*? His wounded eyes stared back, looking for more apology than she could muster.

With an aggrieved shake of the head, he turned back to the TV just as the camera panned across the gang's van riddled with bullet holes.

Reporter Colin Ash, in a jarringly cheerful off-screen voice, summarized one of the police theories. "It is thought that the perpetrators—perhaps a rival gang—drove past the three members of the Violators just as they were getting into their vehicle, this blue Toyota van, and gunned them down in cold blood."

The picture cut to an African-American bystander, a tee-shirted male in his late fifties.

"Reggie Martin saw the shooting as it occurred," Colin said, thrusting a microphone at the man. "Reggie, can you describe what you saw?"

"These three gangbangers were crossing the street right over there. Seemed to be heading for the van, but as they got up to it a car drove by, a white foreign job—don't know the make—and suddenly there was poppin' sounds like firecrackers and the three dudes, they fell to the ground, but one of them pulled out a gun and fired a shot at the car as it was driving away. I guess they died, though, all three of 'em."

"Did you see who was in the car—how many were in there?"

"Huh-uh—was driving away. Sun was in my eyes, y'know? All happened pretty fast. But I seen those three fellas around the neighborhood a lot, sellin' drugs an' stuff, beatin' on people. Can't say they be missed. Someday mebbe these gangs'll just kill each other off, and we'll get the streets back, that's what I'm hopin'. Somebody did the cops a favor here."

Jamie leaped from the chair, startling Kathy. "Turn that damn thing off!"

But the remote was under the sofa. As Kathy scrambled to find it, Jamie steered himself toward the stairway. "Going to take a shower."

"Chicken for supper okay?"

"Whatever."

He stopped halfway up the stairs, just as Kathy found the remote hiding beneath the recliner. "I'm glad they're dead—but I didn't do it."

Seated on the floor, Kathy tilted the remote to switch off the TV but hesitated. Colin Ash was asking a question of another bystander.

"Was a late model Subaru, I'm sure of that," the young woman explained, "just like the one my cousin has, but white."

Just like Jamie's car.

She clicked the TV and stood up. She didn't want to, but she trudged up the carpeted stairway, padded across the linoleum kitchen floor and heard the sound of Jamie's shower starting up. She opened the door to the garage and flipped on the light. The garage was too small and cluttered to walk all the way around the car, so she activated the garage door opener. Creaking and groaning, the old door lifted, and daylight flooded the garage interior.

Kathy peeked at the front of the car; no damage there. She sidled around the right side, looking for some sign, some clue that the Subaru had been at the shooting. Nothing. Stepping into the driveway, she turned to look at the rear end. That's when she saw the shattered right taillight.

The bystander had said one of the downed gangbangers had lifted himself up to fire a shot at the white car. Maybe that's how the taillight got busted up.

She was trembling.

Her phone rang. The noise made her jump. Nervously, she yanked the phone from her pocket and fumbled it onto the asphalt driveway. She picked it up, cursing herself.

"Hello?"

No one there. The call must have disconnected when the phone struck the pavement.

She looked at the call history. *Her mother.*

She could picture her mother in her three million dollar home overlooking the big lake, sipping her scotch and water, stroking her purebred Maltese, knees nimbly tucked beneath her on the fashionable raw silk and wrought iron daybed. Mom gushed incessantly about how much she loved her only daughter but couldn't stop complaining about that daughter's decisions, the worst of which was to marry beneath her station. *And a cop! Why a cop? There's no future in police work. You deserve so much more.* She had never come to visit Kathy in her cracker box suburban home, but one afternoon Kathy had glimpsed her mother Agnes slowly driving by in her Lexus. Not stopping, just passing by disdainfully, assuring mom of the depth of her daughter's downfall. *Such a tiny, common dwelling.* The weekly phone calls mercifully had dropped to one every couple of weeks, but each of those inevitably ended badly, with an alcohol-fortified Agnes crying about the tragic plight of her daughter who was trapped in a relationship without a future.

Kathy desperately had wanted to prove her mother wrong. Happiness, she had earnestly argued, was never the outcome of material wealth and creature comforts. Kathy loved Jamie, and had always believed that their deep, abiding love could conquer anything they encountered. She would be happier than her mother, the trophy wife of a successful Fortune 500 CEO, had ever been. And she would do it her way.

Out of spite, she supposed.

All of her life, Kathy had felt caged by convention and tradition, ruled by the expectations of others, and suffocated by choices imposed upon her—where she would go to school, what career would be best for her, what car to drive, which tutors to hire, what friends to associate with, whom to pair up with.

This was *her* life!

Turning back to the shattered taillight, those words suddenly took on a different meaning.

This was her life.

But…

Maybe there was another cause. A truck might have backed into the taillight in the Home Depot parking lot. It could be the result of a vandal with a slingshot, a rock flung up by a passing car. The world was full of small dings and broken things that remained undetected for days or weeks. There were a thousand and one possible explanations. *Why jump to the worst of them?*

She rushed into the garage and lowered the door—*not* because she was afraid a neighbor might see the broken taillight, but because it was time to get supper started.

She loved making meals for Jamie. And he loved her cooking.

The shower was turned off; Jamie was in the bedroom. Kathy looked into the steamy bathroom and found a pile of her husband's clothes in a heap. She forced a smile—*when will that man ever learn to pick up after himself?* She entered the bathroom and plucked his sweat socks off the floor, then his jeans and underwear. *The things women do out of love!* She lifted up his pale blue shirt with the sleeves still rolled up to mid-forearm and began to wad it up with the rest of his soiled clothes. But she noticed something on the left arm.

A slight smudge.

She didn't want to investigate, but she found her head involuntarily lowering, her nose plunging into the smudge. She breathed in.

And smelled the sharp stench of gunpowder.

CHAPTER 7

The shower didn't revive him. The floor tilted, the square cage of his bedroom threw him against a wall. Hope to God Kathy didn't hear him crash into it!

"You okay?"

"Just clumsy."

He flopped on the bed like a caught fish floundering to find oxygen. He was not so much dizzy as disoriented. Chunks of his day had been cut out of his consciousness, and the edges awkwardly spliced together. It was like the blackouts he had suffered after binge-drinking in college before he dropped out because of the cost. Or because of his lack of discipline.

His friend Rico, he remembered, had pulled him aside and told him he should join the army or something to straighten out his life. Instead, Jamie had followed Rico to the police academy. In many ways, the academy was tougher than college but ultimately may have saved him. No time to get into trouble or feel sorry for himself now that he was alone in the world. Rico's mother had died just a year after Robert Giles, Jamie's boozed-up father, had jumped his car over a highway median killing himself and a teenage girl in an oncoming Honda. Jamie wished that Rico's mother had lived to see Rico and him make it to graduation. Rico had finished third in his class. Jamie had placed sixth. The pay for new cops was lousy no matter how high you finished—a little more than thirty thousand bucks a year, plus $250 for uniform cleaning. Still, a big improvement from his car wash days. Mom would have been proud.

Rico had been like a brother to him, a friend from the old neighborhood who had been called every hateful slur in the book, but always had stood proud with a bright smile. In many ways, Rico had been a role model for Jamie, an example of how to stay focused and lead your life on purpose. The kid had been amazing, especially for a Mexican whose mother had been a "legal" but whose father had been deported back to Mexico when Rico was twelve. Someday, Rico had promised his mother, he'd find a way to bring his father back to Detroit.

Brushing aside the nostalgic remembrance, Jamie tried to piece together his day and remembered driving into the city to meet with an informant at a construction site. *But why?* Jamie was off-duty. He had no reason to be doing police business. He remembered driving somewhere along the canal, heading away from home. Even now, he could feel the sun beating down on the forearm that was sticking out the open driver's window.

But then somehow he was near home. It was like an alien abduction. The time had just been hacked out of his life.

He had pulled into a McDonald's, the one with the big TV in a conversation pit. A pretty fancy place for this neighborhood, he had always thought. But he had parked and gone inside, ordering a large black coffee, then clearing his head by watching the big screen. Management always had Fox News turned on. Jamie was pretty sure that the right-wing franchisee would shoot anyone who tried to switch the channel. But on this day Fox had failed to scoop the competition. A young employee had rushed out from behind the counter and poked a couple of hidden buttons, finding CNN.

"Sorry sir," the kid had said. "Something local's happened."

Sure enough, CNN was broadcasting a tie-in to local coverage of a drive-by shooting. Three gangbangers dead. No suspects in custody. Suspected turf battle.

Jamie remembered calmly watching the story unfold until the reporter identified the deceased. And then he had quietly cheered! He was quite certain that he had known nothing about the shooting until he had seen the TV coverage. He remembered being surprised.

But the stolen chunks of his day's timeline haunted him, as well as the missing motive for meeting with the informant. Maybe Jamie had snapped and picked up an untraceable gun from him, then had driven by the Violators and gunned them down.

Impossible! Not to remember? Ludicrous.

"What do you want to go with your chicken?"

Kathy's voice from the kitchen intruded. He was in no mood to make decisions.

"Just surprise me," he yelled, tacking on a gentle "Sweetheart" to take the edge off the brittleness. What would he do without this woman? With Rico gone, he'd be totally adrift.

Did she suspect he had something to do with the drive-by this afternoon? She'd have to be comatose not to question the timing of his absence and his strange behavior since returning home. Closing his eyes, he tried to calm the buzzing neurons in his brain with deep breaths, to counterbalance any guilt by recommitting to excellence as a husband, but it didn't work. A monster still surfaced from the brine of despair—the monster of doubt. Last week Kathy had accused him of sexual assault; the accusation alone had withered him, but he could remember nothing at all about that evening. Barely a half hour ago, Kathy's fearful eyes had accused him of complicity in the shooting, and again he had been robbed of any recollection.

Jamie could see the pattern, and he was sure that Kathy could see it, too. Out of its element, starved of oxygen, the fish lay still, surrendered to the… *what?*

The madness.

Sleep, like death, began to overtake him. Succumbing to the blackness, he thought of Kathy, could see her innocent face. Faintly in the distance he heard the comforting strains of *Tannenbaum*. The bitter aftertaste of anxiety began to fade.

But then he jerked awake, afraid of losing another piece of his life.

———

After supper I'm going to work out some kinks at the rec center," Kathy announced.

Jamie stuffed his mouth with herbed chicken, savored the deliciousness, and nodded approval. Not that he was in any position to approve or disapprove.

"Sounds good," he said passively, glancing at his wife for any telltale signs of her mood. He had to be careful to keep her happy. If he lost her, he'd probably fall apart.

She seemed calm. If she suspected anything, she was keeping it to herself.

"Terrific meal, Sweetheart," he said. Meaning it.

She gave a little smirk of acknowledgement. Maybe she'd decided in his favor.

By six thirty, they'd finished eating. "I'll take care of the cleanup," Jamie offered. "Go do your thing."

"Well, thank you, sir," Kathy said demurely as she went to the bedroom and returned with her gym bag. "Now you can play your music as loud as you want. I'm taking your car to impress my friends."

He laughed. His car was five years newer than Kathy's beater, which had taken six months of scrimping to save a down payment. On his salary, even the three-year-old Subaru would have been out of their price range if Kathy's cousin Lou, co-owner of the dealership, hadn't taken pity on them and had cut a terrific deal. In the early months of marriage, Jamie had questioned whether Kathy actually could adapt to the radical change in her economic status, but she'd been a champ, never complaining or making him feel guilty about trapping her in near-poverty. Somehow he'd make it up to her.

Now that she'd left, he felt abandoned. For just a second, he feared that she was leaving him, that her gym bag had contained the supplies for an escape and she would never return.

The growl of the closing garage door sent him racing to the tiny picture window in the front room. He caught a glimpse of the Subaru backing out of the crumbling driveway and into the street, then pulling away.

The taillight was broken, he noticed.

When had that happened?

And then a surge of recall zapped him like a stun gun with an image in a car's side-view mirror. Men lying in the street. One rising onto his elbow. Pointing a gun.

Firing.

A small pop. Like flicking a finger at a windowpane.

Jamie's car, marked, like in that old movie, *Chinatown*. The police would be looking for a white Subaru with a taillight shot out. And when they found it, Kathy would be driving.

He had to get her back home right now, so he picked up his cell phone and called her.

Kathy's phone rang in the bedroom. Forgotten.

Only one thing that he could do now—drive Kathy's beater to the rec center and make up some story about needing to swap cars. He hoped she hadn't been pulled over by his brothers-in-blue before getting there.

———

Don't know what we'd do, Lou, if you weren't family," Kathy told her cousin at Harold's Subaru. "It's just so embarrassing, banging up Jamie's car like this."

"Just a little thing, Kathy. Give us twenty minutes and it'll be good as new."

"How much, you know, will it cost?"

Lou noticed a small twitch in his cousin's eyes, the same twitch he'd seen when they were kids playing together and she got nervous about something. He suspected money was tight in the Giles household.

"Not enough to pay for writing it up. This one's on the house."

"You sure, Lou? You've been so good to us."

"You know, I gotta tell you, Kathy—Sharon and I both admire the way you're out there making it on your own. It'd be so damn easy to just ask your mom to fix things now and then, but you and Jamie are doin' it on your own terms. You wanna pay me back? Just keep stickin' to your own principles, know what I mean? Now let me get this little nuisance thing goin' and you can be on your way. You guys should come over for barbecue while the weather's still good."

"We'll do that. I'll call Sharon and work it out."

Just as Lou had said, in twenty minutes the car was good as new. Now—one more stop to make.

On the way home, she drove into a parking space at McDonald's, then unzipped her gym bag, the one genuinely nice thing she still owned, and pulled out Jamie's pale blue shirt, the one with the smudge on the left arm. She balled up the shirt and stuffed it into a white sack. It barely fit. Casually getting out of the car, she walked to the trash receptacle and dropped the whole bag into the garbage.

Now she and Jamie were in it together.

Kathy drove slowly into the small garage, nosing in all the way to the boxes in front so the door would close. It made her think of the spacious three-car garage her parents owned; bigger, probably, than Kathy's house.

Behind her, in the twilight, Jamie studied the glowing taillights. *Both* of them.

He had gone to the rec center, but no one had seen Kathy there. For good reason. She was getting the taillight repaired. Clever lady. Not one to make a scene. Always protecting him.

Suddenly the tail lights went off, and the driver's door opened.

"Nice evening," he said.

"Jamie! You scared me. Yes, quite nice. What're you doing out here?"

"Been out for a walk. Have a nice workout?"

"We all need a little body work now and then."

Jamie turned toward the front door with a slight smile.

"I know what you mean," he mumbled, knowing that Kathy and he were now in it together.

Whatever *it* was.

Inside, as they were getting ready for bed, he cheerfully announced that he was going deer hunting next weekend. Archery season was almost here, and he hadn't been in the woods for, what? Seven or eight years? His tackle was still neatly packed away. Time to break it out, take advantage of his time off. Cheap entertainment. Sit in a tree and wait for a big furry animal to walk by.

"The fresh air will be good for you," Kathy suggested.

CHAPTER 8

The three-hour drive to his favorite deer stand had made Jamie wonder why he had not gone up the night before. Here it was, four a.m. and still two hours to go. Up since 2:30. Tired and hungry. Was that any way to start a hunt?

He tore open a package of store-bought sweet rolls and wrenched off a doughy handful. Scalped. All the frosting was stuck to the cellophane wrap. Carefully, he chose a word from his hockey player's vocabulary.

"Shit!"

He nibbled at the roll. A snowstorm of crumbs fell to his lap. He stuffed the remainder of the roll into his mouth. His fingers were coated with *bakery slime*, as Jamie called it. He licked his fingers and remembered why he had chosen to drive up early in the morning.

Guilt.

Jamie felt guilty when he was away from home for pleasure. His marriage was straining at the seams, ready to burst open—he could see Kathy's raw nerves, exposed by her twitches, flinches, and evasive tactics—yet somehow he had decided that his presence was required to make the relationship work; that if he was serious about it, he'd be away from Kathy as little as possible. So here he was, up at four in the morning instead of asleep in some cozy little northern cabin near the stand, all because he wanted to show Kathy he wasn't so selfish. After all, he was sacrificing his sleep to spend a few extra hours at home with her, and at thirty-one, sleep was more precious to him than ever.

Odd, how his attempts to give a little extra effort never seemed to work out. But then, Kathy hadn't been herself since his drowning. She had grown edgy, tired, short-tempered. God, he wished he could understand what was going on. His death had screwed everything up, he thought. But he knew better, and he blamed himself for most of the problems. He probably had changed more than Kathy had—in other ways, of course.

The car's headlights painted strange patterns on the black terrain. Tall pines became palm trees, the hilly stretch of highway became dunes. Eerie. As if Jamie was in another place altogether.

Numbness set in between his eyes. Road fatigue. He opened the window a crack for fresh air. *I should have come up last night,* he thought. The handful of extra hours that he had contributed to his marriage had produced only a fight. Not the good old-fashioned yelling and screaming type, but the icy, Mexican-standoff kind. The *go ahead and talk but no one's listening* kind. "I don't even know you anymore," she had said. Or something like that. Out of an old movie, wasn't it? "What happened to the Jamie Giles I married?" That was another one. His life had become a cliché. He resented being so typical, so predictable.

The miles wore on, but eagerness for the hunt was bringing Jamie back to life. There was only one part of the hunt he didn't like. And now, as he parked the car on a gravel road, he was about to do the part he hated—a half-mile march into woods black as a tomb, unseen branches clawing at his eyes, night creatures rustling all around him. Spooky as hell. But dawn would be coming soon.

He travelled light. An old compound bow in a camouflage cover, a bow-mounted quiver with four arrows, a knife and assorted survival gear. That was it. He looked at himself in the rearview mirror. Every inch of his face was hidden behind spots and streaks of camouflage stick. His jacket and baggy pants were a leafy clutter of green and brown dyes arranged to make him look like a bush, a tree, a part of the landscape.

The pre-dawn chill had a bite to it and each exhalation forced a dragon-like plume of smoke from Jamie's nostrils. A monster was invading the woods. That's what Kathy would have said. She hated the idea of hunting as much as Jamie loved the practice of it. Christ, they didn't seem to have anything in common these days—an unfair judgment, Jamie admitted.

He unsleeved his bow in the harsh glare of the headlights.

Death is its own reality, Jamie thought. Having experienced it somehow had sapped his fear of it. Almost. Yet the mystery of it remained. Jamie had spent countless hours trying to pierce the veil through which he had caught a glimpse of the unseeable. He had travelled to man's ultimate destination, which was supposed to be a one-way trip. And he cursed himself for not remembering a bit of it. Jamie opened a bottle of foul-smelling deer scent, a milky secretion derived from the musk glands of deer. The label bore a caricature of a lovesick buck surrounded by hearts. The pathetic, cross-eyed creature was leaning nose-first into the scented breeze, so sure of the source, so compulsively attracted to it, yet so totally betrayed by it.

Nothing is as it seems, Jamie thought; but then he discarded the notion like a used Kleenex into the frosty air. Cops don't indulge in philosophy.

Jamie applied a few drops of the scent to his cap, his cuffs, his bow tips. At best it would lure a trophy buck; at worst it would merely mask his human-scent.

Looking like a bush, smelling like a doe, the hunter crashed into the thicket. There was time to make it to his favorite spot before dawn, time for the echoes of his loud march to die in the feeble memories of the deer, time to think. And think he did. About death, mostly. About a large, ripe buck, unsuspecting and fearless, ambushed by the cold sting of a broadhead; the look in the buck's eye at the moment of realization; the defiant hiss from its throat, words almost: *oh no, not now. Not yet.*

He thought about a cop cut down in the prime of life, lured into a watery grave by a group of dim-witted gangbangers; the jarring realization that he was going to drown; the words suspended unheard above the water: *oh no, not now. Not yet.* The long night held only the vaguest memory of dreams at the far corners, dreams that would always vanish under the searchlight of the conscious mind.

Jamie had bought books for the first time since college. *Experiencing Death* by Dr. Alice Mallach was the best. It was a collection of case histories similar to Jamie's. Over one hundred persons had revived from "clinical death" to remember the experience. Vivid passage down a dark tunnel. Out-of-body observations. An assembly of spiritual helpers. A "being of light."

The book had been both fascinating and frustrating for Jamie. Fascinating because it was a colorful guided tour of terrain he had passed through. Frustrating because he had suffered all the risks of passage with none of the rewards. He remembered nothing. "If you can imagine my sense of loss," he had told his physician after reading the book. "It's like being one of the few men ever to land on the moon... and then forgetting to set the alarm. I slept through the most incredible experience of my life."

More of the dark journey into the woods lay ahead. Jamie had been lost in thought and was now unsure how far he had come. Disorientation sent his adrenalin purring. *Panic.* But then, up ahead, he saw the familiar cut of a hill. To the left he heard the faint gurgle of a stream. A clearing, scraped out of the pine, stretched to the right. Yes, he had been here before. The pieces fit together in a way remembered by his instincts. A hundred yards or so and he'd be at the tree where he would set up his stand. Without even thinking about it, Jamie had walked the difficult route to ground zero of his boyhood hunts. Now it was time to settle in.

The morning fog nested like grouse in the hollows. Underfoot, a mitten-thick shag of pine needles hushed the scrape of heavy hunting boots. Tall jack pine from here to heaven stood straight as the teeth of a comb grooming the sky. An October chill rose up to press against Jamie's painted face.

———

Come to me, he thought. *Come to Jamie.*

It was his favorite time, that magic moment, neither night nor day. In the sullen gray stillness, he could hear... yes, he could just make out the thumping of its heart. Or was it his own?

Come to me, he thought.

A twig snapped. Yes, it was out there, a buck by the smell of him. Jamie's left hand gripped the handle of the bow. From behind a leather tab, three fingers of his right hand found the smooth plastic nock of the arrow. Instinct. A small tug at the string.

Keep coming, he thought.

Another step. He could feel the vibrations of it, barely perceptible, but...

There. Behind the fog, a shadow! The hiss of indrawn scent. The black pinpoint of nostril flaring. The twitch of an ear.

Stay as still as a statue, he told himself.

The creature stood. And stared.

With nerves crackling beneath his skin, Jamie turned to stone. The chill vanished, replaced by the flush of heat rising from his body. This was it. Bow versus super instinct.

A squirrel scampered down the side of a tree, scudded across the pine needles, and buzzed up another trunk like the tab of a zipper. Through the fog, Jamie could feel the buck watching.

A rabbit appeared from behind a hairline of bristling grass. It hopped casually toward Jamie, ears flopping, heart throbbing, until it passed nearly over his boot.

It's a damn Walt Disney movie, Jamie thought. Where are the blue-birds, with eyelashes, to tell Bambi there's a hunter in the woods?

Still the buck stared, so motionless itself that, for a moment, it seemed to vanish, to become just another illusion of foliage and shadow, gone as suddenly as a handful of fog.

A maddening, fiery itch began on Jamie's shin; he almost stooped to quench it with a hand before catching himself. With extraordinary resolve, he suffered without making a movement. How long could this stalemate go on?

At last, the buck stepped forward. The confrontation was now in-evitable. Each step improved the odds for the bow. Jamie watched. A magnificent sweep of antlers carved through the fog and made a Jacob's ladder of Jamie's spine. Never had he seen such a rack, so splendidly curved. Thick as a man's wrist at the base.

For a moment, the entire animal disappeared into a swirling cauldron of fog stirred up by the resurrected morning wind. Just as it seemed the fog had absorbed its victim, the ivory symmetry of antlers reappeared dimly, like an apparition, this time impossibly massive, each side the girth of a small tree.

Jamie tasted bitter venom in the back of his throat, the nauseous se-cretion of fear.

The shadowy bulk of the creature followed, its proportions mon-strously magnified, the sagging carcass hideously fat, vast ragged patch-es of hide flapping at its sides. Obscured still by the gauzy mist, the shape flickered like a flame, like a desert mirage, and then seemed to lift a head.

Jamie's heart convulsed, and the clenched fist in his chest drove the air from his lungs in a rasping hiss. The stinging itch on his leg became a white-hot iron that welded him to the ground, scaled as a flame the mar-row of his shin, extended a burning tongue along the arteries of his thigh and turned his bowels to smoldering coals. Looking down he saw that his ankle was a bloody stalk sprouting from the ferocious jaws of an animal trap. The hunter had become a wounded animal, staked pathetically to the ground, each painful movement robbing him of strength and will.

Even before Jamie looked up, he knew.

Even before the smoke was swept away, before the creature screeched in a demon's voice like a thousand dissonant trumpets, he knew.

In some impossible way, he *remembered* what was about to happen. From the smoking chimney of hell in front of him arose the gray hulk of a bull elephant. Two tons of wrath.

Like a swelling gland, fear displaced Jamie's throat and lungs. Each constricted breath seemed to engorge the bitter lump until finally it burst, spreading its paralyzing poison.

The creature turned, its attention drawn by the painful sputter of Jamie's breath. Suddenly its ears fanned out. Wings of terror. Flags of attack. With a terrible, murderous thunder it surged, ivory lances extended. Saplings snapped before it like blades of grass. The earth shook. Still it came, an avalanche of vengeance, collapsing the pocket of space between them into a shock wave.

Jamie stood there, rooted to the spot, trembling.

Still it came, its legs like pistons churning, pumping. Its head an impenetrable boulder of gristle and bone. With great effort Jamie raised the bow. He drew back the string. The arrow felt so slender, so impotent. His muscles quaked. The string slipped off his fingers. The shaft flew.

A prayer for a miracle.

Jamie grimaced, threw up his arms in a futile attempt to shield himself against the deadly collision. He shut his eyes. He heard the bone-crunching impact, the human scream as if from some other lips. He tasted the blood forced out of his mouth.

But he felt nothing.

Then it was gone. The sounds, the taste of his death—they were all gone. Had he died again, this time for good?

A sensation of falling.

Eyes still clenched shut.

Bones rattled as they struck the ground.

The smell of pine.

Afraid to open his eyes.

Afraid to risk finding death. But hadn't he overcome that fear? Hadn't he sought out the answers to that mystery? Here was his chance. Be brave, be bold. Don't look back at life, look ahead to... *what*?

You fool. You'll never know unless you *look*!

Open your eyes.

Open them!

A blur, then a coming together of images. Pine needles. Lots and lots of pine needles. Heaven—or hell—was a sea of pine needles.

No, this was all wrong. He lifted his head. He knelt. His left hand still clutched the bow.

His ankle.

There was no blood on his ankle, no trap. Rubbing it to make sure, Jamie began to admit that he was still alive. Unharmed. Miraculously unharmed.

What about the elephant? A knife-edge of fear sliced through him as he crouched, disoriented but steady. A gray hulk lay slumped on the ground twenty feet from him. Much smaller than he had expected. This was no elephant.

Jamie stood, staring ahead at the carcass. There, nearly at his feet, lay the corpse of a magnificent whitetail buck, the fletched end of an arrow protruding from a wine-dark stain on its forehead.

A perfect brain shot.

But Jamie had seen and heard an elephant. The trees had shaken with the impact of its stride. The thunder of its charge had been almost deafening. The trumpeting, the immense tusks, and the gray ears like funeral flags... they were all gone.

But it had been so real!

And now, after the shattering experience, a word lingered in Jamie's mind. A tiny word that meant nothing to him at all.

Abu.

CHAPTER 9

Kathy Giles soaked. This morning the tub was her confessional. Into the hot, slippery water she poured out the miseries her body had stored. Stress and tension spilled from her body. Warm fingers of water first cupped and then caressed her breasts as she lowered herself further. The water was like the warmth of a man, close and persistent, probing everywhere at once, begging her to yield, to lay there open and submissive.

Jamie had become a stranger. How had it happened? He was usually too tired at night for intimacy—*stress of the job*, he always said. But it started when he missed out on a promotion. His spirit seemed crushed after that. He was so proud of his job. Did he feel like a failure? Was he not bringing in enough money to meet his wife's or his mother-in-law's expectations? Failure could crush a man's libido.

A noise startled her. It sounded like the kitchen door.

Jamie? No, it was only the first morning of his hunt. He wouldn't have come back so early.

The water felt suddenly cold.

Another noise. Someone was in the kitchen.

Kathy shuddered as she stepped from the tub into a thick towel, cold and vulnerable. The large nap of the towel sipped the moisture from her body. She drew a blue terrycloth robe around herself.

Slowly she opened the bathroom door and entered the hall. From her position, she could see the spill of light from the kitchen.

Had she turned that light on?

Another sound. A chair scraping the floor. It sent Kathy's skin rippling like shingles in a wind.

It has to be Jamie, she told herself. Bravely, trying not to be foolish about it, Kathy walked toward the kitchen and stepped into the open doorway. Jamie was seated at the table, his back to her.

"Jamie?" she said, not so much a question of *who*, but of *why*.

Jamie turned slowly. He was seated directly beneath the overhead light, and the downward shadow made black caverns of his eyes. A streak of blood painted an extra eyebrow on his forehead. Kathy stared at him, forgetting if he had replied.

"Jamie, is something wrong?" she asked.

He reached out to her in a strange, childlike way, a boy begging for mother's comfort, both hands extended to show the magnitude of his need.

Kathy walked to him, powerless to resist, concerned for him in some oddly detached way as if he was the child she would never have.

He encircled her with his arms and crushed his face into her belly.

Kathy stroked his hair, a mother's caress. Whatever was wrong, Kathy felt needed. And it felt good.

Jamie began to sob, gently. He clutched Kathy so hard it hurt her, but she said nothing.

"It's all right," she said. "Whatever happened, it'll be all right." She was lying, of course, and she knew instinctively what had happened. Somehow, somewhere, Jamie had seen a glimpse of the madness. It had bubbled up to the surface and scared the hell out of him. No more *terrible nightmare, sorry if I kept you up*. The walls had tumbled down, and the demons were thumbing their noses.

Still, Kathy felt an odd calmness. It was no longer her problem alone. After so much silent suffering, she and Jamie could get help together.

Tomorrow would be the beginning of the healing process. Tonight she would comfort him, hold him...

For several minutes Jamie clung to her, then at last straightened up in his chair with his eyes closed and sucked in a stream of air through his teeth.

"You know, don't you?" A statement.

"Yes," she said.

"You saw it coming on."

"Since the drowning, yes."

"The nightmares were part of it... I'm going crazy."

"Jamie—"

"I'm scared. Kathy, I'm really scared. Today I was out of control, I mean I was *gone*." Jamie stood and strode to the cupboard. Inside he found a bottle of cheap scotch and poured a stiff one. "Cheers... and let's hope I get it down before a gorilla jumps out of the refrigerator."

His speech was gibberish to Kathy, but she sensed a connection to something that had just happened. "What is it, Jamie?" she asked.

He knocked back a slug of scotch and grimaced as the alcohol struck his chapped lips. "I died and my brain turned into tapioca pudding. The doctors can't turn pudding back to brain no matter what they say."

"They said your recovery was amazing," Kathy said.

"Sure," he said, "but did they give me a warranty on parts and labor?"

When he was troubled, Jamie predictably went through stages: silent moodiness, caustic sarcasm, and then, after a sigh and an apology, hopeless indifference.

"I was the one who came back to life," he said. "But the goddamn doctors take all the credit for it."

"Jamie... tell me what happened today."

A pause, then a sigh from Jamie. "I'm sorry. I was just scared, that's all. So who the hell cares? Don't worry about it, I'll be all right."

Kathy heard him enter the bathroom and pull the bathtub plug.

She remembered Jamie's soft, tender kiss before he had left for the woods that morning. Even then she had felt the overtones of fear inside him, but she had known by that kiss that he loved her. It had been both an expression of love and an apology for something he could have known only subconsciously.

It was what she needed. To be loved.

Kathy heard the shower go on. She walked toward the bathroom. Inside, Jamie seemed to be trying to wash away the shock of the day. He was standing there alone, beneath the shower head, probably scared stiff and feeling deserted.

She opened the door and saw Jamie behind the shower curtain. She quietly stepped into the small room, let her terrycloth robe fall to the floor, and slowly pulled open the curtain. She stepped into the shower and put her arms around him.

The water struck the inside of the curtain with the sound of a drum-roll as she said, "I want to keep you."

CHAPTER 10

In the quiet parenthesis of a Sunday morning, after an evening of rare intimacy, Jamie could feel Kathy retreating. If they were going to face this thing together, Jamie couldn't expect Kathy to do it all. He'd have to break some habits, too, maybe open up and talk.

He decided to meet the challenge head on.

"I'm still scared about what happened," he said. "I don't want to wind up in the nut house."

Kathy fleetingly looked away, then withdrew, creating a tiny vacuum between them.

He had been too blunt. The single thread binding them together was too fragile for any such stupid moves, so he added: "But I feel a lot better now that we can talk about it."

He *hoped* they could talk about it. Could they, really?

"Do you *want* to talk about it?" she asked.

Jamie had to think. It was a tough way to wake up. Like having cold pizza for breakfast. And the day seen through the bedroom window was so gray and depressing. Jamie wanted to go to the bathroom. To brush the morning scum off his teeth. To cure his hunger pangs with breakfast.

No, the groaning stomach was not hunger; he knew that. It was fear of confronting the issue. His stomach always waged chemical warfare against itself when he experienced dread, and right now he dreaded any dialogue about his madness. He wanted to get up and jog. Fix the gutter. Clean the basement. Do anything but talk about *it*.

Kathy understood the language of his stomach. He was betrayed by a bit of carbonation in the gut.

"I can't say I really *want* to talk about it," he said.

"But I think we should. God knows it's not too soon."

Jamie smiled warmly, at least tried to, and found it extremely difficult. His lips turned gently upward, but his frightened eyes betrayed the disguise. God, he was trying. His hand moved toward Kathy's thigh, fluttered tentatively above the smooth surface, and then landed. A diversion. Get her attention away from his transparent face.

It worked. She put her hand on his, stroked the broad back of it, looked at it. Jamie knew she was ready to talk.

He wasn't ready for it. What a fool, setting himself up like this!

"You never really told me what happened, you know," Kathy said.

In what seemed to Jamie a rare lucid moment, he spoke. He trampled across the topography of his hunting story, expressing his own incredulity with small gestures of hand and nods of head. For Jamie, reliving the experience revived a sense of terror that drenched his body with perspiration. The more he observed the episode from a distance, the more insane it appeared. Still, he played the faithful tour guide and walked his wife through the entire aberration.

Exhausted, Jamie finished the story. In retrospect, there had been elements of it that Jamie had not recognized at the time. Seen from a safe distance, these elements now seemed far too vivid to have escaped attention.

The heat. The steamy, insufferable heat that had sucked the sweat from his pores and broiled his skin to a bright, puffy pink.

The smells. The dissonant odors that strutted the empty spaces of the clearing to collide in a sweet and sour clash of rotting flesh and flowering trees, sweat and perfume.

And again, at the end, a tiny lingering word, meaningless and naked in his memory.

Abu.

Kathy lay there without moving. Not even blinking. Jamie was sure that the story had sapped her strength and resolve to go on.

No, this was only an illusion because she spoke. "Jamie," she said, "I have to tell you what I've seen."

Kathy, anxious to surrender her solitary burden, failed to detect Jamie's apprehension. She plunged into her eyewitness account.

"It started out as nightmares," she said. "Terrible nightmares that you could never remember, or said you couldn't."

Jamie remembered questions about bad dreams he honestly could not remember.

"The nightmares would grip you and shake you," she explained, "and I'd wake up trembling and afraid. I'd shake you, but you wouldn't come out of it… as if you were trapped inside the dream."

Jamie closed his eyes. That was how he had felt while standing in front of a charging bull elephant. Locked inside a nightmare.

"Sometimes I panicked because I couldn't wake you up," Kathy said. "Sometimes I thought you were dying. But each time eventually you calmed down by yourself. I never understood how you could sleep through something like that and remember nothing about it.

"At first I thought you were reliving the pain and fear of the accident. I grew less afraid and more sympathetic. Instead of trying to wake you up, I'd try to comfort you. Put my arms around you, trying to hold you together. My God, sometimes you'd quake as if your body was trying to shed its own flesh."

A searing pain shot sideways through Jamie's head. He remembered none of this, absolutely none. With the flat tips of his fingers, he rubbed his temples.

"I felt sorry for myself, too, but it was only the beginning," Kathy said. "The nightmares changed. You stopped shaking and started talking."

"Talking?" Jamie said, surprised at the sound of his own voice. "What did I say?"

"I don't know. It was all gibberish, all funny sounding words. Even your voice was different. I can remember going to Pentecostal meetings with my aunt as a little girl. On Sunday nights, the faithful would congregate to pray and receive the Holy Spirit. Some of them would speak in tongues, a sort of *gift* they called it, a flowing, babbling outburst of nonsense syllables that scared me half to death. The talk of maniacs.

"At first I thought that maybe you had received the gift, even though I didn't really believe in it anymore. But it was different with you. Sometimes you'd fly into a rage, screaming and waving your arms, speaking in such… such guttural bursts. At other times, you'd almost croon, with such soft sounds, almost like a new language. I started to worry that maybe I had a split personality on my hands. It was scary, Jamie."

Jamie couldn't think of anything to say. And hard as he tried, he could remember none of this. He spoke no language but English, and felt he didn't speak that very well.

"But things got even worse," Kathy said. Until now there had been little emotion in her voice, but a small tremor now clung to each word. "One night I woke up and you weren't there. The bed was empty, except for me. I looked around the room, and over there," she said, pointing, "on that chair by the closet, I saw a person sitting. I screamed. I thought it was an intruder, someone who had killed you and was waiting to get me. The person was sitting ramrod straight in the chair, feet together, eyes staring straight ahead at me. Jamie, I didn't know who it was. Then I saw he was naked, and I thought, oh my God! MY GOD!"

Tears spilled suddenly down Kathy's cheeks. She sniffed once, twice, then regained control of her trembling voice.

"The scream did nothing. The man didn't move, didn't flinch. All I could do was stare back. His expression was… intense, distorted. And then I saw him, Jamie. I don't know, my eyes adjusted or something, and it was like a puzzle coming together. I saw him, and *he was you!*"

The words stabbed.

"You were somebody else, but still he was you, don't you see?" Kathy said. "My God, I thought, he's moving around now, acting out his nightmares. We stared at each other for five minutes or so, and then you started pacing the floor, ranting and raving, having an argument with some imaginary person. But that speaking in tongues thing was gone... and you were speaking in *German.*"

"Are you sure? I don't speak German at all."

"I took a year in high school, but I couldn't really make out very much of what you were saying. But you were really angry about something. And you kept looking at the window, as if someone was there, and calling out to him. By name. You called him *von Gudden*, and were talking about a lake or something. Wish I had paid attention in German class."

"This makes no sense," Jamie said. "Gobbledygook one night, German another. *Crazy as a loon!*"

"No, no—don't you see, Jamie? The babbling made it seem like madness, but speaking in a foreign language that you don't know—I don't think we're dealing with madness here."

Jamie turned to her, confused.

"Think about it," she said. "Your sudden obsession with *Tannhauser*, a German opera, written by a German composer. And then suddenly speaking German to some doctor named von Gudden. It's like, like— you're living out someone else's life."

"But all that gibberish I was spouting..."

"I don't know, Jamie. But I think that somehow, some way, somebody has taken possession of you."

"You mean like a demon kind of thing?"

She hadn't really thought about demons before, but now she had. "My church—the one I used to go to—believed in demons. And that they could speak many languages. Even had a language of their own, so humans couldn't understand them. The Bible says Jesus cast out demons."

"This is not making me feel any better."

"If it's true, then you're not going mad, you're just maybe fighting off something that's trying to control you. If we could get rid of that thing, you'd be back to normal, wouldn't you?"

"You're talking about an *exorcism*?"

Kathy looked suddenly foiled. "Neither of us is Catholic."

"So can a demon make you do things you don't want to do, or don't remember doing?"

"I suppose so, if it takes you over."

"Then I could hurt someone. *You!*"

"Or maybe those gangbangers?"

Her words didn't feel like an accusation. More like a confession of knowledge.

Jamie opened a vacant, wordless mouth, but then closed it without speaking. What could he say?

"God knows they had it coming," she said, touching him. "It was wrong, but I know you don't even remember it. I got the taillight fixed, the one they shot out."

Since the day of the shooting, Jamie had guessed that he was the shooter, but refused to let the latent images in his mind come into focus.

Kathy's hand, so cool and calm, had a quieting effect. She spoke softly: "It's going to be all right, Jamie, we're dealing with it now. We're talking."

Jamie remained unconvinced. They were not dealing with it at all. Talk could not replace action. But Jamie did not have the slightest idea what action to take. And if he were truly going insane, or was possessed by a demon, how could he trust his own judgment?

"So just to talk this through, why would a demon be talking to a German doctor?" Jamie asked. "Why would it create hallucinations of elephants? Seems like we're grabbing at straws here."

Jamie suddenly hurled his pillow across the room and stood up, the sheets falling away to reveal the strong athletic lines of his back and legs. An idea has seized him. If he stayed in motion, he'd be safe. That was it. The madness, or the demon takeover, always struck when he was motionless. Asleep. Or on the deer stand. So long as he kept moving, he could foil the craziness that stalked him.

But what kind of notion was this? The fancy of a madman, that's what. Could he stay in motion twenty-four hours a day, in perpetual escape from an illness that already had taken root in his brain? It was like running away from himself. No, the answer was... it was in the accident... something to do with his death... There was an answer, yes. There had to be.

Jamie walked into the bathroom. His own face in the mirror startled him. Why was he suddenly such a stranger to himself?

Jamie thought about *Experiencing Death*, the book by Dr. Alice Mallach. In its pages, so many people had remembered so much about dying and returning. Could that be it? Could this madness be not madness at all, but Jamie's repressed death experience bubbling up at last through the fragile surface of his mind? If so, the effervescence could certainly disrupt the orderly flow of perception, creating a world broken by refracted images and the distorted fragments of subconscious memory.

A lot for a beat cop to consider.

But the possibility was refreshing: instead of an affliction, or a demon, his madness was a riddle to be solved. And the solving of it could become his salvation, his healing, the answer to his mystery. He had glimpsed images shot through a prism, refracted into parts. Now he must find the prism itself, for it was one step closer to the unresolved images.

Where to begin?

Obviously, with his dream about the pink hotel.

CHAPTER 11

There was no way it could have been anticipated. Four uneventful days had elapsed with no recurrence of the madness, no misconstrued actions on either side, no outside pressures or crises, not a single demon fighting for control. Life, through Thursday afternoon, had been beautifully banal. *Just like normal people,* Kathy kept telling herself.

But she could not have anticipated Thursday afternoon.

Jamie had gone to visit some friends and came home beaming. His face was a grinning lid that barely contained the good news behind it.

"Come here," he said. "I have something to show you." His exuberant tone infected Kathy with excitement. "Look at this."

He produced a red envelope with a flourish. In white letters it said GLOBAL TRAVEL.

Kathy took the envelope and peeled back the cover. Inside were two airline tickets.

"Nassau?" she said. "I don't understand."

"Read the names."

"Mr. and Mrs. J. Giles." She stared at the tickets for a moment and then looked up. "You're not serious."

Jamie's grin diminished slightly. "Of course I am. Look at the date."

"In three days?"

"Couldn't be clearer. How about that?"

"But Jamie... we can't.

"What do you mean, we can't. We are. A week in the Bahamas, just the two of us..."

"But we can't afford it. Just three days to plan..."

"Objections overruled. It couldn't possibly take three days to pack. And, as a point of fact, we can't afford not to get away. We owe this to ourselves."

"Jamie, that's... that's wonderful." Kathy threw her arms around him, squeezed the breath out of him and withdrew. "But the Bahamas... whatever possessed you?"

"I don't know. We've never been there for one thing. And it's pretty close—not that expensive, really."

"That's fantastic, Jamie!" Kathy sat down, nearly out of breath herself. "But the Bahamas? It's so sudden."

"Nonsense. No *buts*. We're going. And if you refuse, I'll go anyway and take Betty."

Kathy chuckled. Betty, the dispatcher at the police department, was sixty-two. "I wouldn't want that to happen. Poor Betty," she said. And so it was settled.

The next night was also uneventful, except that Kathy was too excited to sleep, and Jamie dozed off almost immediately. Even *eagerly*, as Kathy thought about it. As she lay there, she ran through the game plan of Jamie's behavior. He had been so good-natured. So optimistic and buoyant. It was a change of pattern that seemed almost artificial. Forced.

It was possible, she supposed, that he was trying to prove that his problems were behind them. Overcompensating, maybe. It was also possible that he was trying to cover up something that was still going on. That could account for the pendulum swing of his behavior.

Why was she so paranoid, always looking for the dry rot beneath the surface? The least she could do was to try as hard as Jamie to keep things on a positive note.

No, there was something that rang false. Her soundings had produced an echo that shouldn't be there, a blip that was out of place. Jamie was holding something back, something so big it required a monumental diversion. Such as the Bahamas. The element of surprise. A deft sleight-of-hand maneuver.

But a diversion for what purpose?

Kathy's excitement waned. She began seeing the trip as an elaborate ruse with her as the brunt of a very bad joke. Of course, she could be dead wrong. But she knew in her bones that she was right.

———

That evening, after tossing and turning for a half hour, sleep finally overtook Kathy. If she had stayed awake another fifteen minutes, she might have noticed Jamie's eyes beginning to move beneath their lids, and a sudden but subtle increase in his muscular activity.

A dream was brushing his consciousness, testing for sleep—the same dream that had insinuated itself into his brain the past few nights. The dream settled in, as it usually did, like a fog that would thicken to become a screen for the projection of the mind. A breeze, moist from the sea and gentle as a lover's promise, stroked his face. Behind him was the pink facade of a hotel, radiant in the long golden reach of a dying sun. He could see his own footprints in the white sand, the same cool white beach that sloped beneath him to the water.

Before him was a perfect sea with pockets of midnight blue and soft turquoise and peaks of burnished gold. A thousand sunsets skipped across its surface to dance as reflections on his white robe. Beyond this sea was another shore and a building that pulsed with lights and life.

In a pocket he could feel a thin rectangle of plastic, and he knew what it was. The security card to his room. This recognition caused an image of his hotel door to skitter through his mind, and on that door the number 534. As Jamie stared at these numerals he could see the interior of the room. It was a large suite with a sitting room, bath, bar, and bedroom. In the sitting room was a large overstuffed sofa. No—it was a camel-back daybed plumped with pillows. The fabric was deep cobalt blue with immense white flowers and ferns detailed in beige and grey.

In his dream, Jamie felt intense drowsiness. Without remembering how he had appeared so suddenly in his suite, he walked into a spacious bathroom and filled the spa with steaming water. He stepped into it, releasing his fatigue into the bubbling liquid. *So comfortable.* He could stay here forever. But just as this dream within a dream began to cloud him, he heard a doorknob turn. The door opened.

Jamie woke up, disoriented as always. His first impulse was to look at the door. Probably housekeeping. They always walked in on you. But here he was at home, at night, lying in his own bed next to Kathy.

It hadn't worked. Three of the last four nights he had lived through the same dream. This night he had intended to *will* himself to stay asleep until the door had opened so he could see who was there.

As if he didn't have enough unresolved mysteries in his life right now. The door seemed to hold an important piece of a puzzle. Whoever was at the door would be able to tell him… tell him *what*?

Even though he had failed to stay asleep and identify the visitor, the dream journey refreshed him and reconfirmed his desire to visit the island. The dream had taken place in Nassau. He knew that, just as he knew the pink hotel was the British Colonial Hilton, and the other building was the casino. He had no reason to know these things, but he did. What would he find there? Would it be like his dream? This recurring vision was too much like an invitation to refuse. It held out the promise of tranquility and peace.

If it lived up to his dreams.

Still awake, Jamie again pondered his reasons for the trip. What was he hoping to find? As he searched through the alternatives he found one that fit. If the Bahamas were exactly like his dream, he would know that he was not mad. The dream, then, would have to be some sort of psychic phenomenon. And that would mean the episode with the elephant probably had not been madness but something of greater significance.

God, how he wanted his dream to come true. Since Saturday he had been scared stiff of going mad, of another terror-filled episode. He had tried so damn hard to be brave and normal for Kathy. Had he overdone it? No, he thought not.

It was not like him to lie, especially to Kathy. Yet this time it had come easily. It was so important to reach the Bahamas.

Wide awake, Jamie found himself growing afraid. What if Nassau was *not* like his dream? What if the suite didn't exist? What if the dream proved to be pure fantasy… or madness? What then?

Still, he had no choice. Clearly the dream was calling him to Nassau, to the pink hotel, to suite 534. It promised answers. Peace. He had to take the risk.

CHAPTER 12

The Wisconsin senator was a stout, gray-faced man. Sixty-three years of living—most of it lubricated with gin—had ruined his body the way his state's winters erode streets. As his political career had soared, the senator's choices of gins had improved. So had his frequency of choice. "Alcohol," he was fond of saying, "is the KY jelly of social intercourse." True for many, perhaps, but not for Senator George Harth. For years, alcohol had diminished all manner of intercourse for him.

The stoutness had come from eating more calories than he had expended in hoisting martini glasses, his primary source of exercise. The yellow-grayness had come from the slow poisoning that had reduced his gut to mush. The medical diagnosis had been more precise. Harth had sabotaged his body's most remarkable chemical treatment plant: his liver. In truth, he was far less stout than even a year ago when he would so proudly pat his belly and calculate the number of steaks and lobsters he had devoured to create it.

For Harth, cirrhosis was a death sentence. His body was no longer able to keep its chemistry set in balance. Harth's physician had summed it up. "You know your body is federal property. If the EPA knew what your liver was doing to it, they'd shut it down." Harth had laughed—he was still a politician—yet he knew that the final outcome could only be delayed, not prevented.

As he sat in his office, he wondered if that large faceless mass called the American people would mourn his passing. Would they remember his accomplishments? God, how he had fought for civil rights. His legislation had never passed, his name would never be attached to any of the bills—yet his proposals had served as inspiration and as models for later successful attempts.

All his life, Harth had felt sure that he was ahead of his time. Now he felt behind it. His wife had died two years earlier in an automobile accident. He had no children, and only a scattering of cousins he barely knew and never talked to unless they needed a political favor.

Certainly he had done more good than harm in his years of public service. And if he had sometimes used his political clout for small personal gain—well, who didn't these days? Most of his colleagues looked on such opportunities as mere business perks, informal fringe benefits that helped attract men of their caliber to such relatively low-paying posts. Some politicians, of course, profited more than others. Harth was among that group. Others were stupid or careless; they got caught. Or worse, they were chosen to be the sacrificial lambs of the year. No one cared if you were corrupt, so long as you were corrupt by the rules. Don't let your scam get in the way of CIA corruption. Don't meddle in areas that are politically sensitive or trendy because they're guarded by public watchdogs. Don't make enemies of the wrong people because they'll crucify you even if you're Jesus Christ. Don't commit an act of treason because then no one can help you and everyone will try to bury you.

The American flag stood proudly in its scuffed base behind the senator's desk. He turned to look out the window beside it but found himself staring at the faded red stripes, the small woven patch on the field of blue with its corner jutting into a star the senator felt certain represented his home state, Wisconsin. On the gold fringe was a new visitor, a greenish patch of mildew flourishing among the unkempt strands. The whole goddamn world was falling apart.

Harth never doubted that within the labyrinthine bowels of his country's constipated intelligence system lay enough shit about himself to make the public clamor for a hanging. But he had always felt safe, knowing that it would never be dumped in the public's lap without the laxative of self-incrimination and the dismantling of the rules of corruption. Besides, most of the evidence against him undoubtedly had been gotten illegally. With the current climate of animosity toward intelligence operations and invasion of privacy, the system would be very happy, thank you, to keep its compost heap out of sight.

Occasionally, such information was put to use, mostly as leverage to help align political support. In this way, the intelligence system (such a misnomer!) claimed its right to lobby on its own behalf. But even this inevitable practice had been sharply curtailed in recent years because the watchdogs had sniffed it out.

Senator Harth had prospered financially these many years while he enjoyed a positive, if not heroic, public image. Now, left with only his estate, his good name, and at best a few years of life, he had come to cherish his image above all. Desperately, he wanted to be remembered as one of the good guys.

This is why the senator was baffled and shaken by the contents of a gift-wrapped box that had appeared mysteriously on his desk three days ago. In it he had found a flowing and flawless chronicle of personal corruption supported by physical evidence the courts might suppress as inadmissible, but which the news media surely would turn into headlines. Here was a profile of the worst kind of politician—an annotated, catalogued death certificate of Harth's good name—complete, for God's sake, with a bibliography! There was more of this rotten stuff someplace else.

It made for sensational reading. Harth's "encouragement" of organized crime in the Wisconsin cheese industry (see photos, copies of memos, check receipts, etc.). His accepted bribes (Jesus, two of them had been FBI setups never made public). His minor role in suppressing evidence in two federal investigations. His influence-for-hire record on immigration matters. His conflict-of-interest investments traced through four fronts. His sexual liaisons with numerous big-busted hookers and an occasional Adonis. His misappropriation of campaign funds over twenty years ago (even Harth had forgotten that one).

Recorded phone taps, calendars, financial analyses of his personal records, intimate photographs, testimony of informants… they all combined to paint a vivid, lurid portrait of graft and depravity.

It hadn't been that bad at all, he thought. This is all petty stuff over thirty years' time. It never hurt a soul.

But there it was. Even Harth was shocked by the impact of the accumulated presentation. He confessed to himself that if he had known who this culprit was, he'd have wanted to hang the bastard.

At some point over the past three days, suicide had occurred to Harth, but the cover letter (is that a *formal cover letter*, for Chrissake?) threatened leakage of the information if Harth died before paying. But get this, Senator: you can have this complete report and more in the privacy of your own home for just $1,000,000, paid in five easy installments.

The price of a good name these days.

Small patches of purple hatched on the senator's moist forehead and neck. Against the shell of his body pounded the crashing surf of high blood pressure. He plunged one trembling hand into a shallow drawer and fished out a prescription of pills that would help abate the tide. Two tiny red eyes stared back at him from his open palm, unblinking. He swallowed them.

The manuscript had produced a humid heat that soaked Harth in the juices of his guilt. He dabbed at his forehead with a sweat-stained handkerchief, but still his face bled perspiration. His collar was wet nearly to the knot of his loosened tie.

For the seventh time, Senator Harth peeled back the cover of an airline folder enclosed in the package. He stared at the computer-printed abbreviations that appeared on the ticket. It was a language he read fluently. In his hand was first-class passage to Nassau, Bahamas, ETA 12:30 p.m. Sunday. According to a slip of paper stapled to the ticket, lodging had been arranged in his name at the British Colonial Hilton, Suite 534.

With a touch of sarcasm, the typed message added this postscript: "All transportation and accommodations are provided at no cost to you by your hosts."

At no cost to you!

Only $200,000 this time, and another $200,000 next time. How generous of his "hosts" to cover these expenses in exchange for his cooperation. Except for the damning manuscript itself, the package may have come from a real estate developer soliciting qualified investors by offering free inspection tours.

The stylish package was not the work of the CIA or the FBI or any other cul-de-sac within the government. That much was certain. Extortion was commonly practiced by official agencies, but usually for favors, not cash. Another Justice Department sting? Preposterous. There was no crime in buying information, only in selling it. And compared to the file already compiled, one more indiscretion would be like pissing into the Pacific.

The puzzle, then, was all the more perplexing. Some of the information clearly was from official files—the accounts of two aborted FBI bribery scams from which Harth had profited illegally; the recorded phone taps, each indexed by FBI file numbers; and the photographs bearing grease-pencil legends characteristic of bureaucrats and civil servants, not extortionists.

So who had sent the package?

Harth already had telephoned the Nassau hotel to discover who was paying the bill. Nobody knew. A pre-paid cash account gave the hotel all the guarantees it required. Suite 534 was reserved year-round on such a basis. It was not always occupied, but perpetually reserved. Would the senator be requiring any extra services during his stay? These, too, would be debited from the rotating cash account according to instructions. An odd way for a hotel to do business? Well, the hospitality business had to be flexible now, didn't it? The hotel staff was looking forward to serving its distinguished guest and hoped his stay would be enjoyable.

The senator pulled a silk-lined briefcase of rare gazelle hide across the polished surface of his desk. The leather case had been a gift from a grateful constituent (the specific favor had been forgotten by Harth). The precision-made brass latches opened noiselessly and Harth raised the cover. Inside, beneath a thin layer of official papers, he had placed forty individually wrapped bundles of cash, each containing fifty one-hundred dollar bills.

Two hundred thousand in cash had been relatively easy to get this time. Another two hundred would have been difficult within the allowed timeframe. Not surprisingly, the extortionists seemed to know this. For the fifth payment, Harth would have to liquidate some very non-liquid investments, and that would take time. He was sure he'd be given all the time he needed… and no more.

By the senator's own mental calculation, the million dollars that his "hosts" were sucking out of his estate would milk him to the very brink of a substantial lifestyle change. Apparently, the extortionists had wanted to prevent the arousal of suspicion that would surround a sudden change in the senator's fortune. Was there also the hint of "grace" in the amount demanded, a small inclination to not make Harth too uncomfortable, a flourish of benevolence to match the crisp style of the extortion package? More likely it was a psychological setup. The first payments would be comparatively easy to make, but then…

Until now, Harth had fooled himself into thinking that he might courageously decide to withhold payment. At this moment, though, he realized that there was no decision to make. He could only hope to die before they bled him dry. For the first time, his poisoned body was an asset. In any event, he would not last much longer. His suffering would be short.

With a slight upturn at the corners of his wide mouth, the senator smiled for the first time in days. The message stapled to his ticket held the makings of a joke. Until now, he had seen its unintentional wordplay as the corollary of truth. Surely he, Senator Harth, was the "host," and they were the "parasites."

But now he began to see how his unknown adversaries indeed could become host to a very good joke on themselves.

CHAPTER 13

From the air, it seemed hardly worth all the fuss, this tiny island pasted onto the enormous sheet of turquoise and blue, but it coaxed a smile from Kathy, who sat nearest the window. Jamie craned to see the view. The plastic pane of the window reflected Kathy's face, which floated like a veil between the island and Jamie, superimposing her features on the terrain below. For an instant, Jamie focused his eyes on this likeness of Kathy. In the same instant, she glanced up at the fainter reflection of Jamie and then quickly away. It could have been his imagination, but during the split second their eyes had met, the smile seemed to have disappeared from his wife's face.

Windsor Field Airport was not worth a snapshot, but the taxi driver was. Jamie had caught the driver bargaining with others in the queue for the next pick-up. He was an imposing figure in a steel-gray shirt with a silvery head of coiled hair. His skin, dark as an oil slick, made his white eyes stand out like flashlights. His eyes were aimed for a moment at Jamie, who felt tense beneath their gaze. But then a brilliant, ingratiating smile broke through the cabbie's dark face. *Like the sun coming out from behind a storm cloud,* Jamie thought.

"Welcome to the island of New Providence," he said with a gentle British accent. "My name is Billy Smythe, and my automobile is at your disposal."

The automobile in question was a 1994 black Cadillac limousine with scuffs and scrapes so numerous they looked like decorations on the breast of a five-star general. Still, Smythe seemed to be the luck of the draw. In line behind him were another four cabbies.

"I'm Jamie Giles, and this is my wife, Kathy. Do you know where the British Colonial Hilton is?" The moment Jamie asked, he knew how stupid it sounded.

Smythe laughed. The laughter tumbled out of his mouth in a long, bubbling string, spilling a deep and resonant contagion that caught Jamie and Kathy in its splash. Together they laughed.

"Oh yes," Smythe said at last, "I do believe I can find it for you. I have practiced the journey several thousand times just to be ready for this occasion."

Jamie laughed first this time. But as Smythe loaded the luggage into the trunk, Jamie felt a cold burst of recognition that evaporated so quickly it could not be captured. Instead, he was left disoriented and confused. He had to look around him, at the passenger terminal, at Kathy, at the Cadillac, just to settle his body in space and time. He found himself gripping the limo's open door so tightly his fingers were paralyzed when he let go.

No one had noticed. Maybe it had been a bit of delayed airsickness.

Smythe folded his six-foot-four frame behind the steering wheel and shot a glance into the rearview mirror. For a particle of time, Smythe's eyes were framed in the rectangle, peering into Jamie's eyes as if they were portals to his soul.

"You look pale, Jamie," Kathy said as the limo lurched into motion. "The sun down here should help, but try not to get burned like that time in San Diego, okay?"

"I'll try." Jamie hadn't come for the sun.

The Cadillac bumped along the road. Its front shocks were the vestigial remains of once-functioning original equipment.

"Would you people be liking to see some of the island before the hotel? Very cheap, indeed," Smythe said.

Kathy turned to Jamie with the anticipation of a child in a toy shop. It was good to see her smiling and excited. Until nearing the island, Kathy had seemed resigned to going, as if it were another boring field trip for a dull college class.

"It will help get you oriented. Won't take long," Smythe urged.

"Okay, why not?" Jamie agreed.

They circled the island. Seen from the car window, blue sky simply melted into the turquoise sea. Striated clouds like pulled cotton were mirrored below by gentle white rollers. Everywhere, flowers luminous in the sun burst in bold splashes against exotic green textures. Smythe gave each tree, each blossom a name. Kathy was entranced, but to Jamie it was clear that this was no simple sightseeing tour on the way to the hotel. He wished he had agreed on a price in advance. Nervously, he started whistling the theme from Tannhauser.

Immediately, Smythe adjusted his head to view Jamie in the rearview mirror. "Wagner's Tannhauser!" he said.

Jamie hadn't even been aware that he was whistling. "You know it?" he asked, startled.

"One of my favorites."

Kathy rolled her eyes. "Wonderful! Two Wagner buffs in the car."

Smythe stopped the limousine without another word and climbed out. He walked to a drooping branch alongside the road and tore off several leaves, then tucked himself back behind the wheel.

"Here," he said, handing a leaf to each of them. "Crack the leaf like this—" He ripped a leaf in half and raised one ragged, scented edge to his nostrils. "Can you tell what it is?"

Jamie pulled apart his leaf and sniffed it. "It's familiar, but I don't—"

"Allspice," Kathy said. She was waving the remnant of a leaf beneath her nose. "It smells like allspice."

Smythe laughed again, then started the car with a jerk. Without looking back, he spoke to Jamie. "Keep her, my friend. She has a very intelligent nose. But I suspect that somewhere in your memory was the same answer. Ah, well. Perhaps you merely need to *exercise* your memory. Or perhaps you were just trying too hard. Allspice is very common to the island, madam, but not everyone knows it derives from a single plant."

Smythe was now addressing Kathy, but his remarks to Jamie had been so strange, so out of the flow, as if he had been talking about something else entirely.

A fireball of nausea struck the pit of Jamie's stomach. He had grown very nervous about something. Sick to his stomach nervous. He had always felt this way before a test at school. Before a physical exam. Nervous about the results… and what he'd learn about himself.

But why *now*?

The car bounced on. Conversation between Smythe and Kathy was flourishing like the Bahamian flora, watered by the cabbie's liquid laughter and pruned by Kathy's sharp questions.

Jamie wished they would get to the hotel. Why had he agreed to this tour? He was tired and dirty from the trip, worried about the reservations, anxious to unpack and take a shower.

Suddenly, the limo swerved left into a private drive guarded by two tall stone columns linked together by a wrought iron arch.

"One more stop, if you don't mind. No extra charge." Smythe chuckled. "This is private land we are on now—no one is admitted—but I have permission to come in here. I once worked for the previous owner."

The limo groaned up the steep, tortuous driveway carved through a wonderland of foliage, flowers, and twisted trees. Sunlight stabbed through the small open spaces, slashing the road ahead.

"This is a garden, actually," Smythe said, "and in it you can find every kind of vegetation that lives on the island. Every kind of bird and animal, too. It's my favorite place. I can't imagine a more picturesque scene anywhere in the world."

The crescents of Kathy's eyes became full moons.

Slowly the limo purred through this shimmering, lush fantasy world.

"It's so beautiful!" Kathy crooned. "Why is no one allowed in to see it?"

"The present owner is a very private man. But don't worry, I know him, too. He allows me an occasional tour of his paradise because of past favors."

At last the road slanted up to a house, and Smythe continued past its densely foliated side to park the limo in front. The four-story house looked out on the blue-green sea. Both Jamie and Kathy gasped at the palatial splendor of this unexpected treasure.

It was a castle in miniature. On either end there was a small tower, and emerging from the center was a broader rise that capped a large stone-arched entryway. Two stairways, like the sides of a pyramid, converged in a landing above the stone arch, and on this level a row of vertical windows stretched across the facade. The entire structure was plastered over with yellow stucco and roofed with red tiles.

Jamie had seen this castle before—but where? A magazine, perhaps. Or a film. Surely a number of movies had been shot on the island. Maybe this house had been a location in an old James Bond film, or some other popular movie.

The limo stopped. Jamie and Kathy stepped out as Smythe went for a stroll.

The almost reachable chink of memory haunted Jamie. He squinted noticeably, then opened his mouth in frustration.

Misinterpreting his expression as a look of awe, Kathy said to him, "Really something, huh? Can you imagine living in this place?"

Jamie could, almost. The castle was mesmerizing him. He could almost "see" the interior. He could imagine walking barefoot on floors of marble and mahogany. Listening to the faint gurgle of a stream beneath the first floor. Luxuriating in the sculptures and tapestries, the paintings and European furnishings.

"Over here!" Smythe was calling to them from the far end of the castle and waving a command to follow. "Come and see!" His enthusiasm was compelling.

Kathy took Jamie's hand and dragged him like a loaded wagon to the corner of the building.

Jamie's legs were heavy and numb. Unresponsive. As he and Kathy rounded the corner, another breathtaking spectacle greeted them, this one a glittering terraced garden with winding trails and slab steps, exquisite marble statues, manicured flower beds and sculpted box bushes. A long, cold row of ancient, skirted servants were frozen in relief on a retaining wall while marching up the stone staircase that descended to the garden, one servant per stair, each bearing a gift for someone at the top.

Jamie looked down the staircase.

His head buzzed and throbbed, but he felt an invisible thread pulling him toward the garden. Down he walked, step after step, past the gifts of the servants, around a corner, down a walkway…

There! The statue of a naked woman stood before an ivy-covered wall.

Jamie's breath caught in his chest. "Venus!" he exclaimed. "From Tannhauser." He fought for more breath, felt dizzy but exhilarated at the same time. "Honey, you remember when Tannhauser was on the Venusburg and…"

Kathy had no idea what he was talking about. "Yeah, remember it like my own name."

"And there's a statue here, somewhere, of… of…"

As if remembering something important, Jamie dashed behind the ivy-covered wall.

Kathy followed, bewildered. On the other side of the wall, Jamie was standing before another magnificent statue. This one depicting a man.

A buzzing in Jamie's head blocked out the sound of Kathy speaking to him. The throbbing became a band that encircled his head and squeezed relentlessly. Colored lights fired behind his eyes and he could almost feel the multi-colored rays projecting outward from his pupils. His feet lost all sensation of contact with the ground, as if he were floating, flying, soaring…

"Jamie!" Kathy screamed as he slumped silently to the fitted-stone walkway. Smythe leaped like a cheetah to Jamie's body.

"He's fainted," Smythe said. "Follow me."

The tall cabbie lifted Jamie's 175-pound body and carried him, limp and lifeless, to a water faucet beneath the staircase. He uncoupled a garden hose, turned the valve handle and scooped a handful of cold water onto Jamie's face.

"Is he going to be all right?" Kathy asked.

Smythe's broad silhouette eclipsed the sun. "I think he'll be answering that."

As Jamie opened his eyes he first saw a dark smear across the blue sky. He uttered a single word. "Tannhauser!" Gradually, the smear became Billy Smythe's face. The cabbie's large round eyes had become ovals of concern.

"The statue," Smythe explained to Kathy, "was Tannhauser. Apparently Jamie didn't like it."

Jamie gasped as he stared into Billy's broad face. His body retracted like a turtle's head, pressing itself into the foundation of the castle. Another spray of water brought a deep cough. Jamie shook his head. With open palms, he wiped the water from his eyes and pushed his hair back.

"What happened?" Jamie asked.

"Are you all right? You fainted." Kathy was cradling him.

"Fainted?" Jamie straightened his back against the foundation. "That's not like me."

"Sometimes the travel and the heat—" Smythe offered.

"I think we should go to the hotel now," Kathy said.

Jamie nodded agreement. "How about a hand up?"

Smythe pulled Jamie to his feet.

Kathy studied her husband. "Are you sure you can walk?" she asked.

"Honest, I'm fine."

They started for the limousine. As Jamie passed the carving of the beast and the crowned warrior, he gave it only a sideways glance.

No, those figures couldn't have had anything to do with his collapse.

"I'm sorry about your clothes. I feel responsible," Smythe said as he drove to the hotel.

"Don't be silly. *I* fainted—you didn't."

Jamie's cobalt-blue shirt was still wet from Smythe's vivifying splashes of water. His white slacks were streaked with soil. He removed a white scarf he'd worn around his neck and undid another button on his shirt, baring his chest. The breeze from the open window was cool and refreshing.

Within minutes they were at the hotel. Jamie had seen too many travel pictures of it to separate dream from reality anymore. It looked just as he thought it would.

As the doorman moved Jamie's luggage to the hotel lobby, Smythe glanced across the top of the Cadillac at Jamie and spoke. "I wouldn't think of charging you, not after that dreadful experience back there."

Jamie walked around the limousine to Smythe. "Nonsense," he said, "You were a terrific tour guide. I'm just sorry I scared you." He didn't know how much the tour was worth, so he tentatively handed Smythe two twenties.

Smythe took the money. "I was honored to have you accompany me this afternoon. Perhaps I can make it up to you."

"There's nothing to make up. But I have a feeling we'll see you again."

"I have that feeling too. Good day to you, Jamie Giles."

"Goodbye, Billy Smythe."

CHAPTER 14

The registration clerk was respectful but disorganized under the on-slaught of tourists checking in. The room he had tried to reserve—Suite 534, the mysterious number from his nightmare—was still un-available, the clerk explained. But a suite across the hall from it had opened up.

The bellman chatted amiably—and relentlessly—all the way to Suite 535. Jamie didn't hear a word the bellman said. Neither did he feel the crawling anticipation he would have experienced if the bellman just now had unlocked Suite 534. And so suspense was replaced by shock as Jamie entered the replacement suite.

It nearly knocked him off his feet.

The layout of the sitting room and bar was a perfect mirror image of the suite in Jamie's dream. The decor and furnishings were different, but the layout—

Jamie rushed into the bathroom. Again, a perfect reverse. Into the bedroom. Yes, it was just as his vision had revealed, but turned around.

The bellman cautiously watched Jamie's antics, then charitably asked, "Is there anything I can do for you, sir?"

Kathy sat down on the sofa, mildly confused by Jamie's frantic pac-ing about.

"Yes," Jamie replied. "The suite across the hall... number 534. Is it just like this one?"

"Oh, yes. Just like it, But the color is not the same, and the furniture—"

"No, I mean the physical layout. Is it *just* like this?"

"Yes, I think so."

"Are you *certain*? Could it be just like this, but reversed? Like you see in a mirror?"

"Well, I—"

"You know, the bathroom on that side, and the bedroom over there." He pointed dramatically.

"I see what you mean. That suite is exactly like this one but the opposite."

Kathy couldn't contain herself. "What the hell is going on here?" she asked quietly. "Why don't you just tip the bellman and let him go back to work? You sound like you're casing the joint."

Kathy's presence startled Jamie.

How could he have forgotten she was here? Now he would have to explain.

He quickly offered a tip—a ten was the smallest he had, but no matter—and accepted the security card from the bellman, who left immediately.

The card! Just as he had envisioned.

His dream had come true.

No, no... it had been true all along, but the mechanics of it, the purpose behind it, the meaning of it still remained undiscovered.

Perhaps part of the answer lay behind the door of Suite 534.

Kathy cleared her throat. She was waiting for a logical explanation for Jamie's behavior.

The best Jamie could offer was an explanation. There was no logic.

"Kathy," he said, "until now I thought I was going crazy. Literally. And I know that you'd commit me on the spot right now if we were near an institution. But this room… this *suite*… has proven that I'm not mad after all. I'm going to order up some champagne and then I'll explain the whole thing to you. As much as I know, anyway."

————

While Jamie ordered champagne, Billy Smythe gulped a double rum on the hotel patio overlooking the harbor and, across the water, the casino. He seldom wasted his money on overpriced hotel drinks, but the day's events had overtaxed his impersonation of calmness. Cubes of ice sang in his nervous glass.

Only moments ago, Smythe had peppered Louise with questions. Louise, the afternoon registration clerk, was a distant cousin by marriage. In one sense, she owed her job to Smythe. He had arranged her interview. That had been three—no, four years ago. Hotel management had treated Smythe respectfully in those days. But all that had changed after their boss's sudden death. And Smythe was now driving a cab.

During the dull interludes of encapsulation in his black limo, Smythe had indulged himself with fantasies of such a day as this. Was it possible it would ever come? If so, how would it happen? How would Smythe *know* it was happening?

During his first days of driving the limo, Smythe had invented many scenarios for today's possibility. All of them ultimately had led to the same violent and temporary solution. But none of his fanciful creations had anticipated it happening this way, which seemed so impossible!

He must be certain, *absolutely certain,* that the day's events were connected to that hateful promise. He must question even the most obvious evidence and constantly remind himself that his conclusions were based only on a circumstantial case. His responsibility was immense.

How could it have happened like this? At this time?

Smythe had watched Jamie and Kathy disappear behind the elevator door. Then he had marched purposefully up to Louise, wearing the best look of consternation he could muster.

"Louise," he had said, "there was a man in here just now with a blue shirt. A Mr. Jamie Giles."

"He just checked in. What are you doing here, Billy?"

"Well, I need to see Mr. Giles. Could you tell me what room he's in?"

"You know we're not allowed to do that, cousin or not."

"Louise, the man left some money in my cab. I'm not about to leave it in his message box, not with all the thieves that work here now. Present company excluded." Smythe had smiled coyly.

"I suppose you're looking for a reward."

"At least I'm honest. I could have kept the whole sum. Now can't you give such an honest man the room number?"

"You're impossible, Billy. I don't know what you're up to, but I guess I can trust you."

"The only compliment I've had all day."

"Suite 535," she had remembered.

"Are you sure, girl? A suite? You didn't look it up."

"The man was a bit daft, if you ask me. He got the suite for a discount but complained like a son of a bitch."

"About what, girl?"

"He wanted the suite across the hall. Suite 534."

Smythe had been certain that Louise could see the color draining from his dark face.

Now, on the patio, he was convincing himself with rum that the evidence was indeed circumstantial. More proof was needed. But the only proof at hand was 160, and it burned his throat as it went down.

Anxiety smoldered within him. Fueled by the rum and fanned by the ghostly wings of imagination, it burst into a blistering, suffocating blaze of fear that illuminated a dark corner of possibility. If he had recognized Jamie Giles, then Jamie would soon recognize him. And when that event took place—when Jamie stepped through that thin membrane of understanding—it would be too late.

There was a single element that prevented Smythe from madly plunging ahead with his plan: he lacked any plausible explanation for the mechanics of this phenomenon. By his own calculations, this should not be happening for at least another ten years, probably twenty, and possibly not until many years after Smythe's death. It should not—could not—be a man of Jamie's age in this year. Logic laughed at the notion that Jamie was the man, but the evidence was sober and insistent. Reason argued convincingly for the logistical impossibility of this preposterous theorem, and the innocence of the American, yet Smythe's intuition was compelling.

The question was, if Smythe pursued his instinct, might he be killing a man because a bit of provocative secretion was spit into his buzzing bloodstream by an overzealous adrenal gland?

Another fireball of rum was snapped into his surprised mouth, passing his throat without as much as a hello. Steam vented as a hot breath from his lips. His eyes, once fat white dots bolted into place by rivet heads of gunmetal grey, had become humid yellow slits skimmed with a dull rum glaze.

A minute ago—*was it just a minute?*—the image of this pink American had been so clear, the lines and colors that defined his true shape so indelible. But the vision now was a shimmering mirage, and Smythe drank again as if slaking a desert thirst. He remembered the barmaid's legs like shiny blades scissoring up to him, the bell-like chime of ice announcing another double rum, the scalded streak in his throat after draining the glass, the final decision before rational thought was finally drowned.

He must have more proof, that seemed reasonable, but he would carry the knife at all times. When all doubt was gone, when there was no question of mistaken identity, the knife would do its job.

Quickly.

CHAPTER 15

A gray-faced old man collided with the back of Smythe's chair and groaned a remote "Excuse me," as much to the chair as to the person in it. Smythe barely noticed. It was the hand of fate pushing him onward, or the nudge of conscience propelling him, or the slap-on-the-old-back for a decision well made.

Senator Harth barely noticed, either, just as he barely glimpsed the tall dark man he had jostled. Harth's mind was far away, mentally caressing a past time that in memory was more vivid and colorful than this present-tense chiaroscuro existence. Thirty years ago, in this very hotel, he had been crackling with life, crouching in the starting blocks of his future with dreams of the wonders that lay ahead. His caramel apple tan and sleek, chiseled body had turned the heads of younger ladies and made even his wife look up from her piña colada. His hair had been a blustery, ruddy brown like the thunderhead mane of a buffalo, his eyes an iridescent blue, his lips an expectant slash of pink.

Thirty years ago.

Today he was all drabness. Gray skin and hair. Blue-gray eyes. Black socks and shoes. Gray silk suit and white shirt. Black tie with thin, embarrassed red stripes. Even his voice, once ten colors of baritone, was now gray and metallic.

The senator quickly slipped by Smythe. At the front desk, Harth asked for messages. There were none. *When would they contact him, these Bahamian bloodsuckers? How would they collect their slimy payoff?* Cautiously, of course. Extortion was serious business and those behind this scheme could never be sure that the victim wouldn't decide to purge his soul with confession and set them up. Harth had considered it.

For the payoff, Harth could have brought along a truck full of authorities as witnesses. The cash itself could have been marked, the serial numbers easily traced. It was even possible that an influential, resourceful victim could launch his own private retaliation once the extortionists were identified.

If this scheme were a mass merchandising venture, as Harth suspected from its packaging, the perpetrators would be cloaked in a thick layer of insulation. How could they pull it off over and over again without maximum security? The first part of the plan had been made visible—the island, the hotel. But now what?

The senator walked thoughtfully to his suite. As he opened the door, a frightening thought came to him.

They could be waiting for him inside.

He had assumed all along that they would never show their faces, perhaps never even talk to him directly. But what if he were wrong?

Fear and anger churned in him like oil and water. He was suddenly afraid of a direct confrontation, of meeting the monsters at last, of the unknown being made instantly known. He was also angry. Eager to vent his wrath on a flesh-and-blood target. Mad enough to send a couple of thugs sailing across the room.

In the end, neither emotion won. Instead, they emulsified into a settling dose of ambivalence. What the hell. Nothing mattered anymore. Let 'em come or call or write or send smoke signals. At least he wouldn't be surprised. "What took you so long?" he'd say, if they were waiting.

The faint click of the door unlocking filled the empty hallway like the slam of a bank vault. The door opened with a chirp.

There was no greeting committee. No goons with dark shirts and white ties. No gun barrel to stare down. Only a small envelope that had been slid beneath the door.

So they decided to write.

In his mind, Harth imagined the contents—a cryptic instruction that would send him from one destination to another, then another. Bring the money and wait for a call. Go to this address. Leave the briefcase in the second stall of the men's room. Or something like that. As in a kidnapping. After all, they were holding hostage his good name.

Harth stopped to pick up the envelope. He closed the door before moving to the sofa, a large camel-back daybed plumped with pillows and covered in a worn, deep-blue fabric blossoming with white flowers and beige ferns.

Harth threw off his coat and tie. Only the point of the envelope flap had been cemented, and it popped open with gentle encouragement. Inside the envelope was a colorful brochure touting a casino he had never visited. Harth scanned it, confused. Was this merely an advertising ploy? Had some borderline employable grunt innocently stuffed each hotel room with junk mail?

That was when Harth noticed the address blank on the back page. Neatly typed in the little white square were these words: "Join us at the gaming tables Monday through Wednesday evenings. Play the games of your choice, but please do not lose more than you can afford. We suggest a practical limit of about $70,000 per night."

Of course.

It was brilliant. Harth's lips involuntarily carved a smile onto his face. This was why they had brought him here. To lose $200,000 at the casino!

The scheme was starting to make sense. A casino was the perfect laundry for marked or traceable cash. Chips were bought, chips were sold back. The casino was a money mill that would shuffle Harth's cash and dole it out to hundreds, perhaps thousands of other gamblers in the course of an evening. And while accepting extortion money was a crime, there were no laws here against the house winning from a careless gambler.

If any questions were ever asked, the answer would be simple: the senator had foolishly lost considerable money gambling. Too bad. Better luck next time.

The plan was beautifully impersonal. No contacts. No faces. No license plate numbers. Just a man losing money legally at the gaming tables.

Yet someone, somehow, was at the other end. Harth would lose his chips and someone else would win. Perhaps not even on the same evening. The casino was a money maze that would hopelessly frustrate any attempt to connect the front and back doors. Seventy thousand a night should not raise many eyebrows. That was why he'd been asked to spread the first payment over three days. All so neat and tidy.

Two bill collectors were now standing at Harth's door. The first was exacting payment for a life of hard drinking; the principal and interest equaled his life, and the books were almost clear. The second demanded recompense for a pattern of behavior that once had seemed so clever and rewarding, but now seemed reckless. The settlement of that debt was nearer than the creditors realized.

Senator Harth slumped into the marshmallow softness of pillows. He kicked off his shoes and elevated his gray-stockinged feet.

And fell asleep, dreamless.

———

The champagne bottle stood empty in a bucket of melt-water. For a moment, the room may have been mistaken for a still photograph, so motionless were the figures in this composition. Kathy lay on the bed, face toward the ceiling, the back of her right hand glued to the bridge of her nose as if shielding sensitive eyes from light. Jamie sat bent over the writing desk like a school child, his face buried in crossed arms.

But then Kathy stirred. Her hand moved and her light-struck eyes glistened. "I'm sorry," she said. "I didn't mean to be so hard on you." Not entirely true, of course. "I just thought you booked this trip for *us*."

A muffled, half-hearted "That's all right" came from Jamie.

"And I didn't mean all that stuff about madness and all. I was just hurt."

Jamie lifted his head as if it weighed a hundred pounds, choked the neck of the champagne bottle as he lifted it from the bucket, then let the empty green container drop back into the cold slush. "Maybe you're right," he said. "I should have explained before we got down here."

"It just hurt me that you deceived me. You led me to believe we were coming here for one reason, and it turns out to be some whole other thing I don't even understand."

The surprise of Jamie's explanation had not all come tonight. Kathy had sensed some darker purpose behind the trip from the beginning. It was not disappointment or shock that had inspired her fierce verbal attack of a few minutes ago. It was the venting of pent-up frustration. Jamie had come clean in his excitement over the fulfilled prophecy of his dream. And then Kathy had landed a powerhouse jab with all the grace of a street fighter. She had been waiting days for the opportunity, and when finally it had come, she had knocked him down for the eight-count. Now she could afford to be conciliatory. He knew where she stood.

In the far corner.

"I deserved it," he said. "I was just so afraid I was crazy, you know?"

"No, I don't."

"If I had told you about the dreams and they had turned out to be just fantasies after all, I would have looked like a fool. After all that other stuff, I would have looked like a real *madman* to you. But now I know something else is going on."

"Something's going on, yes. I can see that. I just wish you had been honest with me."

"I know. I'm sorry." His voice was low, earnest. "You have every right to be upset."

"Well—I overdid it a bit."

"I won't say I enjoyed it, but you don't have to apologize. I was unfair. But please, Kathy—try to help me figure this out. That's why I needed you to come along."

He looked so pathetic, pleading for help. Now that she had punished him, she couldn't help but move from the bed and curl her arms around him. He would be honest with her from now on, that she was sure of. And she would reward him with the comfort of her warm arms, the gentle stroke of her hand on his head.

"I'll help," she said. "I don't know where this is leading, but I'll help. Just as long as you're honest with me."

She felt strong. She knew that the coming evening was hers. She was in control. Everything would be fine for at least one more night.

Unsuspecting, then, she had dinner with Jamie and went to bed.

CHAPTER 16

Her eyes turned on. If anyone had been watching, that's how it would have appeared. Her eyelids suddenly snapped open to reveal a moist concaveness that flashed in the scattered night light with the suddenness of a thrown switch. Something had awakened her. Some night spasm, or a nightmare erased by the protective circuit of waking.

The texture of sleep was a rugged badlands of spasms, twitches, tosses and turns, bladder burnings and nerve tinglings, shivers, dreams, and rapid eye movement. The average person would awaken eight times per night and remember few, if any, of those occasions. Kathy would remember this one forever.

She was lying on her left side, her body a crescent from head to knees, the flat of her back toward Jamie. Before the narcotic of wakefulness could deaden those lively senses that inhabit the narrow seam of semi-consciousness, Kathy's body told her that Jamie was gone. The rising and falling nest of heat that should have been comforting the small of her back had dissipated, the slant of the bed was off by a degree or two, the gentle purr that Jamie's sleeping body should have transmitted through the mattress was absent.

The black void of the room began to fill with sharply defined objects carved from the velvet darkness by moonlight. The window overlooking the harbor was unshaded. White light shot through the glass as if it were a projection window in a movie theater. The room was deathly quiet except for the rhythmic hiss of steam from a radiator near the foot of the bed.

Momentary hysteria gripped Kathy. Everything was suddenly foreign. This was not her room, her bed, her house. This was not home at all. The window was out of place. The light from the window was far too white, the quiet much too intense.

Even before she could flinch from panic, the facts tumbled into place. Of course this was not home. It was Nassau, the British Colonial Hilton. Suite 535. A hotel bed. A Bahamian moon.

A trick of the traveler's mind.

But Jamie was not in bed. Kathy knew that without turning. He was in the bathroom, maybe, or getting ice down the hall. (Why would he want ice in the middle of the night?) Perhaps he was reading in the sitting room, After all, this was a *suite*.

Still the goddam radiator hissed. *Like an asthmatic*, Kathy thought.

She felt lonely without Jamie. Afraid. She didn't want to be alone in this strange room in this unfamiliar hotel, vulnerable and abandoned. She wanted to find Jamie and ask him why the hell he had left her like that, and what the hell he was doing out of bed. But then she remembered a terrible thing and her body tensed, trembled, pushing goose bumps through her skin and sending a dreadful ache to the pit of her stomach.

The room seemed ablaze with white light.

Kathy felt frozen in place, too afraid to move, unable to make her muscles do anything but shudder. *Such foolishness*, she told herself, but her *self* was not listening, choosing to think instead about the other reason for Jamie being out of bed.

The madness.

He could be roaming around the suite doing God-knows-what. But she couldn't hear him. She tried, but that goddam radiator was hissing so loudly that it masked everything else.

Oh my God... oh my *God*!

She sensed it now... *knew* it. Her eyes blinked and her mouth turned to sand. A stinging wave washed over her body from the soles of her feet to her scalp like a thousand needles pricking her skin. Her heart crackled and stomped as blood rushed to her face and sweat crept out of her skin. She had swallowed her voice and it lay bunched and quivering at the bottom of her stomach.

There was no radiator in the room. No steam. No manufactured hiss.

There was a man at the foot of the bed. Breathing heavily. Passionately. Staring at her.

She had not moved since opening her eyes. Could not see the man at all from her position. But she could feel his eyes like hands on her body, hear the catch of breath as his blood rose, smell the musky lust of his thoughts.

The madness had followed her.

No! She was imagining this, conjuring up monsters from unfamiliar noises the way night eyes make grotesque things out of slumped shirts and piles of blankets. If she could regain control of her muscles, allow reason to prevail, force herself to turn...

She rolled over slowly, feeling unprotected and frail beneath the single clinging layer of cotton that was her nightgown.

He stood there, grinning madly, eyes dancing like a prison searchlight over her body, chest heaving in and out. It was Jamie, but it wasn't. His features were oddly contorted by his maniacal grin and hot-eyed gaze. He was stark naked and greasy with sweat. His body seemed to sway, to weave and pulsate in the moonlight's crossfire. Sick with fear, Kathy could only knot the hem of her nightgown in her fists and stare— stare at that fearsome, rhythmic madness.

A voice frightened her. It came from Jamie's twisted lips but was heavy, raked over gravel. A ventriloquist's act. Jamie's mouth moved and someone else's voice came out. "I'm so glad you came," it said. "Believe me, the pleasure will be all mine."

The leering, intrusive bending of words made Kathy feel already violated.

She lay there, braced and rigid, breasts pointing up through the nightgown pulled taut by her fists, legs squeezed together in a muscle-aching merger of thighs.

And then he was on her, grunting and snorting like a pig, fingers scratching her neck and finally renting the nightgown from her body.

She fought now, pushing his sweaty face from her breasts. She slapped him hard, thinking that this would startle him, wake him up from the madness and reclaim control as she had done before.

But he was mad-strong and slapped her back. And she knew there was no stopping him this time.

———

Kathy felt as though she had been sutured with flame-threads.

For many minutes she lay there, bent and bleeding, riveted to the foot of the bed by the searing pain of movement. Bruises that would soon tattoo her body began to throb. Her teeth had bitten cleanly through the sheet and her hands each had wrestled a torn, bunched wad of linen from the mattress.

The stabbing pain at last subsided to a prickly throb, as if a spiny bladder were inflating and deflating within the raw heart of her wound. From the size of the hurt she judged the wound enormous—a huge, ragged gash at the joining of her wishbone legs. If she stood, all of her insides would gush through that gaping hole and spill into a steaming pile on the floor.

Jamie stirred. In the painful aftermath, Kathy had forgotten the rutting beast that lay panting beside her. The tangy scent of sweat stung her nostrils as she propped herself up on trembling arms. Beneath her, the rumpled sheet peeled from her sticky breasts and floated to the bed like shed skin. She saw Jamie lying there face down, a dead man in a river of madness.

She straightened her body and found the pain bearable.

Slowly, on hands and knees, she inched toward the bathroom. Even this gentle movement unsheathed the hot knife of pain.

Twice she stopped and fell onto her side, lying there until the agony diminished. Every muscle of her body seemed attached by spider-fine nerves to the wound. Each tiny muscular twitch telegraphed shock waves of pain to her sphincter, which burned like a ring of fire.

She struggled at last to the porcelain cliff of the tub and managed a hand over the side. Lifting herself, she stabbed the plug into the drain and turned the brass hot water valve. The tub began to fill.

The crash of water falling on water relaxed her. Rising steam licked her face. Stiffly, she climbed over the side and lowered her hips and thighs into the hot tide.

Mother of God! She screamed as the scalding water pushed between her legs and molested her swollen tissues like a ball of white-hot steel wool, twisting and scraping the frayed nerve endings. The agony was greater than that of Jamie's vile intrusion itself.

Kathy heard the thunder of water falling from the faucet and the hollow gurgle of the overflow drain. Her chin was hot and wet, her body buoyant and prickly with heat. For a moment, she let these separate realities blow randomly through her mind, but then she became aware that her eyes were closed. Water suddenly filled her mouth and she gagged, choked, arms flailing against the unremitting porcelain. Her eyes would not open, so she fought blindly against the slippery surface.

Now she understood. She had momentarily lost consciousness. The tub had filled. If she could open her eyes, she would find escape. But if her paralyzed eyelids failed to move, refused to acknowledge the full light of consciousness...

She managed to turn off the water. The heat of it enveloped her like a blanket. The darkness was so inviting. Maybe she could float here for just a minute, weightless and painless, before opening her eyes.

A sharp pain attacked her foot. Her toe had struck the faucet and her eyes flashed open. Panic seized her. She managed to get a leg over the tub's side. An arm, then another leg. She tumbled onto the floor, cracking her head on the hard tile. Green sparks sputtered into a black void.

Kathy's next sensation was of intense cold. Ice on her back. Once again she found her eyes closed, but this time she opened them easily. Yes, yes—she remembered the fall from the tub.

The cold squares of tile branded her back with imprints and made her muscles twitch. She sat up.

Kathy could recall the vicious assault, the debilitating pain. She stood. The hot tub had sucked the pain from her and replaced it with a dull ache.

Bearable.

She stared at her image in the mirror. Hair wet and matted. Skin flushed red. Bruises blossoming like tiny purple flowers.

Her fingers sought out the battleground and found it tender but intact. She had not been ripped apart after all.

Again, she looked at herself. The victim. *Or was she?* Perhaps in some way she had provoked Jamie's assault. Maybe she had driven his desire to the brink of violence through her spare rationing of sex. It could be that she deserved punishment and humiliation as atonement for a life of wifely failure and selfishness. In one brutal attack, Jamie had balanced the books. She deserved it.

No, that thinking was sick. Damn it, the bastard had raped her. Was she incapable of outrage? No, it was sick to imagine that she could be responsible for Jamie's crime.

Jamie had attacked her. Nothing could ever justify the inhuman violence he had inflicted upon her. He had become an animal—mad, perhaps, but that was *his* problem.

It came to her just that quickly. She would leave him. *Now.* She must leave before he woke up. But for a miracle, she would never see him again.

It surprised her that she was naked. She could not remember her nightgown coming off. But now she could feel the reddened lines under her arms where the seams had cut into her.

Gliding slowly into the bedroom to keep the knot of pain at a bearable level, Kathy saw the fleshy frown of Jamie's curved body on the tired mattress. His skin was dry. The sweat had evaporated with his passion and rage. The sinewy animal within him now lay hidden beneath the little-boy smoothness of his sleeping muscles.

But she remembered his face as he had come at her. That grotesque, twisted countenance. Eyes, mad with obsession.

She would remember always.

Kathy gathered her clothes in the sullen half-light. She dressed in jeans, sandals and a red halter, then silently threw the rest of her clothes into a suitcase. She counted out half the money in Jamie's wallet and sat down to write a note on hotel stationery.

What do you say to a monster?

She settled on a simple and civilized "Goodbye."

No explanation. No signature. Pure finality.

She left the room without looking back. Outside the hotel she was cheered by the fresh morning air. The sky was beginning to brighten. Seagulls sang their eerie, faraway song. Carrying her suitcase and purse, and taking short, stiff steps, Kathy walked to the private hotel beach and sat down, a solitary figure surrounded by an aimless ocean of sand.

In the end, she decided to go home. She would get a court order forbidding Jamie to come near. In a little while she'd catch a cab to the airport and put a big geographic gap between Jamie and herself. But it was still too early for that, so she'd rest here awhile and give her body and mind a chance to heal. Her brain felt as tattered as her bottom.

CHAPTER 17

At seven a.m., Billy Smythe and his scarred limousine pulled up in front of the hotel. Only a great sense of mission could have roused him so early after the sloshing he had endured last night.

He parked the limo and stepped out. There was little activity yet, and while Smythe was the first in line, he waved forward the two cabs behind him as early-rising guests beckoned. He was not here to accommodate tourists at random. He was here to find Jamie Giles. Should the young American come out, Billy Smythe would just happen to be ready for a fare.

And what a day he had planned for Jamie.

At 7:15, he was seated in the front seat again, legs stretched out like timbers into the driveway. From outside came a soft-spoken voice.

"Airport, please."

Smythe turned to direct the intruder to another cab, but in the golden morning light he saw Kathy's face staring at him through the open passenger window. She seemed as startled as he.

"Kathy Giles," he said. "I never forget a face."

"Billy Smythe." She paused, betraying her surprise. "I wasn't paying very much attention or I'm sure I would have noticed your vintage limousine."

Billy laughed. "Ah—well, that would not have helped. All the other drivers have camouflaged their limos to look like mine."

Smythe could see a purplish discoloration at the corner of Kathy's mouth, another just above an elbow. Her lips smiled but her darting eyes were a ghostly denial.

"You always seem to be around when I need a lift," she said.

"We all need a lift now and then. I'd be very pleased to help you this fine morning."

Billy leaned across the front seat and opened the passenger door.

———

Kathy climbed in, thinking how kind Billy Smythe was not to ask about Jamie. Her pale irises flashed as the limo pulled away from the curb. A kind and gentle man, she thought. Kind and gentle and understanding and the only familiar face on the island and always there when she needed a lift and, goddam it, she knew she was going to cry, and she tried to hold it back but the hot, acidy balloon of tears behind her eyes burst and before she knew it she was at Billy's tiny stucco house telling him what and how and she wanted to kill the bastard and she hurt so badly and didn't understand a thing that was going on.

And then she slept, feeling safer with this near-stranger than she had felt in months.

———

At just past 10:00, Jamie awoke with a tip-toe tumescence ordered by a standing-room-only bladder. Racing with great purpose into the bathroom, he relieved himself with a long, noisy stream. A peculiar soreness lingered, though. Perhaps Kathy's yeast infection had come back. Could that do it? Or maybe he had attracted an airborne herpes virus. He had heard those little buggers could be anywhere.

Where the hell was Kathy, anyway?

He called her name. The hollow silence was followed by that small, gnawing, masculine annoyance at being ignored by one's wife. Or dog. Or waitress.

"Kathy!"

The silence taunted him. He lunged into the empty bedroom and lobbed an obscenity.

The bed caught his eye. Like a ravished corpse, the naked mattress sprawled with its torn bed clothing bunched obscenely at its feet, the obvious residue of some savage violence.

A dark tingling of memory teased him with a faintly etched latent image that remained maddeningly obscure. Jamie's emotional response confused and overwhelmed him. While the scraps of his memory scattered irretrievably, his body responded to the unseen truth. The cover-up staged by his consciousness was flawed. The hot humming in his loins and his heart betrayed the guarded secret. His mind refused to confess a single detail, but every cell in Jamie's body knew that he had done something to Kathy. Something cruel and vicious. He had the scars to prove it. Now he was left to the torture of his imagination.

In the gymnastics of thinking, Jamie pictured himself as a Jeckyll and Hyde, one personality unable to control the other. Dammit, who *was* the other? If there were another person living inside him, why didn't he know?

He gave in to an eerie thought. He was standing in the middle of the bedroom stark naked, and he thought he could hear the *other* one laughing at him. From deep inside his head.

Jamie marched self-consciously to the dresser. His underwear was in the second drawer. On the top of the dresser was a conspicuous piece of paper, which he picked up.

In Kathy's distinctive script was written that lone, cryptic word: *Goodbye*. It struck him with such fierce finality, such mind-wrenching reality, that Jamie nearly fainted. Once he had aligned his groggy brain, he rushed to the closet and found Kathy's clothes gone.

He hoped to wake up from this nightmare and find Kathy's warm, buttery shape next to him. But as he stared at the note again, he knew there was no escape in waking.

Best not to think now, he told himself. Thinking idles the body and offers whole clusters of empty-headed cells the chance to think, to act, and before you know it some of them are spitting out tears and dumping out mucus and convulsing in spasms that rack you with jagged sobs. Better to trick the body, like putting ice on a fresh burn. Keep the body busy. Slide right into one of life's little drills. Mime the motions of a man who is still alive. Those dim-witted clumps of cytoplasm can only do one thing at a time. By the numbers, then. Pull up those jockey shorts and snap the band smartly around the waist. *Thwack!* Plunge into those denim cutoffs and close the old barn door. *Zzzzzzt!* Keep those muscles in step. Rhythm's everything. Forty pushups now, arms jacking up those grief-heavy shoulders. One hundred sit-ups. Ready? Keep up the beat. Make the muscles ripple and purr. Give that body so much to do it won't notice that half of you is gone.

Pant, sweat, count out loud.

Saturate the body with mindless routine.

Call for breakfast, order for two, make the bed.

Shower, shave, steam the wrinkles out of your shirts.

Fill up that ghostly gray gap with activity. Don't stop or the body will turn on you like a hungry lion and feed on your guts—and you know *that* hurts because it hurt so much when Dad left you and Mom, and now Kathy's gone and the volume of pain is so deep and wide that you could sink forever in it and never come out, never find the limits.

Suddenly, the motion didn't help.

And that's when Jamie broke. He was walking to the TV, or moving to the window, or pacing the room. He wasn't sure. He was moving and suddenly he stopped because of the stinging in his eyes and the acid lump in his throat. His head felt stretched over a bubble, a tough bubble that wouldn't burst but kept growing, kept swelling with the bitter gas of grief. His soft eyes ached with tears. His throat seized into a hot, crampy knot pulled tight by fist-like sobs.

For five minutes, he cried. Convulsed violently to the strangled percussion of squeals and gasps. In the end, wrung limp and dry, he sucked in a skinny stream of air, stuttering in staccato chirps. Red blotches speckled his face and a trapeze of wet strings hung from his nostrils, clotting.

He went into the bathroom, paddled cold water onto his face, and toweled off. In the mirror, his puffy eyelids jutted like awnings on a patchy pink facade.

A sharp rap on the door jarred him.

What the hell?

Who?

An impossible thought occurred to him. *Kathy!* But then a muted voice said, "Room service."

Of course. Breakfast.

Jamie glanced at his face in the mirror. He couldn't answer the door like that.

Another rap. Another disembodied "Room service."

Quickly he grabbed a can of Foamy and floated a thick Santa beard over his face from the eyes down. Perfect. He trotted to the door and opened it. In the hallway stood a tall, smiling Bahamian beside a linen-shrouded table on wheels.

"Yes sir, room service," the man said.

"Thank you. Uh—you can set up in the sitting room if you like."

"Yes sir."

As the table squeaked into the suite, Jamie peered down the corridor and was distracted by the housekeeping lady, who was just about to leave Suite 534. The door to that dream-inducing suite was open. Such luck. Perhaps he could catch a quick look inside. Sudden anticipation made his stomach buzz.

He glided easily the five short steps. Backing out of the 534's doorway was a fat lady the shape and color of a coconut. Her droopy arms dragged the carcass of a vacuum cleaner. She shuffled backwards toward a linen cart in the hallway. With great effort she turned, as if the combined weight of the machine and her bulk were taxing her strength to the limit. Her eyes had barely caught Jamie's foam-bearded face when she jumped, nearly in defiance of gravity, and squealed like a deflating balloon. She seemed gradually to sink, and then she pressed a moist palm to her enormously upholstered bosom.

"Lord, you gave me a fright," she said, showing Jamie the white top and bottom of each eyeball.

Jamie gulped before tracing her round stare to his clown face. He had forgotten the Foamy. Now he felt foolish. And to make matters worse, the fat lady's shrill yelp had attracted the occupant of Suite 534 to the open doorway where the gray, somber gentleman squinted at Jamie.

"I'm sorry, really," Jamie said to the man. "I didn't mean to scare her."

Silence from his audience.

"I was shaving and it was, uh, kinda late, and I didn't want her to miss my suite so I came out and, uh…"

"You sure gave me a fright," the fat lady said, laughing.

"Uh, really…" Jamie stumbled for words.

"It's all right. I'm sure she understands," Senator Harth said. "You're across the hall?" He glanced at Jamie's open doorway, which now contained a broadly grinning room service attendant.

"Yes, Suite 535. I'm Jamie Giles." He extended a hand, which was taken.

"Senator George Harth."

"Really? A United States senator?"

"Afraid so. But you'll have to excuse me, I'm late for an appointment."

"Oh—sure. Again, I'm sorry."

"No harm done. I think I'd wipe off that foam, though, before trying to make any new friends."

Jamie laughed awkwardly, then made a limp goodbye gesture as the senator retreated behind his door.

"You sure did give me a fright," the fat lady said again, still chuckling as she pushed the linen cart and the Hoover down the hall.

"Don't forget my room," Jamie called, smiling. "It's the one with the studio audience in the doorway."

As the fat lady bounced away, it occurred to Jamie that he had just met the mystery man, the important personage who had pre-empted Suite 534. So he was a U.S. senator. That made sense. If a senator wanted the suite, the hotel management certainly would accommodate him before Jamie Giles, Detroit police officer. Perhaps Senator Harth was a regular guest.

Jamie stood in the corridor and stared at the closed door of Suite 534. He had not gotten a look inside because everything had happened so fast. The squeal. The senator standing in the doorway. There had been no chance to see—what? It was not a simple matter of matching the appearance of the suite to his dream. It was a *feeling* that behind the door lay a piece of the puzzle that Jamie would only recognize if he were there.

The dream. He had been in the spa—calm, peaceful, secure—and then he had heard someone at the door. The door had opened...

Damn! The next piece was missing. If he could only get beyond that door, perhaps...

No good. The moment had been lost. Jamie pushed his way past the neon smile of the room service attendant and dismissed the bill with a quick flourish of a hotel pen. He washed off the rubbery skin of Foamy and devoured breakfast, barely cognizant of how quickly his grief had been replaced by purpose.

CHAPTER 18

The image of Jamie's father suddenly inserted itself into his mind. The image was of a man younger than Jamie was now. Odd, to think of that thirty-four year old man as Dad, but Vernon Giles had been thirty-four when he had walked out for good, and that was how Jamie would always remember him: eternally thirty-four.

The bastard Vernon Giles had deserted his wife and ten-year-old son—and his bills, which were equal to them in weight, Mom always said. Even now, when he understood that Vernon Giles was a son-of-a-bitch who manipulated everything and everyone to his own selfish ends, Jamie couldn't shed the deeply implanted belief that he, Jamie, had done something to drive his father away.

When Vernon Giles disappeared forever, Jamie's hopes of making amends had shattered. Without Dad there could be no forgiveness, no salvation.

Now Kathy had deserted Jamie, and there was no doubt he had done something terrible to push her away. But Kathy's departure would be different from his father's abandonment because the increasingly intricate puzzle now confronting Jamie could be solved, and in solving it he could somehow earn Kathy's forgiveness—and his own salvation. Solving the damn puzzle had become the most important thing in Jamie's life. Perhaps it *was* his life.

With that in mind, Jamie created a plan. Having had no tactical cloak and dagger experience—he was in law *enforcement*, not detective work, after all—he reached back into thousands of hours of TV shows stored loosely in his brain and came up with a surefire, tried and tested scheme straight from reruns of the *Rockford Files*. Get to know the senator. Lure him away from the suite before housekeeping arrived in the morning. Then just enter the suite like you owned the place.

Simple.

Before you could get to know him, of course, you would have to be where he is. So follow the old codger until the opportunity presents itself.

Jamie tried to think it through. Already he had blown precious time by not having had a plan worked out earlier. Harth had escaped while Jamie had eaten breakfast. No telling where he might have gone.

Think!

Maybe the senator was still in the hotel. A meeting… brunch, maybe. He looked like a man seeking relaxation, not sightseeing. He had been wearing a coat and tie, but then perhaps he wore that costume every-where (except to the beach; *scratch the beach*). Harth had implied that he was due somewhere, but that could have been a ruse to gracefully escape from a madman covered in Foamy.

Jamie put his money on brunch in the hotel. Unless the senator had eaten in his room, that could be his first stop. Jamie gave it a two-per-cent advantage over a wild guess.

He stalked from the room, adrenalin surging. This was like a deer hunt. You always go where the deer will most likely be, and then you make sure you don't miss that one good shot.

———

The corridor to the elevator was long and dark and seemed unusually dim for late morning, unusually constricted. It had not been this dark and narrow before, not in Jamie's memory. Still, his feet moved briskly with the purposeful stride of a businessman late for a meeting—urgent yet dignified. Jamie's mind swam with a multitude of plans for approaching the senator. So much depended on the circumstances.

But something was wrong here—clearly wrong. The corridor... so dim, so narrow. It was suddenly difficult to see. A flutter of uncertainty interrupted Jamie's smooth, confident gait, but only for a moment, as if caused by a catch in the knee or a hitch in the ankle.

Had he taken the wrong hallway? Had the power gone out?

In the darkness, illuminated only by a harsh but dazzling light at the distant end of the tunnel—*why did he think of it as a tunnel?*—the textured walls took on the eerie roughness of stone still ringing with the sounds of a stonemason's copper chisel. A gritty, rasping noise filled the tunnel with echoes, and Jamie turned to find its source. His feet were scraping coarse gravel and sand.

Ahead he could see the ghostly flickering shadows of other men against a growing patch of light. He wanted to call out, but as he sucked in a breath, his nostrils filled with dust and he gagged, tears sprouting from his eyes and sweat cascading down his face.

He had not noticed the heat until now—until that hot, scorching wind had blown through the corridor.

Jamie staggered, squinted into the light, and wiped his eyes with the back of a hand. This was all wrong. The hotel, the corridor...

He heard voices coming from the shadowy apparitions ahead. Gibberish. Strange, distorted sounds, nasal and clipped, almost, almost like...

No, not so strange. There was a familiar rhythm to it.

Damn that echo!

Everything was so hollow-sounding.

Walk, damn it. *Walk.* Get out of here, into the light, into the fresh hot air and out of this dusky, tomb-like tunnel.

The fierce glare that drew Jamie closer became much larger and brighter. In its brilliance, Jamie could at last make out a faint shimmering pattern of shapes, an oddly comforting pattern seen through squinted eyelids.

A thought insinuated itself into his confused mind. *I'll be home soon.*

He stepped into the wall of light, through it, and the heat struck him like a hammer. Blinded and dazzled by the light, drenched in sweat and made dizzy by the suffocating heat, Jamie closed his eyes, clenching them like fists, and leaned against the side of...

A bell.

Jamie's brain sputtered.

Yes, *a bell*.

He opened his eyes. Two dots, one of them glowing orange... *What?* A movement—the walls parting. No, no... an elevator.

Elevator.

The hotel.

Elevator doors opened and a man stepped out.

Jamie glanced up. A green arrow pointed down. Without conscious thought, Jamie stepped into the elevator car. *Senator Harth*, he told himself, *I'm going to find Senator Harth*. And then he backed against the rear side of the elevator to steady himself.

Another bell sounded. As Jamie's elevator began to close, another one opened directly across the corridor. Through the narrowing slit of Jamie's door he could see a man exit the other elevator, a gray sober man in a gray suit and black tie.

Senator Harth.

Jamie's elevator descended with a nauseating suddenness that left his body suspended slightly until the abrupt stop.

The doors opened and Jamie stepped into the hotel lobby to clear the rubble from his mind. He could feel the last dusty chunks of the psychic landfall settling on the floor of his consciousness, and he could feel the accumulated weight. The effort just to move and keep his equilibrium took great concentration.

He sat on a dimpled leather bench and stroked his still-perspiring face with rough palms. The madness had struck again, and Jamie's body had responded to the imagined heat by bathing itself in its own juices. He coughed and realized that his body was still trying to cough up the phantom dust. His pulse was racing, and even now he could taste the acrid, particle-filled air in the back of his mouth. These lingering physiological carryovers were the remains of an experience that seemed momentarily as real as the act of sitting on a leather bench in the hotel lobby. For just an instant, in fact, Jamie's mind vaulted into a fleeting confusion, suddenly unable to distinguish the lobby as tangible reality, and causing Jamie to gasp with the startling conviction that now, at this time, in this hotel, he was trapped within the madness and desperate to escape back into the true reality of the tunnel. This haunting, tortuous mirror-image of a mirror-image provoked a sensation of coming unstuck from all reality, of caroming off one dream into another, of viewing both dreams at last from some unidentified third perspective.

Jamie gripped the edge of the leather bench until his body finally anchored itself in the *reality* of the hotel. Reoriented, he stood up, frightened by the prospect that he might have been dropped off instead in the *other* reality. He had felt so *close to home* in the tunnel.

Jamie convinced himself that it was a trick of the madness to lure him willingly into its dark web. It would have been easy this time to stay there. To go into his dream and not return. Jamie imagined this to be the spell of insanity. He must resist or surely he would be sucked into the black hole of his aberration.

He decided to walk. Outdoors. Sunshine and fresh air would fan the nearly smothered coals of consciousness and revive his sense of belonging to this world.

It worked. Outside, he felt his body sink roots into reality. *This* reality. His strength came back, and so did the memory of Senator Harth returning to his suite.

The plan.

It was possible now. The senator was within reach—if he returned to his suite and stayed there.

Jamie glanced at his watch. Barely eight minutes had expired since he had entered the fifth floor corridor to find Harth, though it felt more like an hour.

Jamie re-entered the hotel and took the elevator to the fifth floor. Walking down that corridor once again gave him a chill of expectancy, as if the environment itself had been the spell caster for the early show and could now be counted on for a repeat performance. But nothing happened.

Relieved, Jamie unlocked his door and headed straight for the telephone. He dialed Harth's room to make sure he wasn't in. After three rings, the unmistakable baritone of Senator Harth grunted an unfriendly "Hello."

The voice surprised Jamie. He had not planned what to say should Harth be in. Jamie felt like a hunter who had moved at the wrong time and caught the coal-black gaze of his quarry. It was unnerving to be confronted by one's prey. Better to remain still and silent, blended once again into the bush.

———

After a few more attempts to raise his caller, Senator Harth finally slammed down the receiver. *Goddam blackmailers,* he said to himself.

He walked to the big camel-back daybed and slumped backwards into its soft blue clouds. The pillows were exquisitely buoyant and submissive. They sensually conformed to the subtle curves and slopes of his broad back and thighs, almost the way his wife had molded her warm pliant body to his on so many cold nights, trying hungrily to absorb him into herself by the sheer volume of their physical contact. And she had succeeded. He knew that now, because he had been so incurably incomplete since her death. She had taken part of him with her; his soul, perhaps. He was left with only his dying flesh, to which he had been mercilessly chained and sentenced to carry on his brittle bones like so much rotting meat. His body's final, abhorrent purpose seemed merely to serve as a disposable container for the foul poisons of his own making, and after that, as landfill.

He missed his wife. *Achingly* missed her. The last flickering patch of blue in his pale irises had been snuffed out, leaving only the overcast gray of a life totally without sunshine.

His eyes were moist, and he felt himself about to cry, so he glanced away from his haunting inner visions of loneliness.

There were just a few more hours of loneliness left.

He found himself staring at the bold white flowers and delicate ferns that spread joyfully across the printed fabric of the daybed. There were more flowers beneath him and around him than most people had at their funerals.

The morbidity of this thought struck him as awfully funny, and suggested the final flourish for his plan.

CHAPTER 19

The hours passed slowly for Jamie. He had changed from jeans into a beige summer-weight suit, which he had put away for the winter until the Bahamas trip had come up. He sat on a chair in his suite that had been relocated near the hallway door. The door had been left open a few inches, more for hearing than for looking out. Several times during the afternoon Jamie had heard a door to another suite open and close, but it was never Harth.

From his chair, Jamie could see the flat panel TV he had switched on. The inane succession of images and the muffled sound—kept low so Jamie could hear the hallway—filled up the hours but numbed the brain. Five times Jamie had caught himself staring almost hypnotically at the screen, unable to recall what he had just seen and afraid that the mental lapse had occurred when the senator had left his suite at last.

What the hell was he doing in there? Was he ever going to come out?

Jamie looked at his watch. It was 7:35 p.m. Maybe Harth had taken ill and decided to stay in. Or perhaps he had escaped while Jamie was mesmerized by the flickering screen.

There was nothing to do but wait.

At 7:40, Jamie went to the bathroom. It took only a minute, and it felt good to move around. As a precaution, Jamie decided to look down the corridor. If the senator had left his room while Jamie was away from his listening post, Harth probably would be still in the hallway.

With little concern for subtlety, Jamie swung open his door and poked his head into the corridor. There, at the distant end of the hallway, was the gray shape of Senator Harth waiting for an elevator.

What a rotten time to take a leak, Jamie thought. He felt his trouser pocket to make sure it contained his security card. His wallet was snugly in place inside his suit coat. He was ready to go.

Just as Harth entered the elevator, Jamie dashed from his suite, racing for the stairs halfway down the corridor. He hoped no one would see him running like a kid through the hotel.

The door to the stairway opened easily and Jamie flung himself down the five flights, gobbling up three and four stairs with each stride. As he reached the door to the main floor corridor, he stopped abruptly and took a deep breath. His heart was crashing through his rib cage—whether from the run or the excitement, Jamie couldn't tell.

He stepped through the doorway, combing back his hair with moist fingers. The senator was getting off the elevator and heading for the main entrance. Jamie followed, desperately trying not to look out of breath.

Outside, the senator motioned for a cab. The second vehicle in a line of four cabs pulled out and dipped into the space in front of Harth. Jamie was only steps behind as the senator got into the cab. Before Jamie could fully raise his hand, the limo in front of the cab line pulled up. Jamie frantically stumbled into it, and then looked up in amazement at the driver.

"Smythe!" he said.

"Mr. Giles, what a pleasure to see you again."

"Look, I know this sounds funny, but I want you to follow that cab." Jamie pointed to the vehicle containing Senator Harth.

"Just like in the movies," Smythe said as he eased the limo away from the hotel. "It should not be difficult. What suite was he staying in?"

"Suite 534," Jamie said, then realized that the conversation had skipped several necessary steps. "Wait a minute. How did you know he was staying in a suite? And that I'd know which one?"

"Oh, he looked like the *suite* type. Expensive suit—a dignified air about him. In my business you learn to make many judgements about people. And you were following him. It's a fair assumption that you'd begin at his room."

Jamie felt a sudden and inexplicable need to explain his actions to this limousine driver. "It's really nothing very sinister, my following him."

"I'm sure it's not," Smythe said, then flashed a smile into the rear view mirror. "You don't look like a spy. Or a hit man."

"Actually, I thought it was someone I knew. An old acquaintance. But before I could ask him, he was in the cab."

Jamie saw a profound hole in his deceit. He had known Harth's suite number. "It was just a coincidence that he was staying across the hall from Kathy and me. I saw him duck into his suite earlier today and wondered if it was old Ben," Jamie lied. "It seems like I'm always just a couple steps too late."

"And how is your *wife*?" Smythe asked.

"Kathy?" Jamie was relieved that Smythe had changed the subject, but this new direction also caught him off guard. More lies. "Just fine, but she had to go home early. Her mother was in an accident. Nothing serious—just some bruises. But you know how women are. Kathy had to make sure that everything was okay."

"What a shame. She had just arrived."

"I know. And it's a bit lonely here without her, but she wouldn't let me go back with her. Said it was ridiculous to ruin both our vacations. That's why I'm kind of anxious to find someone I know. Like old Ben up there, if that's him. Otherwise, I really don't know anyone at all on this island."

"But you know me." Smythe's statement had an odd ring to it, as if it were more of a question.

"Yes, Billy... I do. And maybe I'll get to know you better."

"Our paths do seem to cross."

"They do at that."

The battle-scarred limousine followed the senator's cab to the casino, nosing up behind the senator's vehicle just outside the entrance. From the dark safety of the back seat, Jamie watched Harth stiffly ratchet a leg into the humid space outside the cab's door, then hunch his body and back out of the steel orifice. Slowly, the senator's uncomfortably folded body unfurled itself, and when finally he stood at full extension, he appeared still knotted somewhere, unable to disentangle a kink in the neck or spine. The grayness seemed to have overtaken him, contagiously sucking up the color from everything around him. The senator paid the driver and sadly turned to face the beckoning lights of the casino. He stood there for a moment so motionless that Jamie thought he might have died standing up.

Jamie stopped breathing, waiting for some small gesture of life, but afraid that the frozen figure would instead slump lifelessly to the ground and disappear like the shadow of a rapidly ascending object.

"Is it him?" Smythe's words startled a breath into Jamie's lungs.

"What?"

"Is it Old Ben?"

"I'm—I'm not sure anymore."

"He doesn't exactly seem to be having the time of his life."

"Not exactly," Jamie said. The once-golden prospect of befriending the senator was quickly evaporating.

Then Harth moved so suddenly that Jamie flinched. Walking as a condemned man to the gallows, Harth moved heavily into the casino. Jamie watched, uncertain of his next move now that it was upon him.

"Will you join him?" Smythe asked.

"How about if *you* join *me*, Jamie replied, surprised at his idea but immediately aware that it was a good excuse to procrastinate. "It's a slow night for cabs, I can see that. I'll make you a deal. Stake you one hundred bucks, you forget the fare... and we'll split your winnings fifty-fifty."

"That's a very generous offer," Smythe said, "but you see, it's impossible."

"Why? I'll even pay the fare. Just come in with me." Was he begging? God, he didn't want to beg. Was he afraid of making the next move?

"It really is impossible, as much as I'd like to accompany you, stake or no stake. But it's illegal for Bahamians to gamble in the casino."

"You're kidding."

"True, I'm afraid. The casino is owned by foreign interests. If Bahamians gambled here, they would lose money as almost everyone does, and that money would then be drained out of our economy. It's a good law, I think."

"I'm sorry you can't join me," Jamie said. And he truly was sorry. "Well—I guess I may just as well go in and lose the money myself."

"Perhaps I'll see you again. Do you need a driver tomorrow?"

"I hadn't really thought about it." Jamie glanced at the casino, but a flurry of other images passed before his eyes, jogged by Smythe's presence. The castle. The garden. The fainting spell. Jamie felt an impulsive desire to visit the castle again. "Yes—at noon, if you're free."

"I'm free, of course. Few people make appointments this time of year."

"I'd better pay you.

"You can wait until the end of our next adventure if you like," Smythe suggested.

"No—I'll pay you now. I may not have any money when I leave this place."

Jamie left Smythe and entered the casino. It was a spacious room, though smaller than he had imagined, with shiny legions of robot-like slot machines at either end. A multitude of luminous green surfaces was scattered about like emeralds set out for display. Crowding these gaming tables was a squirming mob of very tan and expressionless people who seemed to be trying their best not to betray any emotions whatsoever. Most eyes intently studied the game before them while hands randomly pumped scotches and rums and mai tais to lips parched by too much sun. At the extreme poles of the room, funny people with frizzy hair and flowery shirts and cups filled with noisy coins gave offerings to the pantheon of three-eyed gods.

Occasionally a sound like chrome-plated water gushing and jingling would decree the beneficence of a particular god and all heads in the room would turn—even those who could not possibly see the wondrous sight—as a small tribute to the dream of winning. The tokens that were zealously spit into a ringing megaphone of metal would broadcast a call for recommitment to the dream. And everyone would go back to losing.

This is how Jamie Giles, who was not a gambler, saw the casino. It struck him as a nursery for adults. Yet the people did amaze him with their diversity, ranging from tourist to tycoon, judging by appearances.

Senator Harth stood in front of the casino cashier. He was handing over quite a lot of money, assuming the four wrapped stacks each contained all hundreds, as indicated by the top bill.

Harth walked away with a small tray of purple chips.

Expensive little buggers, Jamie thought. He stepped up to the cashier and placed a fifty dollar bill on the counter, suddenly blushing with embarrassment. He was totally outclassed. His fifty must seem ridiculous after the senator's casual purchase.

A brief exchange, which Jamie didn't quite understand but got through by replacing words with nods, was followed by the gift of a few chips of several different colors. Jamie couldn't remember which were which, but it didn't matter. He would lose them all anyway.

He followed the senator around the perimeter of the casino. At one point, near the craps table, Harth turned and appeared to look right at Jamie—but without recognition.

A surge of adrenalin shot to Jamie's head. But then the brief confrontation disappeared as Harth cut across the room to the roulette wheel. Jamie followed.

He'd been afraid that Harth would recognize him and begin a conversation. Jamie was not mentally prepared for that yet, not fully in control. It now occurred to him, though, that Harth could not possibly have recognized him. They had met only once, and Jamie's face had been covered with foam.

The senator watched a spin of the roulette wheel. There was only one winner, a gentleman beyond Harth's years who had bet ten dollars on red and was rewarded when the ball nestled into red 14. Harth unceremoniously placed a purple chip on black 33 as numerous busy hands teased the table with bets. A blonde woman frantically consulted a wrinkled chart filled with pencil scrawls. An elderly Jewish lady nervously gulped a gin and tonic. A honeymoon couple clutched hands as if the money for a return ticket was all riding on this one spin. In a wheelchair, a jean-clad Brit drummed his fingers on the arm rest.

It was not until the roulette wheel was spinning madly that someone noticed the small purple chip on the table. It was by far the largest bet. The wheel spun on. Another pair of eyes detected the chip, then another. The staccato trot of the steel ball became a gallop as the wheel slowed. Eyes curiously slid in Harth's direction because the tray of purple chips belonged to him.

"Black 31!"

The chips were cleanly scraped from the felt surface into a hungry slot. Again, the elderly gentleman was the sole winner. He had cannily switched his ten-dollar bet to black. Five players left the game and six joined. Harth remained and placed a purple chip on each of four numbers, all red. This time the betting was serious and a skyline of stacked chips was erected quickly. No one else bet Harth's numbers, as if the small purple wafers were holy sacraments not to be violated.

Harth was the only player who did not watch the chips, the other players, or the wheel as it began to spin. Instead, his eyes scanned the room, stopping hotly on a face here and there, occasionally making eye contact—*forcing* contact, it appeared, with the intensity of his gaze — and then studying the reactions.

When the fickle ball finally tumbled into black 13, Harth seemed not to flinch at all. Numbly he plucked another four chips from his tray and indiscriminately dealt them onto the table. As an afterthought, he recklessly flicked one chip onto the rectangle reserved for green 00.

This time the roulette crowd openly stared at the free-spending gentleman at the end of the table. A few token bets were placed, but attention clearly had shifted to the casual high stakes of the senator's play.

A startling hush greeted the spinning of the wheel.

The silver ball rocketed around the rim and finally fell from orbit to jarringly clack and skip its way into one small notch.

The ball settled. Only the faint whoosh of the wheel interrupted the silence. The wheel was still moving too fast—the ball was a fat blur.

Everyone stared with anticipation at the wheel except for Harth, who again was surveying the casino's population, and Jamie, who closely monitored Harth for some clue to his behavior or motivation. The senator's display of disinterest in losing thousands of dollars was eccentric, to say the least.

A sudden bubbling sigh issued from the crowd, followed by a smattering of muffled applause. Both Harth and Jamie turned. The wheel was coming to rest with the sparkling round marker embedded solidly in Green 00.

Jamie felt a thrilling, exhilarating urge to yell, but restrained himself from even applauding politely with the grinning crowd. He turned to

Harth, who was staring back at him oddly. The force of the senator's gaze almost spun Jamie's face away, but something held his eyes. Yes—there was a slight flush of color in the senator's cheeks, a bright flicker of life in his eyes, the suggestion of a dare on his newly pink lips. The shock of winning had resurrected something within this man.

The croupier, a slender Bahamian woman with green eye shadow and charcoal hair stippled with gold, calmly excused herself from the table and returned less than a minute later with a tray of thirty-six purple chips. Graciously, she handed the tray to Harth, who smiled for the first time in Jamie's memory and immediately placed eight chips on the table, two each on red 12, red 23, black 15 and black 26.

The crowd had swollen to double its former size.

With a flourish, Harth tossed a purple chip to the elderly ten-dollar gambler halfway down the table. The old gentleman fortunately had chosen not to bet a color on the last spin.

"I haven't seen you lose yet," Harth said to the surprised man. "Pick a color and stay lucky. The chip is yours."

The elderly gentleman marveled at the purple chip, tugged the suspenders beneath his boneless sport coat, and firmly planted the marker on black.

"That's good enough for me," Harth said, relocating the glossy chips he had abandoned to red. "Let's see, two on black 4—and two more on black 35. I'm counting on you, sir. You say it'll be black—that's where all my money is going."

The elderly man chewed a quivering lip, blotted his forehead with a sleeve, and glanced at the senator with the corner of a frantic eye. Not another bet was placed.

The wheel spun and the ball seemed to float for ages in the smooth rut above the ridged partitions. At last it dropped, bounced unhappily, changed its mind, sliced a shortcut to the opposite side, rattled like a snake's tail, and went suddenly silent.

Jamie closed his eyes. It wasn't his money on the table—he had nothing to gain or lose—but the suspense was killing nevertheless.

A roar burst from the crowd.

Jamie looked up to see the benevolent ball smugly seated in black 4. The senator grinned. The spectators congratulated each other as if they had shared the winnings. At the middle of the table, the elderly gentleman wept joyously.

It took almost three minutes for the croupier to return with Harth's proceeds, a recess brimming with many enthusiastic retellings of the event. Jamie calculated that the senator had won one hundred ninety thousand dollars on four plays.

One hundred ninety thousand!

And Jamie had yet to place a bet.

———

Senator Harth victoriously departed amid more applause. In five minutes he had transformed into a folk hero. There was a spritely bounce to his step as he entered the casino bar, a large, leafy space overlooking the main floor from behind the slot machines. He set down his chips in the center of a table, pulled out a chair, sat down and decided, *what the hell,* he'd have a drink.

A waitress, whose raven-dark hair was blooming a delicate white flower, approached him immediately.

"A double gin martini with two olives," he said. And then he smiled. He had taken the bastards! Pure bum's luck, but he had done it. And it felt great.

Oh, he had dreamed of winning big all right, as all gamblers do. Last night, when told he must gamble away his payoff, the faint glimmer of this dream had tickled the back of his brain, but had remained just outside the gate of consciousness. Later, in his sleep, his mind had fired fantasies like flares into the dark void of despair.

The clever extortion scheme was not perfect after all! It gave Harth the possibility—the infinitesimal chance—of defying all odds and winning big. Since brunch this morning, the senator's imagination, desperate for revenge, had sweetened the odds of winning until they had seemed nearly even. Before his midday nap he already had convinced himself that fate or God or the demons who surely possessed him would grant this miserable condemned creature his one last wish: *to win.*

Winning would change everything. From the beginning, Harth had planned a different kind of scoffing double-cross. He would come to Nassau, follow his instructions to the letter, but pay off only part of the two hundred thousand. He would lock himself in his suite and swallow the four small capsules he had brought for the occasion. Then he would trigger the chemical reaction with a few sparkling ounces of gin and greet the end as he had lived so much of his past thirty years. Inebriated. The combination of drug and alcohol would shut down the proper biological systems and mimic a death that was "natural" for a man with Harth's diseased organs. No one would suspect suicide. His body would be discovered and the remaining money, so tantalizingly close to the extortionists' covetous hands, would be yanked away at the last moment in a final, small stroke of revenge.

Hah! You thought you had my money, didn't you? The amount paid would appease the bloodsuckers well enough to prevent the release of Harth's file. Or so he had hoped.

But now the gambler's feverish dream had sparked another plan. If he should win, he'd take the money. Screw the appeasement! The prospect of actual revenge, not just the taunting shadow of it, was sweet indeed. And so he would take their money, the thing most precious to them, and tomorrow morning, in front of newsmen and photographers, make a gift of it to the Red Cross in Nassau. The money won plus the money brought. All the booty. Gone forever. Then he'd return to his suite and permanently escape from their threats.

Let them defile his name! He didn't care anymore. At least he'd go out swinging and be remembered by some for his selfless generosity.

He thought back to the start of the evening. It had come too soon and the cab had delivered him to the casino too swiftly. As Harth had stepped from the taxi, the greedy facade had stripped the dream from his soul, leaving him there to stand hopeless, an old fool with a wallet full of money and no chance in the world to win. The death of the dream had felt like death itself. Numbly, he had entered the casino, his body obeying basic instructions of movement but his mind dead with disappointment. He would go back to Plan A. *Lose the goddamn money as fast as he could. Get the hell out of there. Don't let false hopes rise only to crash and burn. Forget the game.*

Instead, he would search the surreal landscape for the faces of those parasites who wanted to bleed him dry. Somehow he would know them. A small look of guilt. The stench of evil. An eye caught staring. A profile too often nearby. He would recognize the bastards and at last give faces to the monstrous shapes he had imagined.

But everything had changed. They would be watching him, nervously wondering what he would do with the winnings. It had been just a fluke, they'd be thinking. He'll go back and lose it all like he's supposed to.

Or would they approach him here? Would they risk exposure to remind him of his instructions? He almost wished they would. Then he could tell them face to face to go screw themselves. He was keeping the damn money. They should've known that fooling around with George Harth was a stupid, expensive, jackass idea.

The martini came and he ordered another. What the hell. Could it shorten his life?

He toasted the purple chips and gulped the drink.

Bring the bastards on! he thought. *Let 'em come and push me! Let me see what a bloodsucker looks like.*

As if reading his thoughts, the man came. He walked timidly, looking around the room as if his course were set only coincidentally for Harth's precise location. He arrived at the table and looked the senator in the eye for the first time. Yes—it made sense. This man was Harth's prime suspect, always glancing at him, following him, watching him play, yet never gambling himself. Let the bastard stand there in his discount store suit until he found his bloodsucking little voice.

Jamie said, softly, "Senator Harth?"

A cold, silent stare.

"I wanted to congratulate you, sir. I'm from your neck of the woods, and I saw you win at roulette. I've never seen anything like that before in my life, and I hope you're going to quit—at least for the evening—because I don't think my heart could take it again. I'd sure hate to see you lose it all back."

So that was how the bloodsucker put it. The senator grinned. "Have a seat, Mr.—"

"Jamie Giles."

———

"Mr. Giles." Harth extended a hand, which Jamie took. The senator squeezed Jamie's hand painfully as he leaned close and said, "You fuck-ing bloodsuckers would blackmail Jesus Christ if you could get a file on him, wouldn't you? Let me put something into that weasel's brain of yours. You and your shithead friends aren't gonna get a nickel back or another goddam penny out of me. Now—" Harth smiled broadly and released his wrench-like grip. "Would you like a drink?"

Jamie couldn't think of a thing to say, so he nodded yes.

"Fine, you're buying." Harth motioned to the raven-haired waitress.

"Scotch and water," Jamie told her. He still couldn't think of any-thing to say. Seconds ticked by uncomfortably in silence. His mind was whirring.

The senator finally spoke. "You don't have to be coy with me. I know what you want me to do."

"I really think you think I'm someone I'm not." Jamie groped for words awkwardly, but then detected a small tremor in the rhythm of Harth's brittle offensive, so he continued. "We only met this morning. I had shaving cream all over my face so you might not recognize me."

Harth's face did not move but the fire in his eyes died. Then, slowly, the hard-lipped smile sagged.

"I'm sorry if you thought I was after your money," Jamie said. "I suppose I did look like someone moving in for the kill."

Still the senator stared speechlessly, with eyes suddenly pale, not sun-bright as they were a moment ago. The senator gripped his temples with his thumb and middle finger and massaged deeply.

Jamie felt a gathering strength. He had not shattered beneath the force of an utterly brutal assault. As he watched the senator's growing distress, Jamie's eyes ignited with a burst of guilty pleasure. His mind probed the dark hidden spaces between spoken words and found a hard rock of certainty: he had been mistaken for someone else, someone who expected money from Harth. The senator was acutely embarrassed because he had realized his blunder. In a minute he would compose himself well enough to offer an apology, perhaps a deceitful explanation of some kind, and then express a desire to pay for Jamie's drink as partial atonement. This desire to redress his wrongdoing would be a moment of vulnerability for Harth, a moment that Jamie could shamelessly seize to help fulfill his plan.

Jamie's mind had never galloped so fiercely, so methodically. There was no compassion for the senator's embarrassment; only a cruel, urgent craving to get on with it, to press the exposed nerves and watch the puppet dance. This was a new appetite, alarming but invigorating.

The prophecy was fulfilled. Senator Harth raised his head from its prayerful attitude, glanced at Jamie with puckered eyes and intoned a gravelly, "I'm sorry… and I'm very embarrassed about the way I treated you. I hope you'll accept my apology."

"Of course."

The scotch came and the senator handed the waitress a ten-dollar bill, telling her with an understated flourish of his hand to keep the change.

"When I came up to your table, you seemed so… imposed upon. I really didn't mean to—"

"No, it wasn't your fault. It's just that there are people in this world who are strongly attracted to big winnings like this, hoping for a hand-out. Winners tend to have an overgenerous spirit, you know. But these people will try almost anything. I thought you were one of them."

"You speak from experience with these... people?"

"They're the same species of parasite that hang around the dying rich. But in your case I was badly mistaken, and I'm sorry. Yes, I remember you from the hallway. Quite a face you had on. I like this one better." The senator smiled, and so did Jamie. "If you had worn your shaving cream here, I doubt that I would have made this mistake. You said you were from my part of the country, as I recall?"

"Yes, from Wisconsin actually. Madison." Jamie felt compelled to lie. Was Michigan not close enough for small talk? "All my life."

"You voted for me, I hope." The senator's tone had quickly become good-natured. Such a politician!

"Apparently a lot of people did, including my wife."

"You're married, then? Is your wife here?"

"Not here with me right now, but yes, she's in Nassau. If she had known I'd run into you here, I couldn't have stopped her from coming. I told her about our conference in the hall and she was very upset that I didn't invite her. She's very political. Worked very hard for your campaign, as a matter of fact, on the telephone."

"I was very fortunate to have so many good people on my side. Perhaps I met her."

"Almost, one time. But she missed you."

"I wouldn't say that she missed much," he said humbly. "I'm just a man, after all."

"You're more than that, I think. To Kathy you're a kind of ideal. She's never forgotten almost meeting you."

"Well—maybe we can fix that for her. After all, we're both in Nassau."

"Would you? I know it would mean so much to her if she could meet you."

"I don't see why not."

"I really feel like I'm imposing on you to even suggest this, but—oh, it's ridiculous really."

"Maybe not. What is it?"

"It's just that tomorrow morning we're having brunch in the hotel about ten o'clock with some friends. If there were in any way—"

"At ten tomorrow?"

"You're probably busy—"

"No, I think it's a wonderful idea. Especially considering all the time your wife gave to me. Afterwards, perhaps you would all be my guests at a little ceremony I'm part of at the Red Cross—if you don't mind newsmen."

"That sounds terrific! We'll just meet you downstairs. I think I'll let this be a surprise to Kathy."

"Looking forward to it." And oddly, the senator *was*. The plan had come to him in a glorious technicolor burst. Why not live out his last hours surrounded by admirers? He would set up the details in the morning.

Jamie drained his glass in perfect sync with Harth. "I do hope you won't gamble that money away," he said.

"Not a chance. In fact, I'm going back to the hotel right now. No sense getting greedy."

Jamie considered sharing a cab, but decided against it. Getting too chummy could be a risk. All Jamie wanted to do was divert the senator from his suite at ten o'clock so he could enter it after housekeeping had unlocked the door. Once inside, he was certain to find the missing piece to this tragic puzzle.

"Is it safe, carrying so much money on you?" Jamie asked.

"Probably not. Too many people saw me win it. I think I'll cash in my chips and call the police for an escort."

"Then I'll see you in the morning." Jamie rose from the table with Harth and shook hands.

"Ten o'clock. I'll be there."

———

Jamie watched the senator move to the cashier. It took only seconds to convert the chips to cash. After the senator counted the bills again, he held a brief exchange with the cashier, who concluded by nodding agreeably, probably confirming that he would call the police escort.

Instead of leaving immediately, the senator walked back to the bar and approached Jamie with a smile.

"Are you staying after all?" Jamie asked.

"No. I just brought a little something back for you." The senator flipped a purple chip to Jamie. "See you at ten."

He turned and was gone before Jamie could react.

The senator was not such a bad guy.

A thousand bucks! Maybe Jamie's luck was changing.

It would be a few minutes before the police escort arrived, and Jamie wanted to leave after Harth, so he decided to kill some time by gambling. Just the fifty dollars he had brought with him, of course. Unless he hit a hot streak. This evening, roulette had acquired a special glow.

Jamie marched to the roulette table and arrived just as the wheel was coming to rest. No winners—a good spin for the house. Jamie put ten dollars on red 14. An impulse.

Seconds later he had lost ten dollars. Try again... Harth had lost twice before winning. Ten on black 2. Not even close, the ball seated itself smirkingly on the other side of the wheel. Once more... *this could be the one.* Ten on red 32. He could hear the number speaking to him.

But it must have been saying, "Don't bet on me." Down thirty bucks so far. Ten on black 15. Watch the wheel spin. And spin and spin. Tough luck... red 3. Okay, one last time. This is it! Ten on red 23. The first four were just practice. *C'mon, ball!*

Zilch.

Jamie looked at his purple chip, then put it into his pocket. *No way!* He wondered if the senator had departed yet, so he walked to the entrance for a look. There, in a splash of light, Harth was hauling his cash-burdened body into the no-frills back seat of a small police car. With a whine of gears, he was gone.

Outside, the cool night breeze fanned small rivulets of nervous perspiration on Jamie's face.

"Jamie Giles!" The voice reached out of the dark and slapped him. "Jamie Giles, over here."

Billy Smythe was disentangling his large frame from the limo's steering column, stepping from the open door, then standing fully erect not twenty yards away.

"Billy, you're still here," Jamie said.

"Slow night. Ready to go back?"

"More ready than you know."

Jamie gratefully entered the vehicle and slumped into the back seat. "It's been quite a night," he said as the limousine eased away from the casino.

"How's that?"

"You know that old fellow I thought I knew? I watched him win a hundred and ninety thousand dollars at roulette. Amazing!"

Smythe seemed to flinch slightly, then said, "He *won*? Are you sure?"

"I was standing right there."

"He must have been placing large bets."

"The way he started, it looked like he was trying to unload a lot of money fast. He just sort of tossed down chips like they meant nothing."

"It must have been quite a sight. Did you ever find out who he was?"

"A United States Senator from Wisconsin named Harth."

"I saw him leave with the police. Smart man, but it cost me a fare. Not to change the subject, but are we still on for noon tomorrow?"

"Twelve o'clock sharp. I'll meet you in front of the hotel."

"One more question," Smythe said. "Did you lose badly in there?"

"If you're wondering about my ability to pay for this fine scenic tour I'm getting tomorrow, the answer is yes, I can. Which means I didn't lose everything."

"Then I will continue driving." Smythe laughed.

Within minutes, Jamie was in his room and only hours away from the answers he sought, answers that would change his life forever.

CHAPTER 20

Kathy awoke at two that morning, disoriented and alarmed. It took a full minute to find reality.

The darkness hid the crumbling plaster walls of the bedroom, the scabs of peeling paint on the two naked windows, the lumpy lacquered arms of the lone straight-back chair, the threadbare braided rug—all the imperfections she knew were there. Beneath her, the mattress dipped and sloped like the hills of Michigan's Upper Peninsula. She could smell the dust that coated the torn lampshade, dimmed the single bulb, filled the cracks between splintered floorboards, and gathered like families of small furry animals around every leg of the bed, the chair, the nightstand, the dresser.

Yet the room, now familiar to her fully awake mind, felt so safe and secure. The madness could not reach her here, not in Billy's tiny house. And if it did, Billy would protect her.

Why did she feel so sure of that? He was, after all, a stranger—this giant black man with hands like steam shovels and a firebrick chest you could shoot bullets at and not mark. She was dwarfed by him physically. By all rights, she should be scared to death. But here she was, sleeping in his house, his bed, vulnerable as a newborn infant but feeling calm and happy.

She felt it in the way he comforted her and held her while she sobbed after trying to be so brave. There was nothing sexual in his smothering, sweeping embrace, just a tenderness and a sadness that could have come only from a deep understanding.

She wondered if this made her a "kept" woman. *Ridiculous!* They had spent barely two hours together and then he had dashed off. Two short, miraculous hours of healing. A brief contact, like the skip of a stone on water that leaves a soft embrace of rings to resonate in larger and larger circles. She tingled now with such a resonance, and with the shimmering anticipation of another skip of the stone.

Being here was so insane… but so *right*! As if everything in her life, every small fragment, had existed to lead her to Billy Smythe. How else could she explain this exquisite sense of completion, this crackling shower of sparks at the very thought of him, this wholeness that swallowed her pain and fed the starving core of hope inside her.

She rolled over and cuddled the pillow, imagining it was Billy. She knew Billy would never be her lover, but he would protect her, and love her in his own way. He would be kind and gentle, wise and understanding. He would hold her when she needed to be held, talk to her about important things, personal things, magical things.

Kathy knew that she would be staying here for a long time, and she was confident that Billy knew, too. Neither of them would have to say it; they belonged to each other now.

Tomorrow she'd clean and paint and put up curtains and make this house a place to share sunny good times and…

She fell asleep, smiling.

———

Senator George Harth awoke. Something about his arm was wrong. It had gone to sleep and the muscles were tingling with a thousand fiery pinpricks.

Like a morning fog, sleep still filled the tired hollows of his mind, but the sensation of needles dancing on his arm kept pricking him awake. Clinging to the gossamer threads of a dream that now eluded him, he opened his eyes and shifted position. *Damn arm!* It would take forever to get back to sleep; it always did.

His right arm felt as if it were fused into an electric circuit, a river of high-voltage current coursing through its bony core. He tried to wiggle his fingers, but they were frozen into a grotesque claw.

Something was *dreadfully* wrong!

Roughly, with his left hand, he rubbed the arm, encouraging blood to return. The arm was hard as a copper wire. With a fist he hammered the arm, trying to wake it up, to loosen the locked muscles and smash the hot cinders that spattered against the raw underside of his skin.

Was this part of the dream? No, no. His arm was ticking, throbbing. He sat up, the sudden horror of reality overcoming him. The river of current broke through the dam of his shoulder, and with a slippery ease began to fill the empty spaces of his body. With a terrible clarity of vision he saw the swollen mass of his heart about to burst. The room filled with pouring prayers: *dear God, not now, not tonight. Just one more day. Don't let it go unfinished.*

There was no answer but the dark, raspy passage of frightened air through the senator's throat, in and out, a tremulous and ghostly sound that Harth was afraid would stop. Each inhalation brought a new surge of throbbing pain. With each exhalation the life seemed to slip out of him. There was just a moment left—he knew that—but the moment stretched into a longer time. And then the growing cluster of pain seemed to congeal into a ball and remove itself from his body, which was still throbbing as if from physical blows, but somehow separate from him. The full physical agony of it was still present, but his mind uncannily was able to sense it remotely, objectively. The ball crackled with pain and tugged on him, gently at first, as a magnet pulls the hand when approaching metal, and then stronger, like the unforgiving force of gravity. As Harth was drawn toward it, the ball moved away.

The pain had become almost unbearable; if it had been inside him, he would have fainted. Yet he was fully conscious, amazingly still conscious and alive. The ball drifted from the bed, pulling Harth to the edge where he tried to stand but instead slumped into a rattle of unsupported bones, his strength gone, his fear swollen with the blinding pain, his prayers unanswered.

So this is how it is to die.

Still the ball pulled at him, and somehow he moved forward, undulating on his left side like some hideous serpentine creature slithering across the floor of a nightmare. His right arm and leg were dead; their useless pulp was now excess baggage. He was dying in sections. But still he moved, wrestling his own carcass across the carpet, pulled by some power into the black cave of the sitting room, reduced in his final moment to a wretched, quivering hulk.

Tears streamed down his face, not from the pain but from this humiliating view of himself.

And then he saw it, just ahead, and at last he understood the purpose of this last dreadful journey. He saw the object of it and his determination grew. The ball of pain was leading him—if he could only make it. *God, please, a few more seconds. A little more strength.*

His left hand clawed the carpet, fingers and toes digging into the nap, arm and leg ratcheting his enormous weight forward foot by foot, until he couldn't go on or his body surely would burst into a bloody splash. But his hand was touching it. He was so close. One last effort, one last impossible gathering of strength. He caught onto it somehow and his body moved again. He was lifting himself, pulling himself up, up...

———

An hour later, the tall figure was still standing in the small indentation that housed the ice chest and vending machines. From this vantage point, no one in the fifth floor corridor could escape Billy Smythe's inspection.

He was very tired. For nearly four hours he had manned this guard post, a lone sentry with only the monotonous drone of the machines to keep him company. It had been a quiet night. Five people had returned to their suites, none had left. The machines had gone unused until now. Billy grabbed a handful of ice from the chest and rubbed his eyes with it. The cold shock peeled back a thin, gauzy film of fatigue and felt good on his drooping eyelids.

Could he have misjudged this whole affair? Had he jumped to the wrong conclusion? Doubt was taking advantage of his exhaustion. It didn't matter, really. He could not take the risk of departing. Not yet. He'd give it until six o'clock and then catch a few hours' sleep before his noon engagement with Jamie. By tonight it would be all over.

For a time.

The soft rustle of trouser legs caught Billy's attention. Another false alarm? At least there was some activity in the corridor. The rustling stopped and there was an odd silence that made Billy's heart beat faster. Someone was standing in the corridor.

At last—the sound of a security card being inserted and the soft thwack of the lock opening. The doorknob gently, quietly turning. The door opening with the faintest creak, and then a soft tick as the safety chain stretched taut.

This was it! Billy looked into the corridor. A short, squat man in a baggy tan suit was leaning against the door of Suite 534. His back was to Smythe and he peered suspiciously down the corridor toward the elevators. The pressure of the man's shoulder held the door open against the chain. As if in slow motion, the man produced a wire cutter that was at least eighteen inches long.

Billy silently slipped up behind the man as the wire cutter's jaws were brought up to the chain. With a dull ping, the jaws closed and the chain snapped. The man slowly pushed open the door.

As he stepped inside, a huge hand clamped onto his neck from behind, steely fingers digging into the tendons just below the skull in a paralyzing grip. The man's arms went limp and Billy took the wire cutter from his hand.

Billy turned the man like a ventriloquist's puppet and looked down at his pudgy face. The man's eyes bulged with pain and fear.

"Did you have an appointment with the senator?" Billy asked, squeezing hard. The man groaned and Billy made his head gesture *no*.

"That's too bad," Billy said, "The senator does not like entertaining visitors without an appointment. You understand, don't you?"

Billy's enormous hand manipulated the man's head up and down.

"But since you came all the way up here, perhaps you'd like to leave a calling card." Billy tucked the wire cutter under his arm and slipped his right hand beneath the man's suit coat, withdrawing a razor-sharp stiletto. "Oh—look at this! Planning to do your nails while you waited for the senator?" Billy dropped the stiletto, then reached into the man's pocket and took out the security card. He released his grip, and the man slumped against the wall.

The man vigorously rubbed the back of his neck, squinting his eyes closed and revolving his head in a tiny circle. He stopped and opened his eyes when he felt something cold.

The sharp blades of the wire cutter were pinching his nose.

"I've got a tip for the people who sent you," Billy said. "Forget it. The senator's well protected, so let him be. And if I see you nosing around here again—" Billy put pressure on the wire cutter's blades— "you won't have a nose to do it with." He removed the wire cutter. Blood started to form along the blade marks on the man's nostrils.

"Now get out of here!"

Billy pulled the man from the wall and booted him down the hall.

Holding his bleeding nose, the man took off running and shot down the stairway.

Billy picked up the stiletto and headed for the elevator. He'd get more sleep tonight than he had thought.

CHAPTER 21

It was a fitful night for Jamie. He woke up twice, aware that he was alone in bed, and called out for Kathy. Both times he relived the trauma of finding the note and imagining what terrible things he had done to her.

Would he ever get used to it? The loneliness was unbearable.

At 9:30 that morning he awoke again. Damn! He hadn't expected to sleep so late. Slowly, he reassembled the plan in his groggy mind. How childish it seemed in the morning light. Could he possibly go through with it? Would it work? He had to try.

The interior of Suite 534 held the critical piece to this terrible puzzle that had ripped apart his life.

He quickly showered, shaved, brushed his teeth, and dressed in jeans and a short-sleeve red and white pullover. It was now 9:50 a.m. Had the senator already left his room? Would housekeeping be on schedule?

Jamie opened the hallway door a crack and began his vigil. The linen cart was in front of Suite 532. The minutes passed slowly. At last the thick-armed housekeeping lady walked out of 532, closing the door behind her. Slowly, she pushed the cart to 534 and knocked. "Housekeeping," she said in a bored voice.

No answer. The senator was gone.

The woman unlocked the door and opened it. She reached for a bucket of cleaning supplies on the lower shelf of the cart and entered the suite.

Give her a minute, Jamie told himself. *Don't be too anxious. Then you can walk in like you were the occupant returning for something you'd forgotten.*

And then it happened.

A high-pitched scream ricocheted through the corridor catching Jamie squarely between the eyes. He was so tightly strung that the scream nearly knocked him over. His knees buckled and a guilty shiver, as if he had been caught in some illegal act, swept over him in waves. He recovered slightly and went to the doorway just in time to see the housekeeping lady racing down the hall.

Jamie tried to pull himself together. Whatever had happened didn't matter. Suite 534 was open and vacant. Still trembling, Jamie walked past the linen cart and through the open doorway. He was several paces inside before he saw the deep blue daybed with its bold white flowers and delicate ferns—and near it, on the floor, the senator, eyes open in a dead man's stare, a defiant smile creasing his face.

A pain struck Jamie in the chest, a burning pain that began like heartburn but burst suddenly into full flame and threatened to devour him from inside. His mouth opened in a sucking gasp and his hand flew to his chest. He dropped to his knees, dizzy and sick. The room for a moment lost its shape and he was floating in a sea of hot bubbling water. He was in the *spa*; his lungs were filling with water, and he was frantically thrashing his arms.

Without conscious thought, his legs carried him toward the open door of the bathroom. Switching on the light, he looked in and *saw* the spa filled with churning water. Impossible. He'd heard no sound. And then he saw himself lying in it, eyes open in a dead man's stare—*no!* It was himself, but the face was someone else. Not Jamie, but some other...

Jamie stood, teetering. He felt old and angry. He stumbled into the front room, crashed into a table, then stumbled and fell on a brief case lying just beyond the senator's outstretched hand.

A thought with no clear source inserted itself into his mind. *Okay, pull yourself together. Remember the ritual. Never leave the briefcase in the room. Make sure the security key is in your pocket before leaving.*

Jamie rubbed his thigh, felt the hard metal shape of his own security card in the pocket. He mindlessly clutched the handle of the briefcase and walked toward the door. Something about the room was wrong, but he couldn't remember what it was. He knew that for some reason he was in a hurry to leave. He could check the room later.

Without looking back, he walked into the corridor, past the linen cart, and into his own suite, closing the door. He set the briefcase on the coffee table and passed out on the sofa, his head whirling in confusion.

Sometime later—minutes perhaps?—Jamie woke up.

Panic instantly seized him. *The senator was dead!*

He heard voices in the corridor, went to the door and looked out. A thick clot of people, some of them paramedics, were standing outside the senator's door. Suddenly, a gurney was wheeled through the doorway into the hall. Someone looked at Jamie and said, "Please, sir— we don't need any more confusion out here right now. Go back inside."

Jamie did. As he turned, closing the door behind him, he saw the brief-case on the coffee table. How had it gotten there? Whose briefcase was it? He walked to the table, staring nervously at the case as if it were an alien life form. A brass monogram gleamed with the initials *GEH.* George E. Harth. But Jamie could remember nothing about how it had gotten there.

Jamie knelt in front of the table for a full minute before slowly trying the latches. It was unlocked! He raised the lid.

Cash! Stacks and stacks of cash. Harth's winnings, obviously.

The rectangles of green crackled as Jamie's fingers obsessively pinched and bent the bound stacks. The fine, curling fibers on the paper's surface could have been the tracings of sparks, so electric was the touch of each bill on his skin. Jamie's heart was jackhammering his chest and perspiration slicked his forehead. And then, with a nervous lunge, he was counting it out, notching up the score with each wet-thumbed stroke, cleaning the carcass of the briefcase in a feeding frenzy of greed. Scattered about him was the scavenged litter of a small fortune: one hundred and ninety thousand dollars! With a circle of arms and fanned-out fingers, he caressed his riches. Lowering his head, he nuzzled the shifting stacks the way he had nuzzled the warm curve of Kathy's neck on past mornings. There was a source of power here, and Jamie wanted to inhale it, taste it, absorb it through every hungry pore. The air was heavy with the perfume of wealth. His body tingled.

A sharp rap on the door startled him. He looked up with the defiance of a lion guarding a fresh kill: *Don't come any closer!*

Another knock slapped him awake, as if he had been dreaming someone else's dream. He looked down. The money was real. They were coming to get it. *They knew!*

Instinctively, he scooped the stacks of bills into the briefcase and dropped it behind the sofa. How could he possibly explain having Harth's money in his possession? He raced to the door, stopped for a deep breath, and then opened it. In the hallway stood a tall Bahamian in a gray suit, the same man who had ordered Jamie back into his suite moments earlier.

"Sorry to disturb you, sir," the man said, "I snapped at you earlier and I wanted to apologize."

"Oh, that's all right," Jamie said, "You were in the middle of some trouble, I can understand that."

What did this man want?

"A medical emergency. The gentleman across the hall took ill. Did you know him?"

Why was this man asking questions? Did he suspect something?

"I really can't say," Jamie replied. "Which gentleman are you referring to?"

"The man in Suite 534, a senator from the United States."

"The senator? Yes—we had talked once, briefly. I hope he's not seriously ill."

"I'm afraid he's passed away,"

"I'm sorry to hear that." *Was he being too casual?* "He wasn't looking very well yesterday. What was it?"

"Natural causes, apparently. We won't know the precise cause for a while."

"Well—thank you for telling me. I was curious."

Surely this man had not come merely to apologize.

"We did find something a bit odd, though. Something that complicates the situation."

This was it. Jamie could feel a nervous flutter in the pit of his stomach. "What was that?"

"The safety chain on the inside of his door had been cut through, neat as can be. I was wondering if you had heard anything during the night."

"The chain was cut? You mean… someone broke into the suite?"

"That's what we're trying to find out. It's probably nothing. I don't want you to be alarmed—or the hotel will be on my back."

"Cut through? That is frightening. Was anything missing?"

God, what a question! It was blurted out before he had thought.

"Not that we know, but then the senator's not here to give us an inventory of his belongings."

"Yes, I suppose it's hard to tell. I really don't think I can help you. I slept like a log last night… a little too much rum."

"Ahhh, the holiday spirits. Well, I won't keep you. Are you here on vacation?"

Jamie nodded. "A very enjoyable one until now."

"I hope this doesn't spoil it for you sir. Good day."

"Yes, uh—goodbye."

Jamie closed the door and walked to the sofa, letting his body collapse into its softness. What did this all mean? The conversation seemed routine. But the cut chain would lead to more inquiries, and soon the authorities would learn of the senator's fabulously good fortune at the casino. A check of the hotel's vault would reveal that Harth had not deposited his winnings for safekeeping, which would mean he had kept the money in his room. Of course, the money would not be found there. If the senator had died of natural causes, the conclusion would be that an intruder had broken into the suite and stolen the money. But had the thief found the senator already dead? It would hardly matter. Unless the police suspected Jamie of burglary, he was off the hook. Any number of people must have seen the senator win at roulette; the list of suspects would be a long one.

But if the thief had cut through the chain to steal the winnings, why had he left the money behind? Had the senator's body frightened him off? Unlikely. Had the intruder failed to find the money? Impossible. Had the senator frightened the burglar off and then died of a heart attack? Possibly.

A sudden horrifying revelation came over Jamie. He was going to keep the money. He had taken it from the senator's suite—that was the only explanation for its presence here—and he had never considered giving it back.

How could he return it without implicating himself? How would he ever explain? Besides, the senator was dead, and nearly half the money had been Harth's for less than twelve hours. The other half probably had been gambling money the senator was prepared to lose. The way Harth had carelessly bet thousands the previous evening seemed to indicate that money was of little consequence to him.

Didn't it?

The gloating pleasure Jamie had experienced while counting those stacks of cash troubled him the most. A sharp pang of guilt stabbed at him. He retrieved the briefcase from behind the sofa and set it on the table. Would the money still be inside? Or was it another of his maddening visions? He opened it.

There, in a soft shaft of sunlight, the reality of the fortune lay before him. A vibration seemed to emanate from the money, looping out and curving back with Jamie's hands in tow. He ran his fingers across the smooth surface of the bills and knew that his conscience had lost a battle. The guilt was replaced with a sense of power that energized him, filled him up, and stroked every pleasure center in his body. He could feel the evolution of himself into something else, something stronger.

And he liked it.

He closed the briefcase and smiled. The senator had experienced good fortune the night before. Why shouldn't Jamie experience it today?

He locked the briefcase inside the largest of his suitcases and shoved it under the bed. In thirty minutes he would meet Billy Smythe. He reclined on the bed, not because he was tired—his body was buzzing with energy—but because he needed to think.

The dream.

Suite 534.

The puzzle remained unsolved. There were now more unanswered questions than before. As with an interrupted dream, Jamie was left with only the reverberation of pieces linked. Something significant had emerged from the chasm in Jamie's broken consciousness and then retreated, like a demon barely glimpsed, into the impenetrable underworld of his mind.

Faint glimpses of his excursion into the senator's room began to taunt him. He tried to relive the experience, but his brain was uncooperative, and only grudgingly presenting snapshots... until the moment Jamie had climbed out of his bathroom hallucination and prepared to leave the suite. The blood on his chest in reality had been the red stripes of his shirt. The sulfurous pain in his chest had subsided. And then a small but sudden snapping had occurred, like a channel being switched, and

Jamie now recalled the oddest mental sensation, as if for a moment all sensory input of the dead senator had been erased, wiped clean from the mind, replaced almost seamlessly by a new continuity. The notions had insinuated themselves into his mind: *Make sure the security card is in your pocket before leaving*—Jamie's hotel ritual. And *never leave the briefcase in the room*—where had *that* come from?

The briefcase. He had grabbed it then, obeying some instinct, some inner voice. *But whose?* Jamie had never carried a briefcase.

Reliving those few horrible moments was emotionally draining. Jamie closed his eyes and tried to relax by breathing deeply. He fell asleep and woke up at five minutes before noon. Thank God for that internal clock! Perhaps the trip back to the castle would produce another piece to this ever-growing puzzle.

As he thought of the fortune beneath his bed, he smiled.

Yes, he could afford Billy Smythe now.

Jamie splashed water on his face in the bathroom, dried it with a crusty towel (why do hotels never use fabric softener?) and walked casually into the corridor.

No hurry. Billy could wait. Jamie could afford *respect* now. Amazing what money could do for one's deportment.

CHAPTER 22

In the lobby, Jamie was seized by an inexplicable urge to buy a cigar. He entered the gift shop and chose two Dutch Masters, one for himself and one for Billy. He had never smoked, but surely the events of the day were cause for celebration.

He could almost taste the flavor-rich smoke curling over his tongue. He placed the cigars in his shirt pocket. Outside, the waving hand of Billy Smythe caught his attention.

"Good afternoon, Mr. Giles." Billy gave him a fleeting smile as he approached. "Are we still going to the castle?"

"I haven't changed my mind."

"Good. I hope I won't be carrying you back to the car this time."

"Billy, I feel good enough today to carry *you* to the car. Let's go."

They climbed into the old limousine and pulled away from the hotel.

"Have you seen the senator this morning?" Billy asked. "I'd suspect he'd be in a pretty good mood today."

"It's funny you should ask." Jamie said, "He got sick last night and died. Rotten timing, isn't it?"

Billy's eyes flashed in the rear view mirror. "He died last night? Are you sure?"

"The police came by and told me."

"The police? Why would they do such a thing?"

"Do what?"

"Come by to tell you a guest had died."

"Well, they said something about his safety chain being cut through. They wondered if I had heard anything."

"Had you?"

"Nothing."

"Did he die of natural causes?"

"As far as they know."

"What about his money. Did they find it?"

"They didn't mention anything about it, frankly. But I guess they had no reason to."

"Death seldom comes when one expects it."

"You turning philosophical on me?"

"I've seen a lot of death in my lifetime. I suppose I'll see more before my time comes."

"You sound sad. Like you lost someone you knew."

"I'm sorry, but at my age you think about death a bit differently." The limousine tentatively eased under the iron arch of the castle's property. The steep driveway slit in half the dense green tapestry of tropical foliage, veering sharply in one direction then another, like a paper tear gone off the crease. Everywhere, flowers like fireworks in a green sky exploded with color.

The exotic jungle paradise slid coolly past Jamie, who sat calmly in the back seat of the limo. "You're going so slow," Jamie said.

"Force of habit. Those few people I take up here usually complain about going too fast. I suspect the path from life to the hereafter must look something like this."

"It would not be a disappointment. But the road seems much longer this time."

"The first time was a discovery. This time it's merely a delay."

At last the limo pulled up in front of the magnificent stucco castle. Like a yellow sunrise, the structure stretched up into the sky, overwhelming the startling beauty of its setting.

Jamie stared in awe. "It's more beautiful than I had remembered," he said. "The man who lives here—he must be very wealthy. You knew him?"

"I did. Very well, in fact. I have a surprise for you."

Billy opened his door and got out. Jamie followed him toward the castle.

"The view from the entrance balcony is an experience to remember," Billy said.

Slowly he led Jamie up the stone stairs that began at the left end of the castle and converged with another stairway at the building's entrance. There, standing on the sun-filled balcony with the fantastic mansion at his back, Jamie looked out at the sparkling sea. A warm breeze ruffled his hair. He breathed in the humid smell of oceans and distant horizons and history heavy in the air. In his mind, Spanish galleons scudded past like clouds and musket fire crackled. Hoarse shouts in undecipherable languages echoed across the water, ricocheted off the castle's wall, and swirled like water devils in front of him.

Jamie felt suddenly alive and alert, filled with a sense of excitement and power. He wanted to hold up his hands and command an army, send ships to foreign lands, issue divine decrees to the gulls who patrolled the seas.

Foolishness, of course. But such a powerful surge of excitement it was. Like a tide.

Jamie turned at the sound of metal scratching. Behind him Billy was unlocking the massive mahogany door, swinging it open with a broad gesture.

"And this is my surprise," Billy said. "Would you care for a peek?"

The slowly opening door allowed a scroll of sunlight to unroll across the marble floor behind it. Jamie's sunstruck pupils could see only a velvety darkness beyond the reach of the sun. The castle's musty breath enveloped him.

Slowly he stepped into the hushed darkness, moving cautiously, as a man newly blind. On the floor ahead he could make out ragged stripes of sunlight projected by a long row of windows covered by imperfectly aligned drapes. The yellow stripes measured a room of enormous dimension.

Jamie's eyes began to see shapes in the dim environment. He moved past a large sculpture and strained to identify it in the murky light.

A loud thrashing sound announced the opening of the drapes. The room ignited in a dazzle of daylight. Jamie whirled around, stunned by the emergence of a fantastic world beyond expectation. Enormous paintings and Gobelin tapestries. Ornate Louis XIV furniture. A delicate rosewood jewelry box in the shape of a medieval castle. Exquisite Chinese vases and porcelain chandeliers. A milk-white marble floor with Persian rugs of burgundy and gold. Brass candlestick holders as tall as a man. A row of short pillars supporting ebony busts of ancient and modern figures.

"It's breathtaking," Jamie muttered, "absolutely breathtaking."

His eyes came full circle to the giant sculpture dominating the room. Chiseled from a single block of purple granite was the massive bulk of a raging bull elephant in full stride, with tusks of genuine ivory protruding like lances from its lowered head. It was a work of startling beauty, but the fierce kinetic beauty of it sent a shockwave of panic through Jamie's bones. This was the beast of his waking nightmare, the killer of his imagined self. Jamie was jarringly drawn back to the sensations of his dream-death: the taste of blood, the piercing scream, the wrenching crunch of bones, the sweet unconsciousness of... of...

He was waking. Had he fainted? There was no cushion of pine needles here, just the cold marble slab of the castle floor. Above him the huge upraised foot of the stone elephant, frozen in time and space, declared once again a reprieve from... *what?*

Jamie tried to move, but his arms would not respond. They were pinned beneath him. He could not separate his legs.

He was tied up!

And then he heard the words: "I'm sorry." It was familiar voice, soft and sad. There, towering above him like a second great sculpture, was Billy Smythe. "I had no choice," Billy said. In his hand was a knife, its blade shining in the sunlight. "There is no longer any doubt."

"Billy, for God's sake what's going on? Why am I tied up like this?"

"I could have killed you before you woke up, you know that."

"For the love of God, are you crazy or what?"

Billy ignored Jamie's words. He seemed lost within himself. "Killing is not easy for me. I couldn't do it, not while you slept. I had to look into your eyes first, into that evil soul to remind me of the reason."

He squatted, leaned over Jamie's bound body, and stared into the fear-struck eyes. "I don't know how you did it, how you came back to me so soon. It seemed impossible at first. But you found a way."

Billy roughly grabbed Jamie by the shirt and seated him upright against the base of the elephant sculpture. "Do you know what I'm talking about?"

Jamie's eyes went blank.

"Of course you don't. Not yet. You wouldn't have come up here with me if you had known. You kept your promise, you know."

"Billy—" Jamie suddenly found his voice. "This is... is some kind of mistake. None of this makes sense."

"You promised you'd come back, and you did. I thought you were crazy, it all seemed so impossible, but I thought if it were true, twenty... maybe *thirty* years it would take. But in just *weeks*?"

"Billy, listen…"

"Look around you. Do you know what this place is? It's *yours*—your home, your monument. Don't you recognize it? Doesn't it comfort you to be back home?"

Jamie, confused and afraid, could find no reply. His muscles trembled.

"Do you know who you are?" Billy was ranting now, pacing back and forth. "You are not Jamie Giles. You were, maybe—but no longer. No, you're not Jamie Giles at all, you're *him*!"

CHAPTER 23

Billy was standing by a column that displayed the bust of a fleshy-faced man with scowling eyebrows and haunted eyes.

"This is you… Bernard Klassen. What's the matter, don't you recognize yourself? Look at those eyes. Even in this bust you can see the devil in them. Oh, forgive me—I am Billy Smythe, your humble servant."

Billy bowed sarcastically.

"And you're Judas," he continued. "Would you like to know how I recognized you?"

Jamie stared, motionless.

"Did you think it was only coincidence that you came to be in my cab? The moment I saw you at the airport I was afraid. The blue shirt, and the white scarf and slacks. That was Klassen! Apparently even death does not eliminate bad taste."

Jamie's mind raced. The shopping before the trip… he had gone from store to store, looking for new clothes. Nothing had appealed to him. But then, as if discovered by an old friend in a foreign land, the vivid blue shirt had reached out to him. And the scarf—he had never worn scarves before. *Where had that notion come from?* Even Kathy had teased him about it, saying it was a bit "Hollywood" for a Michigan cop. But still he had worn it.

"I picked you out of the crowd, let the other cabs move in front of me so I'd get you," Billy said. "In the limousine I felt a chill, but I kept telling myself it could be my imagination. Then, in the limo, you whistled Tannhauser, a favorite of Klassen's. And then I brought you here. There was a glimmer of recognition in your eyes. I saw it, and I thought, *maybe...*

"And then we went down to the garden. You were so absorbed. So distressed. I asked myself, *Was it part of the awakening? Was your soul starting to remember?* And then you passed out. Suddenly you were on the ground, and I remember Klassen staring at that same replica of Tannhauser for such long periods of time. But still, it all seemed so impossible to me, I wouldn't let myself believe.

"At the hotel you insisted on having Suite 534," Billy explained. "When I learned of that—it was like being struck by a thunderbolt. Suite 534 was where Klassen lived while building this ludicrous dream castle of his. This is the only room he finished before his death. Look at me! Even now I'm talking about *him* when I should be talking about *you.*"

Was all of this the manic raving of a man gone suddenly insane, or were the pieces of the puzzle coming together at last?

Fighting the plastic ties that bound him, Jamie stared at the bust of Bernard Klassen, trying to understand the man from his fleshy features. The face was familiar, but only vaguely so. Surely, if it were Jamie's portrait, he'd recognize himself.

"Would you like to know how black your soul is? Let me tell you about yourself. Your early years remain a mystery. But as a young man you went to work for the CIA as an information specialist and were given extensive training. Eventually you helped design the security system that limited access to the volumes of data stored in the network's vast archives.

"American intelligence efforts compile information on everybody, most of it trivial, useless stuff as you might expect. But you suspected that some of it might be embarrassing or damaging to the individuals involved, particularly if they were in the public sector.

"You had helped design the security system, and it didn't take you too long to devise a means of getting through it. Once you had the secret CIA files within your slimy reach, you had the world's greatest source of dirty linen. Blackmail was just a step away. Even the FBI invited you to collaborate on its computer security system. How could you resist?

"Your first victim was a wealthy ambassador to some country I can't recall. Over eighteen months, you collected quite a lot of money from that one—before he committed suicide. But you started worrying about the risks of collection. The money was too easily traced. Someone could set you up. So you took your money and bought an interest in a casino. It was the perfect laundry for dirty money. Before long you owned the casino outright and were on to bigger and better things. Like murder for hire.

"Your information base helped you determine which of your potential victims were worth more dead than alive... and to whom. One of your cleverest murder schemes might sound familiar. A victim would be brought here to lose money at the casino, the traditional method of making payments. But instead, the victim would *win*. For Senator Harth... well, it seems he was on the hit list."

Jamie swallowed hard. Too much of this rang true.

"And then," Billy said, "a thief would break into the victim's room, steal the money and kill the poor fellow. Everyone would be looking for the local riff-raff who did this terrible thing, and no one would suspect the casino. If the money wasn't in the room... well, the contract on the victim's life was worth more than the winnings."

"You mean Harth was murdered?" Jamie said.

"I don't think so, not in this case. But I'm convinced he was marked for a hit. I don't know what happened to Harth, really, but it was your black soul that hatched the scheme to kill him. I have no idea how many deaths you are responsible for. As for me, I was responsible for only one. Yours."

Billy rubbed his face nervously. "You had more vices than extortion and murder. Besides gluttony, your biggest appetite was sex. I went to work as your driver ten years ago. My daughter became your personal secretary three years later. Or so I thought."

Billy stopped for a moment, turning his back on Jamie. When he turned to face him again his eyes were moist. "She was a beautiful girl, my one and only." He stopped again, memories clouding his speech. "She was my pride—my *life*, after my wife died. We were so close... and I had no idea what kind of an animal you were. I was always naive beyond my years."

Billy wiped the moisture from his eyes with the back of a huge hand.

"She moved into the hotel. To be close to you. Her job demanded it, she said. And I believed it, of course—she was such a good girl, a sweet girl. But you had a power over her. You told her my life would be cut short unless she fed your appetite. I only saw her once more, in that last year. In the hospital. She was so badly beaten... I barely recognized her..."

Tears filled his eyes.

"She wouldn't talk to anyone but me. She told me the things you made her do—*unspeakable* things—and the blackmail schemes, the murder, all of it. But then they made me leave and I never saw her again until four months later. You took her away, and then she was found on the beach. They said it was an overdose of heroine... such a shame that local black trash like her had to give the island a bad name and end up polluting our beaches in front of the tourists."

Billy closed his eyes and fought back the tears. "I plotted for months to get you, even though I was sure you were going insane. You kept telling me that when you were a child you had visions of lives you had lived before, and now you were meditating and remembering and gathering around you artifacts from those lives. And you said you were close to a secret that would make you a king once again, with all the glory you had known in those other lifetimes.

"You were obsessed with building this monument to your delusions of grandeur, and with your meditations, which would go on forever. And I was obsessed with revenge. With stopping you from doing more of your evil. I pulled together the whole nasty story of your operations, but I could prove nothing. You bastard, I wanted you dead!

"Early one evening, I was waiting in the limousine for you, the same limousine I have now, and I got drunk from a flask I carried to help me tolerate your presence. I got to thinking about Tia, my daughter, and the other lives you were destroying, and I was drinking rum, too much of it, and when you finally came back to the limo you had that evil sneer across your face, the leering smile that always followed your perversions.

"I wanted to vomit, but I yelled instead, telling you for the first time that I knew about Tia and the others and I couldn't let you go on, even if I had to kill you. And you laughed at me and said I was through, that I could never hurt you, and even if I killed you you'd come back to find me. *You promised you'd come back!* And then you got out and told me to take the car away, it had the stink of black trash about it and you never wanted to see me or the car again and I was lucky to be alive, just don't cross you, that's all.

"But I was now a student of Bernard Klassen. I knew your habits and behaviors. I worked fast, and two days later it was all set up. You took your stroll along the beach... "

Jamie felt his mind beginning to unreel the dream he had come here to resolve.

"...as you always did—a long walk in the sand—and then you went up to your suite, number 534..."

Yes, yes ... Billy was describing Jamie's dream perfectly.

"...and went in, leaving the door unlocked, because in a few minutes your favorite whore would be joining you."

Was this it, Jamie wondered? The door would open—he could recall the dream in such vivid detail—and would it be a woman?

"But this time," Billy continued, "it was not Maria, your favorite, but someone else. It was me! It happened fast, almost before you knew it, a hand pushing down into the water and it was done. The body of Bernard Klassen lay there dead."

There could have been no conclusion to Jamie's dream. Klassen—*Jamie*—had been killed.

"It can't be true," Jamie screamed, knowing that he believed it but wanting desperately not to.

"You still doubt it?" Billy asked quietly. "The elephant behind you. I saw the effect it had on you. Do you know why Klassen commissioned it? All his life he suffered from a terrible fear of those creatures, the way some men are afraid of snakes or heights or water. Pictures of them made him turn away, carvings made him tremble, but at last he conquered his fear by uncovering the roots of it, he said, and had this sculpture made to celebrate his success. He called it Abu."

Abu! The strange word that had crept into Jamie's mind during his waking nightmare at the deer stand, that reliving of some...

"I saw your fear of it," Billy said. "The cure was not lasting, was it *Klassen?*"

"*I am not Klassen.*" Jamie screamed. "I am not! I am Jamie Giles—not the sex fiend you make me out to be."

"Oh, I see. Maybe we should ask your wife about that."

"Kathy? You've seen her?"

"I drove her to the airport," Billy lied. "Would you like to hear what she told me... how you—?"

"No, don't say it!" Jamie paused for a moment, thinking of Kathy, thinking of the acts he must have unconsciously committed, the loss of control, the impossible struggle he faced with the soul of some other person clawing for supremacy. If all this were true...

"It isn't possible, it just isn't!" Jamie shouted. "We lived at the same time. He died just a few weeks ago, you said..."

"I know, September 23rd, I'll never forget it. The feeling of relief."

September 23rd. The date of Jamie's accident. The date that he had clinically died. Could the soul of Klassen...?

"My God," Jamie said, "while I was dead, his soul was somehow born again in my body..."

Jamie looked up. Billy was standing over him, turning the knife slowly in the sunlight, mesmerized by the power of the cold blade.

"This will be for Tia," Billy whispered, "and for all the others."

His huge body coiled into a crouch and he sliced the air with a vicious arc of the blade, bringing it to rest on Jamie's neck below the left ear.

"Goodbye, Klassen."

Jamie felt the cold sting of the knife edge, imagined his throat filleted like a fish on a Michigan lakeshore. His guts seized up in absolute fear. "You're not a killer, Billy," he said softly, carefully, his neck riding the razor-sharp blade. "And I' m still Jamie Giles."

CHAPTER 24

You're *Klassen!*" Billy roared. The knife-edge bit into Jamie's skin with the motion of his outburst, bright blood lubricating the shallow nick.

Jamie's neck tightened into a basket weave of flexed muscles. His eyes hid behind squeezed lids. Through a tightly clamped jaw came half-swallowed words: "But the body is still Jamie Giles."

"The soul is Klassen!" Billy stared at Jamie's concealed eyes. "I've already killed you once. How can it be murder to kill you again?"

Jamie opened his eyes and stared at Billy. "Then do it. You can kill Jamie's body, but you can't kill Klassen's soul."

"Don't try to sway me with your cleverness." Billy was trembling.

"Listen to me...!" Jamie pleaded. His eyes suddenly flickered with energy. "Klassen's soul is trapped in this body. For God's sake, don't free it to come back in some unknown form."

"Shut up. Those are *Klassen's* words! I won't listen!"

"Those are Jamie's words, Billy. There is still some of me left. Help me, Billy. I'm as afraid of him as you are. *Help me.*"

"I should kill you!" Billy's knife still pressed against Jamie's neck.

"Help me, I *need* you." Jamie's voice was a low whisper.

"Shut up!"

"There must be a way, a better way."

"I don't know…"

"Billy… help me, *please!*"

Billy was silent for a moment, then he withdrew the knife. Suddenly he hurled it across the room. "Damn it. *God damn it!*"

Jamie took a deep breath. "We're in this together," he said. "I need you to watch me... watch every move. You can't dare lose track of me. God, I'm tired…"

Jamie's head sagged to his chest as if some great life force had suddenly escaped.

Billy picked up Jamie's limp body and carried it to a sofa, laying it down and untying him. He bent over Jamie's lifeless face, studied it, then whispered to the limp form: "Jamie's out cold, but I have a feeling *you* can hear me, Klassen. Don't try to get by with anything because old Billy Smythe'll be watching every move you make. I don't know why you picked on Jamie... It isn't fair, not after a fellow's all grown up, but that's your style—just reaching out and grabbing whatever you want. I'm serving notice, Klassen. I let you out of the bottle last time, but this time I'm keeping you stoppered up... and the bottle won't be leaving my sight."

Jamie may have squirmed ever so slightly, but Billy couldn't be sure.

———

The scream vomited from Jamie's throat in a thick, uncontrollable eruption. He jackknifed into a sitting position, sweating and panting, eyes torn open wide, hands flying to his neck. Billy leaped out of his chair and stood there as Jamie slowly awoke and swung his feet onto the floor.

"Did you sleep well?" Billy asked.

"Some joke," Jamie replied, still panting.

"Bad dream?"

"A nightmare. Some weirdo was slashing my throat with a knife." Jamie submerged his face in cupped hands. "God! Maybe you should have done it. Is this all a dream? I can't tell my dreams from reality anymore."

"Could be it's all a dream. Or maybe... maybe it's all reality."

"Why didn't you do it? Why didn't you cut my throat?"

"One of you talked me out of it."

"Jesus!" Jamie slumped against the back of the sofa. "Damn!"

"I don't understand any of it, really."

"It's—" Jamie wasn't fumbling for words, he was hesitating, as if afraid to say what he was thinking. "It's reincarnation. My God, I always thought that stuff was just superstitious Hindu crap, but—"

"But now you know. You've lived before."

Jamie shivered, looked down at himself. "It's spooky, knowing that someone else is living inside my skin. So who am I? Jamie or Klassen?"

"I'm sure we'll find out."

"But if I'm not *me* anymore... where did I go? And how can I remember everything about Jamie Giles—*feel* like Jamie Giles—if I'm not him?"

"You're talking to a dumb Bahamian. I don't have a single answer, but I can guess."

"Then do it."

"Each of us has a soul. Some of us—maybe all of us—have a soul that's lived before in some other time, some other body. Probably more than once. This soul is... is... *life*! It's the *life* part of you."

"It seems to have a life of its own. And its own mind."

"I don't know. I've been thinking about it since you blacked out again. A person's body and brain are the other part, the physical part. I would think that the soul and body together make up the personality. Which one has the greater effect? I couldn't guess."

"But in my case, I died—literally died. Just weeks ago. All I can imagine is that my soul knew a good thing when it happened and flew the coop. And maybe that was precisely when Klassen died."

"The son-of-a-bitch didn't waste any time. He even found a way of escaping all the wasted time of childhood."

"God, it's creepy. So how about me, anyhow? My soul bailed, and Klassen's soul immediately set up housekeeping in my body."

"It's got to raise hell with your mind," Billy said. "After thirty years, I think your body, brain and soul would have worked out a nice living arrangement."

"I'll tell you what it's like. *Dreams*—which must be memories of those past lives. *Fears*—which might be old reincarnated phobias. And weird behavior I can't even remember a lot of the time—which just scares the shit out of me."

"So tell me, Mr. Giles—I hope you don't mind me calling you that."

"Please don't ever stop."

"So tell me... what's your plan?"

"Plan? Are you kidding? I mean… a few minutes ago I found out my brain was on a time-sharing plan with some psychotic sex-fiend murderer. I don't know what the hell to do. Exorcise him, maybe."

"That's for demons. And if you found a way to expel Klassen's soul, it would undoubtedly kill you. Which is probably the only way to get him out of you anyhow."

"Catch-22, huh? I can't even trust myself. You want a plan? I'll give you plan. I'll hire you—pay you whatever you want just to stay with me, watch me every minute, until we figure this thing out. I've got money, don't worry about that."

"The senator's?"

Jamie nodded.

"And if I do this… what then?"

"Like I said… then we figure it out. Learn everything we can about this thing. About Klassen, about other lives before him. There's got to be an answer somewhere. If I stop believing that, I may as well cut my own throat. What was that you said about a secret Klassen was onto?"

"I'm not sure. He was obsessed with it, though. Said it would make him rich and powerful, more than any of his other lives."

"The guy was apeshit."

"More than you know. And paranoid."

"How's that?"

"He told me once that he knew someone was stalking him."

"What?"

"In all his other lifetimes. He said another person had been one step behind him in discovering the secret."

"Another person… as in *singular* person? The *same* person? You mean Klassen and some other soul have been battling it out from one lifetime to another?" Jamie stood up and started pacing. "Mother of God! You mean there's another one like me? Like Klassen?"

"He was convinced of it. In fact, it seemed as though that was the only thing he was afraid of. Even death didn't frighten him. I guess we know why. But the prospect that this other soul would discover the secret before him…"

Jamie had paced to a large jewelry box carved out of rosewood and inlaid with pearls and semi-precious stones. It stood three feet high on a Louis XIV desk, had the appearance of a small castle, and presented a maze of drawers and compartments. Jamie pulled several drawers and found them empty.

"They inventoried everything that was in it," Billy explained. "Went over the whole thing looking for a will."

"In a sense, this is all mine, right?"

Billy hadn't thought about it that way, but he nodded.

Jamie pulled a narrow brass-knobbed drawer entirely out of the case, fondling it gently for a minute, inspecting the wood and masterful construction. And then he turned the drawer upside down and inserted it knob-first into the vacated slot as if *remembering* a secret maneuver.

Billy watched, confused but fascinated.

As the drawer went all the way in with a sudden click, the top of one of the castle's towers opened up, the concealing pieces so perfectly crafted that detection had been impossible.

Billy stared with eyes the size of softballs.

Jamie reached into the concealed space and removed a small, folded piece of paper. He opened it and turned toward Billy, reading. "*If you have found this, you know who you are.*"

A shiver shot through Jamie. He felt like he was reading his own words from beyond the grave.

"There must be more!" Billy said. "Go on, read it."

Jamie stared at the hand-scrawled note again. "*This will be our only direct communication. The existence of this note means that I have failed in my search for the secret, but the discovery has only been delayed until your lifetime.*"

"The secret!" Billy said. "Does he say what it is?"

Jamie continued reading. "*I urge you to trust no one, because Nehsira hunts you.* Who the hell is that?"

"Just keep reading, dammit."

"*Locked inside you, in your own secret compartment, is the key. With his cunning, though, Nehsira may steal it without your knowledge, and then all is lost. To victory! Yours in spirit, Bernard Klassen.*"

Jamie turned to Billy and saw only a vacant, uncomprehending stare. Jamie understood. He had just communicated with the presence that was struggling for control over his own mind and body, and felt entirely confounded by the message. Who was this man named Klassen who was inhabiting his body? And where was *Klassen's* body, now that it had been shed like a snakeskin.

"I don't know why, but I need to go to Klassen's grave."

Billy flinched. His eyes narrowed. He was clearly surprised at Jamie's statement. Finally he said, simply, "All right," and then looked away, as if second-guessing himself.

CHAPTER 25

A brisk twenty-minute drive whisked Jamie to a slight rise of land—*a local Boot Hill*, Jamie thought. But there was no cemetery sign on view. Just a small brick building with an expansive lawn uncluttered by grave markers. Billy parked the limo in front of the building, and Jamie read a small sign next to the front door: NASSAU NURSING HOME.

Jamie turned to Billy with a sour face. "I thought we were going to Klassen's grave?"

"Patience! There's someone here you need to meet," Billy said, hoisting his large frame out of the front seat.

Jamie followed the cabbie past a reception desk—where an attendant looked up at Billy with a familiar nod—and then down a dim corridor to a windowless door. Billy's hand dwarfed the doorknob as he turned it and pushed.

Jamie's vision was blocked by Billy's broad back as they entered the room. His first impressions were of sounds and smells. First, pulsating whooshes and asthmatic, mechanical gasps punctuated by staccato beeps. And then the stench of disinfectant and body fluids mixed with the sweet breath of flowers.

Billy stepped aside, revealing an oversized crib with raised sides. Lying in the crib was the withered, motionless shape of a man curled in a fetus position. His eyes were closed and crusted over. His chest rose and fell to the rhythmic beat of a hissing ventilator that piped oxygen to tired lungs. Plastic tubes fed into him, and out again, indiscreetly porting urine to plastic bags. Electrodes like leeches clung to his body, sucking out electrical signals and transporting them through a web of wires to beeping and blinking machines. The man's translucent, parchment skin shamelessly exposed a delicate mesh of blue veins.

Billy sighed. "Jamie, I'd like you to meet Bernard Klassen."

The words at first didn't register. Jamie kept staring at the pale, monstrous, organic growth at the end of the squirming tendrils of technology, but then it hit him.

Hard.

He was looking at himself.

Too weird. Time to get out of there.

In the corridor, Jamie uttered his first words to Billy since entering the building. "Christ, he's not even in the ground yet!"

"The machines keep him breathing."

"But he's dead, right? Otherwise how could he... how could his..."

"His soul be in you? The wonders of medical science keep his body going. His money will keep those machines working a long, long time. He has no relatives that anyone knows of."

"So this was part of his plan? To keep his body alive?"

"I don't see how. His brain was damaged from lack of oxygen. What good is a body without a brain? I think his Living Will called for extraordinary measures, and when they defibbed him and got a faint pulse, they had no choice. You know, I've often thought..." Billy pauses.

"Thought what?"

"Too bad he parachuted out at the last minute. Otherwise, I would have had him trapped inside that living corpse in there, unable to do anything about it. If only he had *almost* died, but *not quite*..."

"I've got to get out of this place. Just too creepy."

In the lobby area, a leggy, beautiful Hispanic woman was chatting amiably with the receptionist. A purple orchid sprouted dazzlingly from her black hair. She looked up, startled to see Billy.

"I'll meet you in the car," Billy whispered to Jamie, then approached the woman as Jamie slowly walked past the woman.

Before going outside, Jamie looked back. Billy was talking to the woman, who was staring at Jamie.

————

Her name is Maria," Billy said, agitated. His foot was riding the gas pedal hard, and the limo was lurching twenty miles per hour over the speed limit. "She's the woman Klassen was expecting to enter the bathroom when I—*surprised* him in the spa."

"His favorite whore?"

"More than that. The one woman who could always get what she wanted from the bastard. A lot of his property was jointly held by Klassen and Maria."

"She still comes to visit him. Must have cared for him a little."

"Bullshit. As long as Klassen keeps breathing, his property is in a legal tangle. If he'd die, like a good boy, she'd collect on his life insurance and own a lot of property outright. Plus, she's probably in his will for a good deal more. I think she visits mainly to figure out how to pull the plug on him."

"She kept looking at me as I was leaving." The image of Maria danced in his mind—the perfect bronze skin, the raven hair, the ever-present orchid...

"She asked who you were. Just to piss her off, I told her you were related to Klassen. Let her stew over that complication for a while." He chuckled. "Another heir."

Jamie didn't get the joke. The fragrance of orchids was enshrouding him. It was the distinctive bouquet that always aroused Klassen—and now Jamie—when Maria was near. The sway of the limo made Jamie dizzy. Suddenly he was displaced into the back seat—Klassen's seat. Maria's bare, silky leg was gliding over his lap. He could feel her humid breath on his neck, hear her purring into his ear, feel the tingle of her nails teasing his thigh…

"Are you with me?"

It was not Maria's voice—*Billy's*. A large black hand gripped Jamie's knee, shaking it.

Jamie snapped out of it. "Yeah, I'm here. I'm okay."

———

At the hotel, Billy successfully parked in a space that Jamie judged to be shorter than the limo. Like a chauffeur, Billy ran around to the passenger side and opened the door.

Jamie pulled himself out of the limo. "Let's go to my room."

Moving through the lobby, Jamie spied the gift shop and steered a new course. "Get me some ibuprofen," he barked.

Bristling at the Klassen-like command, Billy nonetheless led Jamie into the gift shop and located an assortment of over-the-counter drugs.

As Billy waited in line to pay, Jamie wandered to the bookrack, drawn by the familiar cover art of *Experiencing Death* by Dr. Alice Mallach. Very popular, it seemed. He pulled the book from its wire basket, exposing a second book by Mallach entitled *Another Time*. The jacket promised stories of people who had been reincarnated.

He handed the book to Billy, who paid.

"I'm expensing it to your account," Billy said.

Heading for the elevator, Jamie grabbed the bottle of ibuprofen from Billy, cracked the tamper-proof seal and fished out a wad of cotton. Adult dosage was two tablets. As the elevator doors opened, he dry-swallowed four.

He had the headache of two adults.

———

Kathy considered the note and the money. *Go home*, it said, *and visit your parents. Let them take care of you while I sort out things here.* Billy, it turned out, was generous to a fault. *I will keep you informed of our progress.*

Progress? What kind of progress could Billy Smythe hope to make? He had shared with Kathy the facts of this outrageous dilemma—and she appreciated his candor—but there seemed to be no hope in this case. Billy had put on a confident face when he'd spilled out the facts to her, but that was probably to keep her calm. If only it were just a *demon*—there was always the prospect of finding a specialist for that kind of thing. But for another person's soul to be taking possession of one's body—who do you call for that?

Billy didn't know that Kathy couldn't go home to her parents, could never admit to them that she was having *difficulties* in her marriage. *Hadn't they warned her? Over and over?* She sure as hell couldn't tell them about Jamie's affliction.

Affliction? My God, she didn't even know what to call it. *Visitation? Possession?* No, her husband had been… had been *hijacked.*

And she wanted him back. The *real* Jamie, not the monster.

Until then, she couldn't go home, where an unpredictable Jamie might find her. She couldn't go to her parents' house. The most obvious place was Becky's. Kathy and Rebecca had grown up best friends. Now Becky lived in a two-room New York City apartment. She waited tables in a deli while learning what Kathy and others had always known—that her singing and dancing talent would never get her onto Broadway. Or even off-off-Broadway. Kathy's theater friend offered the perfect hideout until Billy made enough progress to… maybe… Whatever!

She picked up her cell phone and called Becky. Got voice mail. Left a rambling message about coming to New York, and please call back, and how great it would be to get together, and by the way, have you got a couch I could use for a night or two?

A night or two.

How she wished.

CHAPTER 26

The remnants of two room service dinners lay on a portable table. Billy lounged in a chair reading *Experiencing Death* by Dr. Mallach, while Jamie sat on the sofa with *Another Time* by the same author.

"Listen to this!" Jamie sat up, bringing the book closer to his face. "There was a case of an American soldier in the Korean war who was killed and came back to life. When he got home, he started playing jazz saxophone, even though he'd never played before."

Billy stood, walked to an ice container on the dresser, and chunked some cubes into a half-full glass of water. "So what's the punch line?"

"Turns out that a famous sax player had died at exactly the same time the soldier was killed on the battlefield."

Billy gulped the water. "Sounds like you and Klassen."

"So it's happened before. The musician's soul jumped into the soldier's body just after the soldier's soul had vacated the property. For a time, the soldier kept his own personality because it was stored up there in the conscious part of his brain."

"Or so the author believes."

"But more and more, the musician's personality took over because it now occupied the soldier's *sub*conscious… and somehow it kept leaking out—*spilling* out the way it does in dreams—until it totally took over."

The thought that Jamie could be completely hijacked by Klassen's personality stopped him cold. Even the usual *fuck* froze in his throat.

Billy's eyes drilled through him. "All right, so the soldier changed. He took on the personality, and the skills, of the musician. Did he ever go back to being himself?"

Jamie set down the book and rose from the sofa. It took a long time, but finally he said, "No."

"I'm trying to understand this," Billy said. "Is Dr. Mallach saying that my *soul* is my *personality*?

"What she's saying is that your soul remembers every experience you had in every previous life. And it brings to *this* life all the personality traits you had then."

"Then I must've been a real son-of-a-bitch."

Jamie began to pace. He was catching ghastly glimpses of how this might work. "Think about it! In my case, my adult brain still remembers Jamie's personality—and now *that* personality is battling Klassen's for control of Jamie."

Billy's dark skin seemed to blanch. He collapsed into a chair. "You just referred to yourself in the third person."

Jamie swiveled and looked at himself in a mirror. "So tell me… who am I?"

"All right, let's think this through. Does Mallach say how long it took for the musician to completely take over the soldier?"

"Yeah. About a month."

Billy's bloodshot eyes rolled sarcastically. "Oh—well… then you have about a week to solve your problem before you totally disappear and become Klassen. In which case I'll have to kill you again. Thanks for the heads up."

"You don't think good triumphs over evil?"

The intensity of Billy's gaze made Jamie avert his eyes.

At last, Billy spoke. "So, as we agreed, you can't be left alone."

"Agreed."

"Ever."

Silence. To Jamie, this suddenly sounded like a life sentence.

Billy reaffirmed his own statement with a nod.

"Unless—" Jamie picked up the Mallach book "—unless this woman, this author…"

"Dr. Mallach," Billy prompted.

"Yes, Dr. Mallach. She uses hypnosis to regress people into their previous lives," Jamie continued, gathering his thoughts. "She can track a soul through those lives like a detective. Maybe she can do the same for me. Bring out Klassen's soul."

"And what? Interview him?"

"I don't know. Maybe uncover that secret."

"And if she finds out that secret, by that time you'll *be* Klassen."

"Dammit—you really suck at giving moral support. You want me to just give up? Just lie down and let that bastard's soul take me over? Hell, I never even believed in souls before this."

"Me neither."

Jamie shuddered. "I have to say, I'm kinda scared. What if he actually takes me over for good? Which is stronger anyhow? The body and brain, or the soul?"

"Well, Mallach said the musician's soul took over the soldier." Billy blew a gale of wind through his lips. His brain could take no more thinking about the unthinkable. "You can take the bedroom, with its own bath. I'll sleep out here in the sitting room." He noticed that Jamie did not move. "That means now! I'm tired."

Like a spent marathoner, Jamie shuffled to the bedroom door and pulled it open. "There's no lock," he said. "You trust me not to take out Klassen's revenge on you during the night?"

Billy pushed Jamie into the room and shut the door. He said, "Sleep well," and then dragged the sofa over to prevent the door from opening.

"What if there's a fire?" Jamie yelled.

"Then you'll burn."

———

At one-thirty in the morning, Kathy's cell phone buzzed, waking her from a light sleep on Becky's sofa. Quickly, she silenced it so Becky wouldn't wake up. The poor girl had to be at the deli at 5:30 to serve breakfast to New York's early risers.

Kathy thought it might be Billy responding to her text about going to New York. But glancing at the screen, she saw it was Jamie—his fifth call since she had escaped the hotel room. She couldn't bring herself to answer it. Didn't know what she would say. Suddenly, she wanted to pick up and blast him with her rage, but finally decided to let the call go.

For five minutes, as she lay in the dark, curiosity gnawed at her. Finally, she broke down and checked for a voice message, even though Jamie had left none after his earlier calls. Still, maybe…

It would be interesting to hear how he'd explain himself.

One message was waiting. Nervously, she touched the icon, entered in her passcode, and put the phone to her ear. Jamie's voice startled her.

Kathy, really wish you'd pick up. I totally understand why you had to leave, and I'm so, so sorry, but I wanted you to know I've got a plan, and a friend who's helping out. I'm just so… shit. You know that wasn't me that did that, right? I'd never hurt you. I just need to hear your voice, know you're okay. Text me if you don't want to talk.

A long pause gave tears time to well up in Kathy's eyes. She could hear Jamie's breath on the phone, trying to hold back his own emotions. And then he spoke again, desperately trying to be more upbeat, but failing miserably.

You'll never guess who's with me right now. Remember Billy Smythe, the limo driver? Long story. Hope you don't mind if I call once in a while and let you know how things are going. God, I miss you. And I love you. Gotta go.

Kathy knew that it wasn't Jamie who attacked her in the hotel room. But he looked just like Jamie. And every time she thought about that rape, which was almost every waking moment, she saw Jamie doing it. How could she ever get over that?

———

In the darkness of early morning, Billy was asleep on the couch that blocked Jamie's bedroom door when the door quietly pushed outward a few inches, stopping abruptly against the back of the sofa. With a faint scraping sound, the couch moved an inch, then another, and suddenly— with a jerk—two inches more.

Sleeping lightly, Billy woke up as the couch moved another inch, accompanied by a grunt from the bedroom. The prisoner was attempting an escape.

Billy lay there, certain that the combined weight of the heavy sofa and his own substantial carcass would prevent the door from opening. He listened to the sounds of futility coming from the bedroom. It amused him until Jamie—no, until *Klassen*—grew frustrated and began slamming the door repeatedly against the sofa. An explosion of guttural gibberish erupted from the prisoner. If this were a movie, Billy thought, there would be subtitles so he'd know what all that babble meant.

There was a brief pause in the action, as if the captive had just remembered to breathe.

And then, suddenly, a raging cacophony of crashes. Jamie's room was being destroyed. Billy could imagine the mirror, the lamps, the table, all being thrown and shattered. In seconds it was over, but Billy, despite his tremendous advantage in size, felt terrorized by the fury caged up behind the door.

Then, absolute quiet again.

Except for the sound of his heart pounding.

A startling crash brought him to his feet. A chair exploded against the door—an exclamation point, in case Billy hadn't gotten the message that Klassen was angry.

He shoved the sofa back, and the door closed with a solid whack.

Billy had unleashed this beast. Was solely responsible for it. And as keeper of the beast, he had tethered himself to it for life.

Obviously, he had not thought this through.

CHAPTER 27

Billy shook his head as he walked through the bedroom. Jamie lay unconscious on the bed. Shards of broken glass and splinters of wood and plastic littered the floor. Softball-sized holes decorated the walls, exposing ragged edges of plaster. Thousands in damages, he guessed.

Reaching the naked mattress—the linens had been stripped off and cast aside—Billy pulled out his knife. With the other hand, he shook Jamie's shoulder.

Jamie jerked awake.

Holding his breath, Billy stepped back, wondering which person he'd be confronting this morning.

Jamie focused his eyes on Billy. For a moment he seemed confused. He glanced around the demolished bedroom. "Holy shit! What happened?"

Billy let out his breath. "Klassen got out."

It took a few seconds for Jamie to untangle this statement into a logical thought.

"Damn! Don't remember a thing."

"Good morning, Mr. Giles. Nice to have you back." Billy's words sounded sarcastic.

"Interesting evening for *you*, I'll bet. How am I going to pay for trashing this joint?"

"The senator's money, remember? That's also how you'll pay for two tickets to New York."

"What's in New York?"

"Dr. Mallach. I reached her office this morning. They want us to come right away."

Jamie rubbed his eyes. He'd leave this very minute if he could.

"There's a flight in two hours," Billy explained. "I charged two tickets to your credit card. Hope you behave yourself in public."

"Seems like Klassen's a night person."

Billy knew better. Kathy had told him about the daytime slaying of the gangbangers in Detroit. Billy also knew that he wouldn't be able to carry a knife on board.

As if thinking about that same Detroit incident, Jamie said, "Watch yourself, okay? Klassen's a killer."

———

One of the hotel guests, a black-haired woman in sunglasses and a large hat, took a particular interest in a conversation at the cashier's station. A tall, muscular Bahamian was blaming room damage on a drunken party. A younger companion was offered some papers to sign, and then seemed to have a dispute over his credit card. Exasperated, the younger man counted out a lot of money in cash, then offered even more when the manager balked. Finally, the negotiation was over and the two men threaded their way through the crowded lobby without noticing the woman.

Maria.

The younger man—Bernard Klassen's long lost relative—was wheeling a small suitcase. Maria guessed the two were heading to the airport.

———

Late that afternoon, Billy tipped the bellman at the New York Waldorf

Astoria, closed the door to the two-bedroom suite, and whistled. "Never stayed in a place this nice," he said. "Under different circumstances, I could really enjoy this."

"I saw a men's store downstairs," Jamie said. "I think we should buy some clothes. Nothing we brought along fits this setting."

Billy marched to the larger bedroom and inspected the door. No lock. "I have a couple more things to pick up. A length of chain, a padlock…"

"Total buzz kill, Billy."

"A knife…"

Billy's phone rang. He answered, mumbled a few words of agreement, and hung up.

"Let me guess who that was," Jamie said. "Klassen's arch rival, Nehsira. He's in New York for a few days and wonders if we'd like to have cocktails."

"It was Dr. Mallach's assistant, Robert Schmidt. He'd like to take us out to dinner. And by the way, don't make fun of this Nehsira character. He may be the key to solving our dilemma. Besides Klassen, who else knows what this is all about?"

"Then we'd better do some shopping before dinner. My treat."

Jamie started to wheel his suitcase into the larger bedroom, but stopped and turned. "So if they want to publish our story in a book, I'm thinking they should buy the rights. How much do you think it's worth?"

Billy knew Jamie was joking, but still it unnerved him. "You're sounding like Klassen. Do I have to lock you up right now? And by the way, you can leave me out of it."

"Just asking. And just so you know, I'm thinking you should get fifteen percent of whatever. You're my agent."

More like a jailer, Billy thought.

———

The small Italian restaurant seemed even smaller, squeezed by a hundred celebrities and dignitaries hanging on the walls in an assortment of picture frames. The Asian waiter, who oddly spoke Italian with a Sicilian accent, explained the delights of the fusion specials that blended the best of various cultures into culinary delicacies. Finally, he handed out menus to Billy, Jamie, and Robert Schmidt.

Schmidt had that distinctive *assistant professor* look. His tweed coat didn't match his trousers. Though he was at least thirty-five, his hair was tousled like a young boy's. His wire rim glasses were probably de rigueur on most college campuses. Jamie hadn't seen Schmidt's shoes, but suspected they were sneakers, which would complete the academic ensemble.

Schmidt watched the waiter disappear, then turned to Jamie. "Mr. Smythe certainly piqued my curiosity on the phone."

"You must get a lot of calls," Jamie replied.

"Oh, yes. Dr. Mallach's books are very popular. She's sold in over 37 countries now. We've researched hundreds of apparent stories of death experience and reincarnation. Her far-flung reputation is like a magnet for people with stories to tell. Have you read her works?"

Jamie and Billy both nodded.

"Then you've read accounts of the best documented stories that we have. Unfortunately, only a small percentage of the stories that come to us can be verified scientifically. And even then, the scientific community often refuses to look at our documentation before dismissing the evidence. It's not an easy field to be in. Your story, however—if I understand it correctly—would be a first. We've never come across a claim of someone being reincarnated into a younger person."

The waiter returned with a white wine for Schmidt, and beers for Billy and Jamie.

"You can call it a *claim* if you want to, but it's true," Billy interjected.

"Personally, I don't doubt that you believe every word of it, Mr. Smythe."

"You can call me Billy."

"But we need verification, don't we, *Billy*, to prove it to the rest of the world. The scientific community has a fetish about verification and documentation."

There was so much to cover, Jamie was growing impatient with the exposition. "Dr. Schmidt—" he said.

Schmidt raised his hand, cutting him off. "Please, just *Mr.* Schmidt. I'm a PhD candidate in psychology. Not there yet. Sort of got sidetracked into this alternative channel."

Jamie didn't care. "You should know, Mr. Schmidt, that we are not here just so you can document our story and have it as another book to sell. If we're going to give you the most amazing reincarnation story of your careers, we want something in return."

Schmidt was not used to having such a hard-edged business conversation with his subjects, and not sure how to handle this new wrinkle. He took a long sip of wine and said, "Are we talking money here?"

"Mr. Schmidt, I may only have a few days left to live, and I desperately need some help. I can give you all the proof you need, and you can have the story, if you help me."

"Fair enough. But we'll need to know *how* we can help you."

"I need you and Dr. Mallach to track down an old acquaintance."

———

That evening, after locking Jamie into his bedroom with the padlock and chain, Billy had curled up in his own king size bed with good intentions of finishing Mallach's book on reincarnation. But he was distracted by the anticipation that Klassen would make an appearance at any time. Billy was not physically afraid of Klassen—it was just the general creepiness of knowing a monster lurked in the next room. And who knew, really, whether the evil spirit-force of Klassen might animate Jamie's body with super-human powers.

In this way, then, Billy freaked himself out until he was unable to read or sleep until sleep finally overtook him about four o'clock. This was why he struggled to wake up when Jamie pounded on his locked door, shouting that he was hungry and wanted out.

Dragging his bone-weary carcass out of bed, Billy staggered across the sitting room to the other bedroom, fumbled for the key, and opened the door.

"Klassen didn't trash the room this time," Jamie said. "Maybe he's given up."

"Fat chance." Billy rubbed his eyes. He could have used another four or five hours of sleep.

"I'm starved. What time's our first session with Mallach?"

"At ten. You're dressed already?"

"Those are really ugly pajamas. Hope you change. I'll meet you downstairs for breakfast." Jamie started for the hallway.

Billy grabbed his arm. "Not alone. For all I know, you're Klassen pretending to be Jamie. Maybe you're on good behavior so I'll cut you some slack. That would be just like Klassen."

"Then put on some pants, man... I'm hungry."

Billy dragged the younger man into the bedroom and started dressing.

"I'm not Klassen right now," Jamie said. "I have no idea why he stayed under wraps last night. Wish we could predict his appearances."

Billy pulled up gray trousers and began threading a belt through the loops. "Until he takes you over, I think you're in a battle for control. Sometimes you come out on top, sometimes Klassen."

"Makes sense, sort of. When I fall asleep, I lose some control. Maybe that's why he usually comes out at night—when my brain is parked. But why, then, no appearance last night?"

"I told you. The bastard doesn't want to be predictable. It's not very hard to lie low for an evening."

Billy finished buttoning a shirt, thought about putting on one of his new ties, then dismissed the idea. Throwing on a sport coat, he said. "What are you waiting for? Let's go eat."

Jamie tore a label off Billy's sleeve and followed the large man out of the room.

CHAPTER 28

After breakfast, a taxi dropped Billy and Jamie off at the address on Schmidt's business card—a tall, tired office building in midtown New York. They stepped out of the elevator on the eleventh floor and walked halfway down a featureless, carpeted corridor to a door marked MAL-LACH RESEARCH INSTITUTE. The lobby was just large enough for a receptionist desk, a sofa, and two chairs. This could be a physician's office, or an accountant's.

Robert Schmidt, in jeans and a dark green turtle neck, was chatting with a middle-aged receptionist as they entered. With a "Good morning" he reached out and Billy instinctively shook his hand, as did Jamie. "I hope you're not too apprehensive," Schmidt said. "What we do here is painless, you know."

Schmidt started to smile, waiting for a predictable nervous laugh. None came. To Jamie, the line seemed rehearsed, probably offered to everyone who arrived for a first session.

Schmidt's smile faded. "Well—" he said, "Dr. Mallach is expecting you. We appreciate your punctuality. The Doctor is very busy. I must ask that from this point on, you follow her instructions absolutely. To the letter. And best to just answer her questions. What she needs to know, she will ask."

Jamie didn't like Schmidt's condescending tone. In fact, he didn't like Schmidt, who had suddenly ushered them down a narrow hall and into Dr. Mallach's office.

"Here they are as promised," Schmidt announced.

"Thank you, Robert." Dr. Mallach, an attractive woman with perfect posture, sat in a high-backed executive chair behind a polished, uncluttered desk. She was in her fifties, according to information Jamie had found on the web, but didn't look it. She stood up, and her tailored suit made it obvious she was proud of her figure. She had black hair with all inevitable signs of gray chemically obliterated. No discernible wrinkles on her face or neck. A confident stride as she approached Jamie first, then Billy. No hint of racial prejudice as she firmly shook hands with the shiny black Bahamian, nor any sense of intimidation when her hand was engulfed by his.

"So nice to meet both of you," Mallach said. "Robert, leave us alone for a few minutes, would you?"

Schmidt deferentially backed out of the room and closed the door.

Mallach smiled warmly at Jamie. "Well, I think we should get started, don't you?"

Jamie nodded.

"I would like to hear everything you can remember, Jamie, from the time of your drowning. And then I'd like to hear about this other person who you believe has inhabited you. What's his name again?

"Bernard Klassen," Jamie responded.

"Yes. He is, after all, at least half of what we're dealing with here."

"What do you mean, *at least* half? I would say *exactly* half."

"You and Klassen make two, but there may be others as well."

Jamie whipped his head toward Billy, who shrugged.

Mallach reacted to Jamie's astonishment. "Ahh, that surprises you, does it? Well, we've found that in many cases of reincarnation, the soul that moves forward has lived many lives before."

"I—I guess I knew that, from reading the stories in your book. But I hadn't thought that maybe Klassen had lived before…"

"That's what we're going to find out, Jamie. If you don't mind, I'd like to record everything. Video and audio. Is that all right with you?"

"I suppose so."

"Then if you'll be seated in this nice comfy chair right here…"

Dr. Mallach guided Jamie to a recliner in the center of the room. Jamie wondered why he hadn't noticed it before. But now, as Mallach manipulated a black remote, lights came on above the chair, illuminating it. Jamie looked up at the ceiling and was surprised by the array of lights attached to an electric grid, and by the video cameras—he could count four of them—mounted on the walls of the office. Like a spider on a strand of silk, a microphone dangled just above the chair.

"You'll soon forget about all the equipment, I promise you," Mallach explained, moving Jamie gently into the chair. "Feel free to use the controls on the left side to make the chair more comfortable."

Jamie started to fiddle with the controls. "I'd like to have this at home," he said, laughing nervously. So far, nothing is what he had expected.

Mallach turned to Billy. "You'll be able to observe from the room next door, if that's all right."

Billy nodded, completely mystified by what was happening. He glanced at the right-hand wall and noticed a wide mirror scattering light back into the room.

"Yes, a one-way mirror," Mallach explained. "From the other side, you won't miss a thing." She smiled and turned toward the mirror. "Robert, would you come and get Mr. Smythe?"

Seconds later, Schmidt opened the door and Billy walked into the hall.

Now it was only Jamie and Dr. Mallach.

———

The bald, dour man at the Waldorf registration desk didn't look up as the woman approached and placed a passport and credit card on the counter, pushing them forward to attract attention.

The man looked at the passport photo, glanced up at the woman, then lowered his eyes again. "Reservation in your name?"

"Yes."

The man's eyes moved to a computer monitor. His unseen fingers clacked away on a keyboard as he studied the information on his monitor, frowning once, then brightening.

"Ahh, yes. There you are."

He inserted a blank security card into a box, and it was instantly spit out, ready to unlock her room. He placed it into an envelope and handed it to the new guest. "Fifth floor. Elevators are over there."

"Can you tell me if Mr. Giles has checked in yet?"

The man prodded the computer into action and replied, "Yes, yesterday afternoon."

"Thank you."

Maria strode toward the elevators. Her slender fingers combed long, raven hair around a fragile orchid. A number of heads turned as the dazzling woman wheeled a small suitcase through the crowded lobby.

———

The control room, which viewed the regression room through a one-way mirror, looked like a living room with soft chairs and a long sofa. Billy watched from the sofa as Robert Schmidt—apparently an electronics expert as well as a psychologist—sat down at a console and manipulated various camera controls. Multiple monitors showed the visual effects of his jiggering. One camera zoomed in closer on Jamie's face, another framed a waist-high shot, and yet another a picture of Jamie's entire body. Billy noticed five audio controls. Looking hard, he found five suspended mics, not just one, positioned to pick up voices anywhere in the room.

Mallach wrapped a blood pressure cuff around Jamie's left arm, and attached numerous electrical leads to various points on Jamie's body and head. The wires swept upward into a moveable track above Jamie's chair. If Jamie were to stand up and walk around, he would look like a marionette but would not get tangled in the wires. On a black, hand-held panel, Dr. Mallach tapped some controls and the lights in the room dimmed.

"Are you comfortable Jamie?" Mallach's voice sounded natural coming through the high-end speakers in the control room.

"Very much."

"Then we will get started."

"Should I close my eyes?"

"It doesn't matter, Jamie. But if you want to, that would be all right." Dr. Mallach's voice had become soft and soothing, its register lower than her normal speaking voice.

"Are you recording this?" Billy asked Robert.

"All of it," Robert replied.

Mallach took a short step toward Jamie, who had not closed his eyes, instead keeping them trained on this woman who was about to guide him through some strange ritual. "All right, Jamie," she said, "I want you to raise your right arm."

"I don't feel hypnotized," Jamie confessed.

"No problem, just follow the instructions. Very slowly now, raise your right arm toward the ceiling."

Billy watched Jamie's arm begin to reach upward.

"That's right, Jamie," Mallach continued. "As you raise your arm, you are going deeper and deeper relaxed. Deeper and deeper relaxed."

Jamie's arm was now straight up, his fingers extended.

"There… now your arm is stiff and rigid. Just as rigid as a bar of steel. If you wish to go even deeper relaxed, let your arm drop to your lap."

Jamie's arm fell with velocity.

"That's fine, Jamie. Very good."

Billy stood up and walked toward the one-way mirror. "Is he under already?"

"Getting there," Schmidt explained.

Mallach walked back to her large chair and sat down. "Now, as I count to five, you will go still deeper and deeper relaxed. And as you go deeper, your pulse will slow down. It will slow down from—" Mallach glanced at a readout on her black panel— "from 80 beats per minute to 50 beats per minute, and you will go still deeper relaxed. One..."

Billy glanced at Schmidt's console and saw a digital display labelled PULSE. It read out at 80, then suddenly dropped to 74.

"Two..." Mallach said. "Deeper and deeper relaxed as your pulse slows down."

Billy watched the readout drop to 68.

About five seconds later, Mallach said, "Three."

The pulse display changed to 62.

"Four," Mallach said.

Jamie closed his eyes and his head slowly started to drop. The motion caught Billy's attention.

"Five."

Jamie's chin was touching his chest. His arms were limp. Billy turned to the pulse readout as it bottomed out at 49, then suddenly bounced back up to 50.

Astonished, Billy again turned his attention to the regression room, noticing that Dr. Mallach was consulting her watch.

"All right, Jamie. You can let your pulse go back to normal. You will now have easy access to your memories."

Jamie lifted his head but his eyes remained closed.

"I want you to reduce your brain wave activity to five cycles per second. As I count to five, you will slow your brain waves to five cycles per second. One... two... three... four... five."

On Schmidt's console, another digital readout dropped to five.

"This is just too spooky," Billy blurted out. "Some kind of parlor trick? What's the point?"

Schmidt turned smugly and said, "We've found that five cycles per second is the ideal state for recalling previous life experience. I'm writing a paper on it."

Mallach rose from her chair and walked over to Jamie. She leaned over him and spoke. "Now you will experience the sensation of rising from your chair… rising up and lifting through the ceiling, all the way up… up… up to a cloud. You have left this lifetime now, and you are going back to the life you lived before Jamie Giles."

Billy felt a nervous rise of bile in his throat.

"I want you to find a vivid event in this previous lifetime. Find it now, and concentrate on it. You may open your eyes, if you wish."

Jamie's eyes blinked open. Billy flinched.

"I want you to tell me who you are. What is your name?"

Jamie cocked his head, eyes focusing on Dr. Mallach. He seemed to be considering whether he should speak.

"Tell me your name," Mallach commanded.

At last, with a coarse voice that sounded raked over gravel, Jamie said, "Bernard Klassen."

CHAPTER 29

The taxi battled traffic on the way to Robert Schmidt's apartment. Seated next to Jamie in the back, Billy was deep in conversation with Schmidt, seated in the front.

"Don't worry, you'll be able to verify everything," Billy said.

"The hell with verifying it!" Jamie was hyped up, energized by the regressive hypnosis, just as Dr. Mallach had said he might be. "I'm running out of time here, you know? We've gotta make something happen fast."

Robert didn't like to argue, but he was frustrated with Jamie's insistence on speeding things up. "And what might that *something* be?" He couldn't hide his exasperation. "For one thing, the answers you're looking for may be in lives previous to Klassen."

"So why'd we stop? I could've maybe recalled other lives."

"We've learned that taking a subject back through more than one life at a time tends to cause some disorientation, and can produce jumbled, unreliable recollections. You need to let us go through the process here. I'm sure we'll get the answers you're looking for. By the way—what *are* you looking for?"

Jamie was stumped. What *was* he looking for? "Honestly, I'm not sure."

"Then maybe you found it, and you don't even fucking know it."

Schmidt, looking straight ahead, had seasoned his retort with the vinegar of arrogance.

Jamie didn't like the taste. "Trust me, I'll fuckin' know it!"

Schmidt quickly softened his tone. "I'm just saying, we're all feeling our way here. We've never had a case like yours before. We understand that you're afraid this Klassen entity might take you over permanently, at any moment. The clock's ticking, right? Just remember, Dr. Mallach and I are on your side. We'll move as quickly as she thinks we can. But it would help if you had any clues as to what you—*we*—are looking for. *Specifically*, I mean."

"*Nehsira*—the person who is trying to track down Klassen for some reason. That's *who* we're looking for. If we could find Nehsira, maybe he'd have some information that would… that could…"

"…that could help you get rid of this monster?"

"I guess. Or maybe keep this guy from killing me, if that's what he's after. Maybe it's about revenge for something. That would be some grudge, huh? I don't know. *Damn*! I don't know anything!"

Schmidt twisted in the front seat to look directly at Jamie. "Jamie, you're fired up right now, but you're going to crash in a little while. I guarantee it. And releasing Klassen to cough up his story might have stirred the pot, so we don't exactly know what the consequences of that might be. Relax the rest of the day, will you? And if you need me before our session tomorrow morning, just call."

The taxi pulled up in front of Schmidt's apartment building.

"See you two in the morning, okay?"

Billy nodded, but Jamie just looked away as Robert climbed out. The car lurched into late afternoon traffic, narrowly avoiding an accident.

"That prick, Schmidt, wants to get famous," Jamie said, "and I'm his fuckin' ticket."

"He and Mallach will have to fight over who gets their name on your syndrome."

"I'm just a goddam paper at a psychology convention. Jesus!"

Billy looked at the despondent younger man next to him. "It's only the first day."

"Yeah, but one of these days will be my *last* day, partner."

———

At 1:30 a.m., Billy's cell phone lit up and beeped. He had yet to sleep, his mind like a meteor hurtling aimlessly through a universe of frightening possibilities. Squinting dry eyes, he sat up and saw that the caller was Kathy, so he connected.

"Are you okay?" he asked, omitting any greeting.

"Fine, just lonesome. My friend is gone most of the time so I'm just lying low and reading books. She has lots of those. Ever read *Pale Fire* by Nabokov?"

"Never heard of it." He lay back down on the pillow.

"I found a line in the book that says what I've been thinking. *Dear Jesus, do something*."

"Well, in case He doesn't, I'm doing my best to fill in."

"Figure anything out today?"

"Just a little bit. But we're picking away at Jamie's recollections—may take some time."

"I'd like to be there, in the background."

"Not a good idea, I think."

"Please, Billy. I can't just be sitting here wondering what's going on."

The sound of breaking glass startled Billy. He sat up, listening, afraid that Klassen might be on a rampage again.

"Billy? Are you there?" Kathy asked.

"I'll think about it, I promise. I've got to hang up. We'll talk tomorrow."

He disconnected the call as he heard Jamie calling out, "Billy! Billy, please... c'mere!"

At least it sounded like Jamie, not Klassen. That was good news.

Billy stood up and straightened his pajamas, then walked to his open bedroom door. Across the sitting room, Jamie's bedroom door was still securely shackled.

"Billy, for God's sake, I need you!"

Panic had crept into Jamie's voice, prompting Billy to race to the credenza, switch on a lamp, and retrieve the padlock key. Running to the door, he slipped the key into the lock, fumbling once, then getting it right. The padlock opened and Billy removed the chain.

"Billy! Hurry!" The voice was a hoarse whisper now.

But as Billy gripped the doorknob, fear seized him. He had no idea what was going on behind that door.

"Billy? Are you there?"

Billy's huge hand rotated the doorknob, then cautiously pushed open the door, revealing a dark room illuminated only by hazy street light filtering through the curtains. He stepped into the room, his eyes slowly adjusting to the darkness. He could make out the bed now, empty.

"Where the hell are you?" Billy said.

He took another step, and the door slammed behind him. He turned to his left, where a dark shadow now masked a man-shaped section of the glowing curtain.

From the shadow came the rough voice of Bernard Klassen. "Over here, Billy."

Instinctively, Billy took a step backward. "You!"

"I came back, Billy, like I said I would."

"You son-of-a-bitch. How many times do I have to kill you?"

Klassen laughed. "My dear friend, you really are dumb as shit, you know that? You can't kill me. On the other hand, it's time for me to even an old score."

Billy's eyes had adjusted, and he could make out the dark face of Jamie staring at him with glistening, angry eyes. "And you are a demon from hell."

"Well, not exactly… but I take that as a compliment."

Looking around the room, he saw that the dresser mirror had been shattered. He felt the padlock key between his fingers and wondered how he could get out of the room and chain up the door with Klassen loose.

"I never told you about your daughter, did I, Billy?"

Billy stopped thinking about the chain.

"She was a good fuck for a while," Klassen said, "until she got worn out. And then she was just a dirty whore."

Klassen's words ignited Billy's fury.

"Couldn't ever get enough," Klassen said. "I tried to give the bitch what she craved. Rough, crude sex… dope… booze. God, what an appetite. And she liked to be hurt—did you know that, Billy? She wouldn't let me stop until there was blood…"

Billy was almost out of control. "You sick maniac…"

Klassen was amused. "Oh, you brought her up just the way I like them."

Billy stepped menacingly toward the shadowy figure. But he stopped suddenly when Klassen held up a jagged shard of the broken mirror.

"I want you to know, Billy, that she begged me to kill her. Those appetites of hers, they were just too much. In the end, she knew that only death could satisfy her. You should thank me, Billy. Really you should. I gave her everything she wanted."

This was too much. Billy lunged for Klassen, who slashed out with the hunk of broken glass, but missed. Billy shoved him into the dresser, but somehow the shadow slipped away and Klassen managed to get behind him, pressing the brittle edge of the shard into Billy's neck. With one python arm, Billy kept the shard from slicing his neck.

Klassen was incredibly strong for a dead man.

With his other hand, Billy maneuvered the room key so its pointed end protruded from his fist. As the glass shard began to draw blood, he stabbed the key into Klassen's thigh.

There was a terrible scream as Klassen released his death hold. Like a dancer, Billy swiveled and landed a huge fist into Jamie's gut, sending him halfway across the room. But with nearly superhuman strength, Klassen rebounded and tackled Billy. Sent him reeling to the floor. Put a hard fist into Billy's jaw. Then another.

A knee in the crotch toppled Klassen and suddenly Billy was on top. Three hard blows to the face, and Klassen stopped moving. Mad with rage, Billy found another shard of mirror on the floor. Holding Klassen's head in one hand, he raised the glass blade and readied himself to plunge it downward.

But then the shard reflected a shaft of light onto the face of his adversary, and he saw it was not Klassen. It was Jamie. *Of course* it was Jamie—a young man innocently inhabited by the evil soul of Bernard Klassen.

Klassen had been right when he'd said, *You can't kill me.*

Billy angrily threw the shard against the wall. It shattered into a hundred glistening pieces. He painfully stood up and looked down at the bloodied face, which in his battered brain seemed to blur from Jamie's to Klassen's.

"Fuckin' maniac!" he said.

And then he left the room and chained the door.

CHAPTER 30

Through the one-way mirror, Billy watched as Robert Schmidt ushered Jamie into the regression room. Jamie seemed to notice the stunned expression on Mallach's face as she looked at him. His left eye was dark and puffy, his left cheek bandaged, his upper lip swollen, his chin bruised…

Billy saw his own reflection in the glass. He didn't look much better.

Mallach did not question Jamie about his bruises. Instead, she simply said, "I'm glad you came back. Not everyone does."

Jamie had been in a foul mood all morning, refusing to speak to Billy. His disposition carried into the regression room. "Let's just move on, all right?" he suggested curtly. "I don't think we can learn any more from that bastard Klassen. I'm tired of him."

"Then let's go to an earlier lifetime, shall we?"

Jamie gave a look of approval as Schmidt entered the control room, nodded at Billy, and took his seat.

Mallach gestured to the chair, and Jamie sat down, adjusting the controls slightly. Mallach lowered the lights and quietly shuffled closer to Jamie, carrying her black control pad.

"Just sit back and relax."

Jamie wriggled slightly, but kept his eyes trained on Dr. Mallach.

"Yesterday, I left you with special instructions—that you would immediately go into a deep state of hypnosis when I said the word *mindspan*."

Jamie immediately closed his eyes, and his head fell forward.

Billy was impressed with the effectiveness of this technique.

"You are going deeper and deeper relaxed now," Mallach said. "Your brain waves are slowing… slowing down to five cycles per second."

She checked the digital readout on her black pad.

"That's right, very good. You are now leaving this lifetime. And you are backing up past the life of Bernard Klassen. I want you to concentrate on a life you lived before Klassen."

Mallach hesitated for a few seconds. Billy suspected she was allowing time for the inhabiting soul to recalibrate, or something.

"Now tell me," Mallach said, "what is your name?"

Jamie lifted his head, cocked it a few degrees, and then dismissively looked away from Mallach.

"I said, tell me your name." Mallach's voice now crackled with authority. She was taking charge.

Jamie abruptly turned his head. In one of the monitors on the control panel, Billy could see a close-up of Jamie's face, eyes staring haughtily at Dr. Mallach. And then Jamie spoke—in German.

"Wer will meinen namen wissen?"

Mallach was stunned.

In the control room, Schmidt turned to Billy. "Does he speak German?"

Billy shrugged. "His wife told me he didn't speak anything but English."

"Well, I was born in Germany. Dr. Mallach…"

She turned toward the one-way mirror, putting a finger on the hidden earpiece that allowed her to hear Schmidt.

"He wants to know who's asking for his name. In German—ask him to speak English. *Sprechen in Englisch.*"

Mallach repeated the German command.

Jamie smiled. "Who wants to know my name?"

"A friend. I am a friend. My name is Alice Mallach. Please tell me… how old are you?

"I am ten years old. How old are you?"

Alice glanced at the control room. She didn't like giving up her age, but relented. "I'm fifty-four."

"Are you from one of my dreams?"

"Dreams? Do you have dreams, child?"

A shadow seemed to pass over Jamie's face. He grew suddenly angry. "I asked if you were from one of my dreams."

The force of Jamie's voice sent Mallach backward a step. "Yes," she said. "Yes, I am from one of your *good* dreams."

"I have no good dreams! I pray, to the Holy Mother, that she will take my dreams away."

"Please, child, I want to help take your bad dreams away, but I have to know your name."

Jamie turned away.

"Please tell me your name." Mallach urged. "I love to hear you say it."

"My name…" Jamie stopped, looked down. "My name is…"

"Please, child, tell me your name, and then I'll help you get rid of your dreams."

Jamie started weeping. The demanding child had suddenly become a frightened little boy. Jamie curled his legs up in the chair. "No one will want a king who dreams terrible things."

"Are you going to be a king some day?"

"Someday."

"If you tell me your name, I can help with your dreams."

"*Everyone* knows my name."

———

After ninety minutes, Dr. Mallach needed a break. She reminded Jamie of the *mindspan* command and then brought him out of his trance. He was allowed to use the men's room first; Mallach didn't like her subjects having contact with anyone but her during a session.

In the men's room a few minutes later, Schmidt was scrubbing his hands under hot water as Billy entered. The two glanced at each other. Both of them looked drained.

"Good time for a break," Billy said. "So, you seemed to know who this person was, this other life of Jamie's."

"They called him *Mad* King Ludwig," Schmidt replied.

Billy splashed some water on his face. "A *real* king?"

"The king of Bavaria. That's where I was born. Everyone there knows the story of the mad king who built the fairytale castles. Ever hear of Neuschwanstein?"

"Rings a bell, but I'm not sure why."

"Neuschwanstein is a fantastic castle that Ludwig built in Bavaria. So fantastic it was used as the model for the Disney Fantasyland castle."

"Was he truly *mad*?"

"He suffered from a hereditary mental disorder. Went mad… schizophrenia, probably. He was eventually removed from office and put in the custody of a psychiatrist."

"The world, I think, has a lot of leaders in that same condition."

"But there was something different about Ludwig," Schmidt said, half-sitting on a sink. "As a child, he had bad dreams. *Terrible* dreams."

"Visions, you think?"

"Just like Jamie's, perhaps."

"Do you think—?"

Schmidt nodded. "Maybe Ludwig's madness wasn't hereditary after all. Maybe he went mad trying to resist the memories of his previous lives."

Schmidt pitched a wadded-up paper towel into the trash bin and left.

Billy lingered, staring at himself in the mirror.

CHAPTER 31

Hooked up again to the tubes and wires, Jamie instantly went under when Mallach spoke the word *mindspan*. Robert and Schmidt took their places in the control room, focusing their attention on Dr. Mallach as she began her questions. Immediately, Jamie put up his hand to quiet her, then stood up and began to walk around the room, eyes wide open. The wires tracked with him, as they were designed to do when a patient became ambulatory.

"All right, Ludwig, what are you doing?" Mallach seemed confused by his pacing. "Are you nervous about something?"

Again, Jamie silenced her with an authoritative hand signal, and a look of irritation. He continued pacing.

Mallach watched for a minute, then impatiently commanded, "Jamie, you will tell me now—in English—what is happening."

Jamie stopped pacing and turned toward the one-way mirror. He seemed to be staring directly at Robert Schmidt, but Billy knew it was impossible to see through the mirror.

"They sent an arrest commission," Jamie said.

———

For Jamie, the regression room has transformed into a gray stone chamber. He recognizes this place—the Tower Room in Neuschwanstein castle. A shaft of sunlight penetrates the darkness, slashing across the floor and a large wooden table and bench.

A voice in his head speaks to *him*—to *King Ludwig*. "Why did they send an arrest commission?"

Ludwig is insulted by the question. And yet the voice ironically is the answer to the question posed by the voice.

He answers, as he always does. "They think I'm mad, and they want the throne taken out of my hands."

Ludwig knows that, to the commission, the voice in his head will confirm his madness. Is he truly mad, then? Or are the voices real—angels, perhaps, or demons. He has never known for sure. Most of his life he has spoken with the voices, but this one is different. This one is new.

The voice presses the inquiry. "What are you going to do?"

"I have already done it," Ludwig says. "I rounded up all the members of the commission upon their arrival. They can think about their traitorous behavior in that stinking gatehouse."

The sunlight dims, and Ludwig considers how dreary the Tower Room is without light. He vows to illuminate the interior as soon as he takes care of the traitors in the gate house. And some hanging art would make the room more to his liking. He decides to commission some new works from that artist—what is his name? He had done a magnificent job creating works to accompany *Tannhauser*, the masterpiece that the composer Wagner had created under the sponsorship of the Bavarian King. Oh, how Ludwig loves that opera.

There is always something to do in a castle.

A long-haired, beak-nosed man of about thirty trudges into the room. Ludwig recognizes him as Weber, his valet. The man approaches the king but stops four paces short, staring dumbly at the floor.

"Well, speak up!" Ludwig shouts angrily. "What news do you bring?"

"Your highness, we found a note on Dr. von Gudden, the neurologist from the asylum, who was among the members of the commission. It says…" Weber seems to have lost his tongue.

"Go on, now. Give me the news."

"The note says that your uncle has already been named regent."

In an outburst of anger, Ludwig overturns the immense wooden table, then tosses a heavy bench on its side. He knows that the naming of a royal family member as regent means that he has already lost his title. He is no longer king. "Dr. von Gudden! I appointed him myself to the asylum, a generous promotion! And now he has the audacity…"

Ludwig marches over to Weber and grabs the man's shirt, nearly lifting him off the ground.

"Here is what I want the captain of the gendarmes to do with the traitors in the gate house," Ludwig says. "I want them skinned alive! Scalp them, cut off their tongues and hands, and flog them! Then blind them. Place them in heavy chains. And throw them into the deepest dungeon to starve. Am I clear on this?"

Weber silently stares at his king.

Ludwig releases his grip and shoves the man backward. "Do it! Your king commands you!"

Weber flees the room just as the voice speaks to Ludwig.

"I want you to take a seat now and make yourself comfortable."

Ludwig sees no harm in that. What else is there to do? He has declared his punishment for the traitorous bunch downstairs. It may be time to think about how to deal with this *regency* plot. Damn his uncle for going along with it! The old man must have been tricked. Or threatened.

He uprights the heavy bench and sits down.

The voice speaks to him. "Ludwig, I want you to move ahead now, to some *later time* of special significance."

The voice slithering through his brain makes no sense at first. What does *later time* mean? But then the room tilts and the stone walls melt away and Ludwig is suddenly outdoors. To his right is a familiar body of water—Lake Starnberg, on the grounds of Berg Castle, a favorite place. Neuschwanstein is his personal masterwork—a fantastical showpiece of the first order—but Berg castle is his place of rest, a comfortable retreat for a busy king. Why, then, does he not feel relaxed? It's a beautiful, sunny day, the birds are singing, an old friend is at his side. He is wearing an overcoat to fend off a morning chill.

——

Through the glass, Billy Smythe watched Jamie walk around the perimeter of the regression room, Mallach accompanying him on the right. After several minutes of silent, side-by-side walking, Mallach said, "Ludwig, tell me what you are doing. How is this walking around important to you?"

Without hesitation, Jamie replied, "I'm walking along the shore of Lake Starnberg with Dr. von Gudden. They have put me in his custody at Berg Castle, which is now my prison."

Jamie suddenly stopped and looked up into remembered trees, raising a slender finger to his lips. "Shhhh! Do you hear it? The song of a nightingale." He closed his eyes and smiled, apparently finding joy in the song of a bird that lived nearly 130 years ago. "Even my protégé, Richard Wagner, could not write such a beautiful melody. It's one of the few things that keeps me sane here."

"Ludwig, how can you walk so peacefully beside the man who certified you insane?"

Jamie grasped his head in both hands. "The voices in my head betrayed me. Can't you stop and let me enjoy a peaceful afternoon?"

"I'm sorry, Ludwig, but von Gudden…"

"Is an evil man!" Jamie angrily shouted to the ceiling. But then he spun around as if hiding a smirk. "But he does not know that *I* know who he really is. Or that I have a plan."

"A plan? What kind of a plan?"

Jamie wheeled to face Mallach with a steely glint in his eye, and a mischievous grin. The intensity of his gaze seemed to unnerve the hypnotherapist.

"Doktor von Gudden, es gibt keine wachen die uns folgen," Jamie said. "Sie waren sich bewusst, das?"

Startled, Mallach sucked in her breath and took a half-step back.

In the control room, Schmidt stood up. "This is unprecedented!" he said to Billy. "In all of our regression, no subject has ever spoken to Dr. Mallach as if she were a participant in the scene. He called her Doctor von Gudden."

Mallach gathers her composure. "Ludwig, you must speak to me in English even when you are speaking to another person."

———

On the serene bank of Lake Starnberg, Ludwig stares deeply into the eyes of his adversary. After a brief hesitation, he says, "Doctor von Gudden, no keepers are following us. Were you aware of that?"

"Yes, I know. You see, I'm not afraid of you." The psychiatrist touches Ludwig's arm in a familiar way.

Ludwig starts walking again, studying the grass. "Can I be cured, then?"

The Doctor catches up. "I'm afraid there is no possibility of that. You must remain under my care."

Ludwig stops, his face swollen with rage. A full six inches taller than the squat von Gudden, his shadow eclipses the doctor. "Do you think that I'm stupid? I know what you're up to."

"Now don't get agitated. Let me help you… that's what I do as a doctor of psychiatry."

Ludwig grins and shakes his head. "I know much more than you think. You signed the paper declaring me insane."

"You've known that for some time."

"But I also know why you did this—so that I would be under your direct influence as you opened my mind to extract its secrets."

"Again, that is what psychiatrists do."

"But the voices in my head have helped me understand that there is one secret that you will stop at nothing to get. Am I not right—*Nehsira*?"

Ludwig watches the doctor's face turn ashen and his hands begin to tremble.

"That's about enough!" von Gudden roars. But even in shouting, his voice quakes. "Come with me now, we're going back to the castle."

He forcefully grabs Ludwig's arm, but the ex-king seems rooted to the spot, staring back at him.

"I said let's go back now!"

The doctor looks around for help, but finds none. As he desperately swivels his head to the right, a leaden fist smashes his jaw, sending von Gudden and a tooth separately into the reeds.

Ludwig watches blood drool from the doctor's mouth, the man's eyes droop and close, the feeble attempt to rise only to fall back into the water. The captive king looks left, then right, expecting the hands of a keeper to pull him back into manacles. But no one is near. His eyes search the surface of the lake. Then it occurs to him. The water can be his escape—not just from this prison-castle, but from this ill-fated life.

Ludwig throws down his hat and strips off his jacket. He splashes into the lake, hoping he has the courage to drown.

Von Gudden rises slowly, like a hulking monster, slimy weeds hanging from his arms. He slumps onto dry ground. "You cannot leave me now!" the doctor calls out. "Not after I've found you!"

Ludwig does not turn back.

Von Gudden stumbles into the black water. Using his hands as paddles, he chases Ludwig deeper into the lake, catching up to the taller man as the water reaches chest-high.

The two men begin to thrash about. Ludwig wraps his hands around the doctor's neck and pulls him underwater, his long fingers beginning to strangle the life out of...

Dr. Mallach tried to wrench Jamie's vice-like grip from her neck. Schmidt and Billy Smythe rushed into the regression room. Billy peeled Jamie away from the woman, embracing him in a fierce bear hug. But Jamie wrestled free, falling to the ground and gasping for air.

At first, Billy thought he had injured Jamie. He stooped to see what was wrong. Robert pulled the big man away as Jamie began gurgling and turning white.

"My God!" Mallach said. "He's drowning!"

Robert turned to her, confused. Jamie was lying on the carpet, not a drop of water in sight.

"He's still in his past life—drowning in the lake!" Mallach screamed.

Robert immediately began doing CPR, compressing Jamie's chest. But Jamie, eyes bulging, grabbed Robert's arm and fought it.

"He thinks you're Gudden!" Mallach said. She looked at the digital readouts and saw that Jamie's vitals were plummeting. "No, no—not yet." she muttered. "Jamie! Jamie, listen to me. You will obey me now and leave this time—LEAVE THIS TIME!"

Jamie's vitals continued to falter.

"Jamie! You are going to another time—far in the future. Listen to me!"

Jamie drew in a long, painful breath, gagging and sputtering as if lake water had filled his lungs.

Billy reached out for Jamie's limp hand, aware that he had developed a fondness for the young man who was housing the malevolent soul.

"Please, Jamie—you are going to another time," Mallach urged. "There is no need to die here again. You are going deeper and deeper relaxed. Your pulse is returning to normal."

Jamie stopped breathing and let out a long sigh.

"Is he dead?" Billy asked.

Mallach glanced at the black panel, saw Jamie's pulse rise a few digits.

"He's coming back… coming back to me," she said.

Jamie opened his eyes and looked around—confused, afraid. He rolled over on his side and coughed, then seemed surprised that he had expelled no lake water. Looking around at the faces staring down at him, he crawled to Mallach's desk, sitting upright against the front panel.

Dr. Mallach approached him, but he pushed her away with a hiss.

"Jamie, it's me, Dr. Mallach. Do you recognize me?"

Jamie frowned and seemed to struggle with focusing his eyes on her face. Then he nodded, and looked down.

"I tried to kill you," he said hoarsely.

"It wasn't your fault."

"I thought you were—someone else."

"I know, Jamie. But look at me. I'm all right… no damage done. Except to my pride. I've never so… so successfully regressed anyone before."

Jamie turned back to Mallach and cocked his head, as if he were still struggling to see her clearly. Looking confused, he glanced at Billy, who was seated on the floor near Schmidt.

"I've tried to kill two of you now," Jamie said. "I'm losing control of this *thing* in me."

"This was my fault, Jamie." Mallach said. "I regressed you too deeply without any precautions."

Billy noticed that Dr. Mallach and Jamie seemed unable to make eye contact with each other. *Wounded pride on Mallach's part, perhaps? Shame on Jamie's part?*

Too much to process.

———

Gino's Italiana served a veal scaloppini that Robert Schmidt claimed was the best in New York. He insisted that everyone try it. When it arrived, he anxiously took a forkful of meat and sipped some wine before noticing that Billy and Jamie were picking at their food.

"Not hungry?" he asked.

His companions ignored him. Jamie absently stared out the restaurant window at the rain-slickened street.

Robert changed the subject. "I guess it was a pretty stressful afternoon. By the way, Dr. Mallach said I should pick up the tab. She felt badly about how things went. She'd be here with us, but had a prior commitment. I was thinking… maybe we should induce hypnotic amnesia after these sessions to…"

"No way!" Jamie said. "I want to remember *everything*."

"I just thought it must be difficult, reliving all that—horrible…"

Billy put his huge hand on Schmidt's arm. "Robert—shut up."

Robert stuffed another bite of veal into his mouth. "Look, everything that happens in that room is absolutely confidential. No one needs to know—" he glanced awkwardly at Billy "—anything at all."

"Why are you looking at me?" Billy shot back. "I'm not the subject."

Robert swallowed. "It's just that I've never known anyone who literally killed someone."

Billy stared back, hard.

"I mean, like you killed Bernard Klassen, right?" Schmidt suddenly realized that he was on dangerous ground.

"Shut up, both of you." Jamie seemed to be in no mood for bickering. "We need to jump forward or I'm going to run out of time."

Schmidt considered this statement. He had never understood the urgency of unraveling the tangled details of this case. "I don't get it. What's the rush?"

"How long did it take that sax player's soul to take over the soldier?" Jamie asked. "In Mallach's book—remember?"

The pieces tumbled together for Schmidt. Jamie sensed that he had a limited amount of time before the soul of Klassen/Ludwig/*whoever else* completely took over his body and Jamie Giles was erased forever.

Schmidt nodded slowly. "And you think this 'takeover' is imminent, in your case?"

"Imminent? Christ, you sound like a scientist. This is my *life* here! There's a little piece of me left inside this body, but..." He glanced at Billy.

Confused, Schmidt turned to Billy, too.

"Why is everybody looking at *me*?" Billy complained.

Still staring at Billy, Jamie said, "Last night Klassen was loose in our room."

"What?" The revelation startled Robert. "Shit. You weren't under hypnosis then."

"It's happening fast now," Jamie said. "He's taking me over a few hours at a time, and there's nothing I can do. I don't even know if I can make it until the session tomorrow."

Jamie gulped down his glass of wine and peered at Robert.

"You're watching me disappear."

———

To all but one, the individuals seated in *Gino Italiana* appeared to be three businessmen out for dinner. But for that one particular observer sitting at the window table of a coffee shop across the street, two of these men were targets of intense scrutiny.

The observer sipped a small dark roast and watched the men rise from their chairs and head for the door. Outside, two of the men hailed cabs. The tall black man and a slender white man climbed into a cab together, waving at the third man.

The observer knew where this pair was headed—back to the Waldorf Astoria. The observer's eyes, though, stayed on the third man who'd been left behind.

Maria still didn't know what Billy and the surprise "heir" to Klassen's fortune were up to, but she hadn't lost the scent.

As the third man stepped into the busy street to hail a cab, she knew it was time for her to leave, too.

CHAPTER 32

Billy detected a shift in Jamie's demeanor. Who wouldn't be going through an emotional disturbance, after such agonizing revelations? But then, Billy always worried that Klassen was worming his way to the surface of Jamie's consciousness again. The previous evening had rattled him.

He was still surprised at his own feelings—the way he had felt compassion for Jamie as the young man had gone through his near-drowning. And how he had wanted to reach out and touch Jamie, to let him know that he understood the kind of torment he must be going through.

The cab lurched around a stopped car. Billy reached out to touch Jamie's arm, but Jamie pulled away as if shocked by a cattle prod.

"I don't want to be around that prick anymore!" Jamie said.

"Who? Robert? He's part of the team."

"Gives me the creeps. There's just something about him… Keep him away from me."

"Jamie, be reasonable…"

Jamie's nostrils flared, the way Billy remembered Klassen's doing when he flew into a rage.

"I gave you a fucking order, Billy!" Jamie said indignantly. "I don't want him near me!"

The outburst caused the cab driver to glance at Jamie in the rearview mirror.

Billy grew rigid in the seat, fearing that Klassen was gaining control. "Jamie—fight him, dammit. Don't let him take you over."

Jamie glared at him. "You think only Klassen gets mad?"

Jamie pulled out a cell phone and called Kathy.

Billy could hear the phone ringing in Jamie's ear.

No answer.

Jamie hung up. "What did you do with her, Billy? I know you did something." He was suddenly not angry. Tears loomed in his eyes and his voice softened, almost pleading.

"She's safe, Jamie. That's all I did. Helped her get to a safe place. You really scared her."

Jamie shook his head. "Just tell me where she is. How I can get in touch with her. Please, Billy. I have to talk to her. She doesn't know—I have to explain…" He hammered the phone on the back of the driver's seat. "I need to hear her voice."

"Let's get through these sessions first, okay? Then I promise…"

Jamie's glare interrupted Billy. "Maybe I've been thinking about this all wrong."

"What do you mean?"

"I remember that Nehsira, alias Dr. von Gudden, held the keys to Ludwig's freedom. And who now who holds the keys to my freedom?"

"You're in big trouble when you can't tell your friends from your enemies."

"Nehsira is someone close to me. I can feel it."

Jamie's phone chirped.

Billy jumped.

Jamie answered. "Kathy? My God, are you all right?"

Billy could hear Kathy's voice faintly rattling, even as Jamie put the phone to his opposite ear.

"No, I just… well, I needed to know you were okay," Jamie said. "And that… damn, I'm so sorry for what I…"

Billy could hear Kathy speaking, but couldn't make out the words. He could see Jamie melt into his seat, dripping with remorse, tearing up at the sound of his wife's voice, but also slowly brightening as Kathy soothed him with something. Forgiveness? Understanding? Billy couldn't tell, but the conversation showed Billy that he was sitting alongside Jamie, not Klassen.

"Okay," Jamie said finally. "When Billy says it's all right, we'll meet."

He hung up, and the cab arrived at the Waldorf Astoria.

———

The hotel lobby was throbbing with people. Billy and Jamie pushed their way across. Billy's hand seemed fastened to his sternum.

"If New York has such great food, why can't we find where they serve it?" he said, steering for the concierge, who was mercifully unoccupied.

"I need antacid—fast," Billy explained.

The Concierge smiled and raised a finger. "One moment, sir, and I'll get you some."

Grateful, Billy scanned the crowd as the concierge left his post.

"Seems like a convention just arrived," Billy said to Jamie.

There was no response.

Billy looked around, then jerked his head left and right in panic, realizing that Jamie had disappeared.

The concierge returned with two pink tablets entombed in plastic bubbles.

Billy grabbed the tablets and said, "Don't go away. I may need more."

———

Robert Schmidt didn't go home after the session. He was one of about two hundred other singles, or pretend-singles, to fill up Buster's for happy hour. He'd been fortunate to grab a table in a shadowy corner of the lounge, where he and Maria were in rapt conversation, oblivious to the slow-moving horde circling around.

———

Jamie couldn't stand it another minute—being a prisoner. He knew the risks of being alone, but he needed some time and space to gather his thoughts, so he had abandoned Billy when he'd had the chance. The conversation with Kathy had jarred him awake, confronting him with the personal consequences of his/Klassen's actions.

Who was responsible for what he did? If he were arrested and convicted of spousal abuse, who would be guilty—Jamie or Klassen? Or maybe Ludwig? They'd put Jamie's body in prison—the other guys were dead—but was Jamie's *body* at fault?

It was all too complicated. He didn't know who he was anymore. Maybe Jamie had receded to be just the whisper of a memory, a residue of consciousness lingering in his cells. It could be that he was fighting a battle that was already over, and he had lost.

He stumbled into a deli and ordered coffee, black, and a piece of apple pie.

Huh. That was an order Jamie would have placed.

So maybe Jamie was still around someplace.

At the register, he paid for the food and found a reflection of himself in a mirror behind the cashier. He didn't recognize himself, and it scared him. When he moved, the reflection moved, but the body was someone else's.

And that's how he knew that he was now Klassen.

CHAPTER 33

He walked as if pulled by instinct to an obscure Manhattan street in the 20's, and found himself staring at a building that looked ready to be torn down. If someone drilled a geological core through the posters on the exterior walls, it'd go back maybe thirty years.

Klassen, enjoying the agile body of Jamie Giles, entered the building and followed a rough staircase down to a basement. He knew where he was going. He'd been here many times during visits to New York. The raucous mash-up of laughter and cussing and heavy metal, punctuated by an occasional scream, assaulted his ears.

And aroused him.

An unlocked door, painted with the words BRIMSTONE CLUB, blocked his path. He pushed through and the noise became deafening. To his left was a freakish assortment of S&M enthusiasts clad in everything from three-piece suits to obscene costumes that would give the Marquis de Sade nightmares. They sipped drinks, eerily watched the proceedings, or engaged in crude physical acts using a collection of fiendish apparatuses.

To his right, a tall, bald man with a bare chest above tight, black-leather bikini shorts, looked up with a scowl. Klassen knew this man—Ace, the proprietor—but Klassen knew Ace would not recognize him in this younger body. Hell, in the deli, Klassen had been shocked when seeing his own upgraded image in the mirror, and during the long walk here he'd been sorting out the pieces of what was happening. In the end, he'd figured that he had successfully achieved his goal. The confusing array of dream-like scenarios he'd been experiencing had been of this new life as a younger man, glimpses that had broken through the new host's consciousness.

"Ace," Klassen yelled. "Good to see you." His hoarse voice was neither his own nor a young man's, but a harsh mix of the two. He was amused as Ace clearly failed to recognize him.

Ace thumbed a large metal spike on a wristband. "What can I do for you, Big Guy?" he shouted.

Klassen removed a wallet from his hip pocket and cracked it open, startled by the driver's license photo that greeted him. On it was the same face that had stared back at him in the deli mirror. The face of the body he was operating right now. He looked at the name on the license—Jamie Giles—and then removed five one-hundred dollar bills.

Mr. Giles was about to finance a night of pleasure for Bernard Klassen.

Klassen handed the money to Ace, who guided him to a curtained doorway. Klassen followed him into the club wearing a cold, cynical sneer.

The Brimstone Club featured S&M at its organized best. This could have been Sodom and Gomorrah. The population of the smoke-filled hellhole ranged from professorial types in tweed coats to steel-studded bikers. Klassen looked at home here. He laughed and marched through a tangle of jaded humanity in various degrees of undress performing creative acts of simulated torture with terrifying apparatuses right out of a horror movie.

Klassen slipped into a back room where various sweaty sadists were taking turns whipping a young woman strapped to a crucifix. Klassen shook his head. This was ritual more than torture—as if the idea of it was more titillating than the act. Klassen laughed at each gentle lash of the leather strap on the naked woman's back.

He would show them how it should be done.

———

In his hotel room, Billy Smythe paced, muttering to himself about the stupidity of letting Jamie escape. It was Billy's job to keep him safe. To keep others safe from him. An escape meant that Jamie was under the control of Klassen… or one of the other entities.

His cell phone rang. "Hello."

It was Kathy. "Me—just checking in. How's our boy?"

Billy couldn't bear to tell her Jamie was loose on the streets. "Resting," he lied. "We made great progress today, but these sessions wear him out. Reliving all this ancient stuff. Do you need anything?"

A pause, then Kathy said, "I want to be there with you. He wouldn't have to know. Billy, I have to see for myself that it wasn't Jamie who did these things to me. I need to believe it was someone else. But it's hard, Billy, when I have nightmares with Jamie's face in them…"

"I can't let you be there," Billy interrupted. "It could be dangerous. If somehow he saw you, I don't know what kind of reaction that would provoke."

"You could make it work, Billy. Please…"

"I'll think about it. But not tomorrow, all right?"

"Okay."

"Do you need money? Anything else?"

"No, I'm good. Lonesome's all. Can you get away and meet me somewhere, just the two of us? I need to see a friendly face."

Billy looked around the empty suite. "Not tonight. He could wake up any time," he lied again. "He's my job until we get this thing figured out."

"Then hurry up. I'm getting a little squirrely here."

"He loves you, Kathy. Never meant to hurt you. But he's got this monster in him…"

"I just wish I could understand it better."

"Soon, Kathy. Soon."

———

Even for the Brimstone Club, Klassen's brutality was over the top. Ace grabbed a fistful of his hair, ironically shouting, "You some kinda pervert or what?" He looked at the two muscular men who had subdued Klassen and shook his head. "Throw the asshole outta here!"

Klassen was hauled to a back door and shoved into the alley. He fell against a dumpster, then shielded himself as his shoes and clothing were tossed at him. Angrily, he pulled himself to his feet and rushed to the closed door, banging it with his fists. He bellowed, "I'll get you, you son of a bitch! Nobody fucks with me like that!"

Klassen angrily dressed, unconcerned by the danger in the neighborhood. At two in the morning, the streets were owned by crazies—druggies looking for a score, dealers keeping score, pimps supervising the rain-slickened streets, a legion of whores descending like locusts on the few johns looking for action.

Klassen paced down a side street near the bus station. A black hooker in silver shorts a size too small brazenly approached, molesting his fly with the tip of her parasol.

"Say, Honey—whatcha got in there?" She gave a lewd smile. "A present for Mama?"

He stopped.

She looked down at his crotch, bugging her eyes out as if willing his arousal. "Oooeeee! We better get to my place quick or all the blood's gonna rush outta your head and you is gonna faint!" She chuckled, then looked up at his face, hidden in shadows but faintly showing the outlines of a grin.

Suddenly Klassen grabbed the parasol so fiercely that the hooker leaped backward. He found the handle, then pointed the parasol like a weapon at the hooker, pushing the tip into her chest and forcing her against a rough brick wall.

The woman looked scared—*surprised*, like she hadn't bargained on this guy being the violent type.

Klassen thought about plunging the parasol into the woman's chest, but instead maneuvered the tip of it into her blouse and pulled the material away from her chest for a look at her professional equipment.

As he peeked, he erupted in a big, uproarious laugh, then held out the parasol for her to take.

She snatched it angrily and watched him step away. Turning, she saw two druggies watching with hazy grins, multiplying her humiliation.

She turned back to Klassen, who was disappearing down the street. "You gotta pay to look, fool!"

Klassen stopped walking. With his back to her, he held out a paper bill.

The hooker turned to the druggies with a triumphant snort. "That's more like it!" she called out, then pranced to the outstretched hand, making a show of it.

As she reached out to take the money, Klassen turned to face her, something hard and cold in his eyes. And then his other hand shot out like a snake's tongue and grabbed her blouse, renting it from her body. Even this street-toughened whore instinctively tried to cover her breasts. The druggies howled with laughter.

Klassen dropped a one-dollar bill on the sidewalk. "Fair market value," he said before wheeling and walking off.

A few minutes later, Klassen spotted a pretty but skinny Hispanic girl who could be Maria's sister. He stopped and stared at her. She looked him over.

———

Robert could hardly believe his good fortune—that a beautiful woman like Maria would be turned on by him. His hands fumbled with a bra clasp as he and Maria lay on the sofa in the Mallach Research Institute control room. Her genuine curiosity about his work had made her easy to bait. And so what if he had bragged a little about the sensational Jamie Giles sessions? Of course, then he had to show them—just a few minutes' worth would do it.

The footage had worked better than a romantic movie, and soon she was compliant to his needs, with the video seeming to heighten her passions.

Hypno-porn, he thought. *Who would've thought?*

With the video session chattering in the background, Robert finally released the bra clasp.

On the video, Dr. Mallach said, "I want you to tell me who you are. What is your name?"

Maria turned her face toward the monitor. Robert did not notice—his eyes were elsewhere.

"Bernard Klassen," Jamie said through the speakers.

And Maria sighed.

———

Paint flaked from the walls, which were pockmarked with holes left from some past violence. The odor was overpowering—like a mix of piss and sour wine. At the bottom of a ramshackle stairs, a door opened. The Hispanic girl led Klassen through it, then led him by the hand up the stairs.

A white-haired gentleman in a suit but no tie bumped into them on his way down the stairs, refusing eye contact. Obviously a john with his business completed.

On the landing above, two meaty black men were drinking from a whiskey bottle and talking secretively. One of them, probably the girl's pimp, watched the girl as she dragged Klassen into a dim bedroom.

"You be good to him now!" the pimp hollered. "Looks like a big tipper."

In the room, Klassen looked around. The squalid mattress, covered by a loose, stained sheet, could be the comfortable home for numerous kinds of life forms. This was an odd choice for a man of means. He could have hired an expensive call girl, yet this skinny but beautiful whore had reminded him so much of Maria that he just had to have her.

"My name is Susana," she said, holding out her hand for the obligatory financial exchange. "One hundred," she said.

Overpriced for a street walker, Klassen knew, but he didn't care. Never taking his hot gaze off her, Klassen reached into his wallet and withdrew a hundred dollar bill, briefly exposing a thin stack of bills left in the wallet.

"Take off your clothes," he demanded.

She took the money and started to remove her clothing. Before she got very far, he was on her. Savagely.

———

A few minutes later, Susana rushed out of the room in panties and an open blouse, carrying the rest of her clothes and a police baton. She looked like she'd been through the spin-dry cycle at the laundromat. For a few seconds, she just glowered at her pimp, then angrily slapped the money and the baton into his hand. There was a lot more there than a single hundred dollar bill. And the baton was smudged with blood.

The pimp pocketed most of the money, smiling greedily, then handed her the rest.

She flew down the stairs, pausing at the bottom just long enough to step into her tight shorts. And then she was gone.

The pimp heard some angry banging and crashing in the vacated bedroom, like a wild animal trashing its cage. He and his friend decided not to hang around. As they started down the stairs, two whores and their johns started up, blocking the path.

Klassen's door suddenly burst open. With a trickle of blood on his forehead, Klassen emerged, raging. Clearly, the girl had knocked him out with the baton, but now he was conscious. And mad.

The pimp turned to view the landing above him. "Sayyyy, brother, I wouldn't do nothing now—I got lotsa friends here."

Klassen's glaring eyes searched for Susana. Not finding her, he focused on the pimp. "She took my money. I want it back. Now!" He held out an open palm.

The pimp laughed and started up the stairs. He was bigger than the man up there, and his friend was bigger yet. He just didn't seem to like Klassen's tone of voice.

The hookers and johns backed down the stairs.

"The way I see it, my friend, the girl earned it," the pimp said, reaching the landing and stopping. "Did you see the way she looked? Oooooeee! You are some animal! Can't blame a girl for defending herself, right?" He stepped forward until he was right in front of Klassen. "Now why don't you go back to your hotel or whatever and…"

With a muscular thrust of arms, the pimp shoved Klassen back into the bedroom, then dusted off his hands, a dramatic gesture for the benefit of the others. He wheeled and started down the stairs.

But Klassen emerged again, this time holding a rickety chair. He furiously slammed the chair against the wall and held one leg like a weapon in front of him. He now had everyone's attention again. This time, though, his posture and countenance were startling in their mad but regal authority. He extended a finger toward the pimp, then fearlessly walked toward him. His palpable fury surprised the pimp, who backed down a step or two.

Then suddenly Klassen issued a torrent of guttural utterances, unintelligible as words, but with clear intent. The scorching threat smashed into the pimp with fierce impact.

"The guy's nuts!" the pimp shouted. No one, it seems, liked being around an insane person. Before running out the door, he took one last glance up the stairs and found Klassen imperiously looking down on him.

———

Just after five a.m., Ace walked out the front door of the Brimstone Club and pulled it shut, making sure it was locked. He stepped back, staring at the faded lettering on the door. One of these days, he would have it repainted.

As he started walking south, a shadowy figure caught him from behind, pulling him to the ground. Before he knew it, a knee kicked him in the groin. As he painfully rolled over, just before a fist smashed into his face, he saw the grinning face of Klassen staring back at him.

Klassen roared a string of syllables that made no sense, then pressed down with an iron bar on Ace's neck.

Ace fought the bar, but it was useless. Klassen was too strong. But before he lost consciousness, Ace heard the *whup-whup* of a police siren, and through half-closed eyes saw the street ignite in a blue-white beam of light. The pressure on his neck eased. He heard the iron bar clank on the sidewalk as Klassen ran away.

CHAPTER 34

Hey buddy, wake up!" The voice was unfamiliar. Jamie tried to ignore it and continue sleeping, but then hands shook him. "Hey, I got more fares this morning, fella. Let's move it."

Jamie opened his eyes, recognizing his hotel. The back door of the cab was open. The driver was leaning over him. "It's your hotel, so let's get out now. Nine bucks."

Jamie pulled himself out of the cab and stretched. "How much you say?" He reached for his wallet, patting all his pockets.

"Nine bucks. Let's move it along, okay?"

"Shit, my wallet's gone."

The cabbie shook his head. "So what're we gonna do here?"

"Look, I'm staying with someone. I'll go inside and get some money."

"Yeah, like I haven't heard that one before. Think I'll come with ya." The cabbie slammed the back door and followed Jamie into the lobby.

———

Snoring loudly, Billy shifted his uncomfortable body on the sofa, then woke suddenly at the sound of voices outside. In the dark, he staggered toward the door to hear better, but was startled by the scraping sound of a security card followed by a metallic click. He ducked behind the door. As a man entered, Billy's big arms imprisoned him.

"Hey!" Jamie shouted. "It's me!"

Billy let go and switched on a light. He'd expected that it was Jamie, but didn't know which entity might be controlling him. Jamie's bruised face and soiled clothes surprised him.

"Take care of them, will you?" Jamie said, glancing at the open door.

A bellman and a fortyish man in a sweatshirt and jeans stood in the hall. "Nine bucks for the ride. Another five for the bother," the cabbie said.

Billy fished a twenty and a ten out of his pocket. He handed the twenty to the cabbie. "Here, you deserve more." He stuffed the ten into the bellman's hand, slammed the door, and turned to Jamie. "What the hell?"

"I don't know—really."

"Have a nice time out there?" Billy was livid.

"Like I said, I don't know."

"Well, you look like hell. You lose your wallet or something?"

"Wish I knew. Damndest headache ever."

"Someone worked you over. You're probably lucky to be alive."

Billy followed Jamie into the bathroom. He watched as Jamie started running hot water into the sink and looked down at his bloody right hand. Jamie's eyes gazed into the mirror, seeing his torn and filthy shirt, his swollen and bruised face, and caked blood like a dry river streaking his forehead. He looked horrified.

"Did you hurt someone?" Billy asked.

"Not sure what I did."

"You remember nothing at all?"

Jamie closed his eyes. "Maybe a few things. Blurry, disconnect things, like in a dream. Not much."

"Better get cleaned up. You can't go see Mallach looking like this."

Jamie turned at the mention of Dr. Mallach. "There's something you can do, Billy. Get a copy of all the videos they've made of me, and a computer to watch 'em. The answers we're looking for are in there somewhere. I want to go over every second of every session."

Billy sighed. "Anything to keep you at home."

———

Robert munched popcorn at the control board and Billy slouched on the sofa, both of them watching through the glass as Dr. Mallach interrogated Jamie. Ties were loosened, shoes were off—the two men had been here for a while.

The intercom chirped and Robert picked up the phone. After a pause, he said, "She's here? Just a minute." He glanced at Billy, who shot back a helpless nod. "Send her in," Robert told the receptionist. He stepped to the door and opened it.

As Kathy nervously entered the room, Billy stood up and gave her a hug, then sat down and patted the sofa next to him. She took a seat there.

"Thank you for letting me come, Billy."

"You have a vested interest, I know." Billy said, then gestured to Robert. "This is Robert Schmidt, Dr. Mallach's assistant. He's videotaping the sessions."

Robert and Kathy nodded to each other.

And then Kathy looked through the glass and saw Jamie. She hadn't imagined the emotions she would experience upon seeing him for the first time since he had brutally... No, better not go there. She was also unprepared to see him connected to countless wires like a fresh victim caught on long spider threads. He looked so frail, so vulnerable in that room, with the hypnotherapist pacing around him and his vital signs betraying his body's reaction to every change in his environment, both real and imagined.

God, she was glad that there was a thick window between them. She was not ready to be in the same room with him. The pain and humiliation of that night in the Bahamas came flooding back, making her want to retaliate. Fear and anger overwhelmed her. She fought to repress these feelings so no one would see her giving in to them, for to give in would mean that she had lost her battle for normalcy just as Jamie was losing his own fight.

"So, have we solved the mystery yet?" she asked, wondering if her casual tone was too light-hearted.

"Not yet," Billy replied. "But we're learning a lot about Jamie's past lives."

"Like good ol' Mad King Ludwig, right?" Kathy shook her head. "From a distance, it all sounds kinda goofy. But then, I was on the receiving end of some of his behavior."

Studying Jamie more closely, she noticed that his face was badly bruised, and a gauze pad covered part of his forehead. "My God, what happened to him?" Kathy asked with a note of compassion that surprised herself.

"Mugged," Billy replied, "in New York. Can you believe it?"

"You were there?"

"Unfortunately, no. A long story. But it won't happen again, I promise you."

She stared at Billy for a moment, then nodded.

Through the speakers they heard Dr. Mallach addressing Jamie: "Once again now, Darius, when you are ready, when you have chosen some memory to anchor yourself, please let me know."

Kathy turned to Robert and asked, "Who is this *Darius*?" If she stuck to the facts and asked questions, maybe she could keep her emotions in check.

"Darius the Great," Robert explained, "the third king of the Persian Empire, who ruled until about 480 BCE, when the empire was at its peak. He controlled a vast amount of land that included much of the Caucasus, part of the Balkans, Central Asia, much of west Asia, large chunks of Africa including Egypt, Libya, Sudan and Eritrea, most of

Pakistan, northern Greece, and the Aegean Islands. As you can imagine, immensely wealthy and powerful."

Billy smiled. "He's like a walking encyclopedia."

"Actually, when Jamie mentioned Darius," Robert confessed, "I just looked it up on Wikipedia."

Kathy stood and approached the glass for a closer look at Jamie. "So my husband comes from royalty—Ludwig and Darius. You'd never know it from our humble home. I wonder if they left him any of their money." There—she managed a little joke.

Robert smiled. "Would you care for some coffee?"

She nodded and he poured a cup, which she took with a polite smile.

Dr. Mallach paced impatiently. Her voice came through the speakers again: "Jamie, when you have chosen some memory to anchor your…"

"I must kill them all, as before!" Jamie shouted.

At these words, everyone perked up.

Kathy and Billy stood by the glass, watching Jamie tilt his head back.

"Three thousand men," Jamie said. "I will kill them before they talk to others. They know where my secret is hidden. They brought it here!"

Suddenly, Jamie stood up and commanded, "Now!"

————

The carnage surrounds Jamie, who is reliving a drama that had played out thousands of years ago. It makes him gasp—the thrill of it, the invigorating sense of power. He is Darius! His command is law, and defiance treason.

Row after row of sweating workers stand on the edge of an immense pit they had dug, their backs to a phalanx of archers. Suddenly, they begin to topple into the pit as arrows penetrate their chests and necks, spattering the ground with blood. Three hundred archers, ten executions per archer.

But even then Darius is not finished. Responding to a pre-arranged signal, his eighteen captains order their archers, all but thirty of them, to set down their bows. The archers push the corpses that had remained topside into the mass grave, and then begin the arduous task of filling in the pit. Before the archers finish, the thirty armed archers kill the others, and then the captains kill the thirty.

———

Dr. Mallach looked upon Jamie's intense gaze into a world she cannot see. The man was standing ramrod straight, chest billowing ancient air, eyes wild with exhilaration.

"It's done," Jamie said, closing his eyes. "All but my eighteen captains. They believe they are safe, but I will slaughter them when we arrive home. And then there will be no one to betray the secret."

Jamie sat down in his chair, as if on a throne. "I know who Nehsira is," Jamie continued. "Nehsira's not so clever after all. I could not have chosen three thousand workers to hide my secret unless I knew that Nehsira was not among them or my captains."

Jamie leaned back as if going asleep.

Mallach interrupted. "Darius, please tell me where you are now. Are you still at the hiding place?"

"The hiding place is a very long journey from Persepolis." Jamie paused, turning his head and opening his eyes. "I am looking at my favorite concubine, Tarka."

———

With the eyes of Darius, Jamie sees Tarka lying asleep beside him. She is fantastically beautiful. Her long hair flows across the pillows. Watching her chest breathe in and out gives him a surge of pleasure.

"I loved her," Darius thinks, then realizes he is speaking. Confessing, it seems, to the gods. "I loved her until I learned her treachery. She had bought a potion from my alchemist, hoping it would drug me, but he betrayed her. She wants to learn the hiding place of my secret—because *she is Nehsira!* But she could never get the secret without the symbol."

———

In the control room, Kathy pressed her palms against the glass as Mallach leaned toward Jamie and asked, "Darius, please tell me—what is the symbol?"

Jamie laughed. "You must know it to get it." Then he grew serious. "And now Nehsira must die."

Kathy flinched as Jamie leaped from the chair, tearing off some of the electrodes and sending wires into a mad dance above. He knelt down on the floor, and Kathy could imagine Tarka lying there beside him. Suddenly, Jamie raised a clenched hand, which seemed to hold an imaginary object—a knife!

Kathy flashed back to that awful vision of Jamie in their bedroom, holding his trophy above the pillow like a knife, ready to stab it.

In a furious blur of movement, Jamie pounded the edge of his fist on the floor, plunging the imagined blade downward, over and over, spewing rage and revenge.

Mallach stepped backward, startled by Jamie's display of hostility. The observers could only stand and stare until Mallach regained her composure and brought Jamie out of his trance. Jamie was left sitting on the floor, winded and confused.

Kathy turned to Robert. "Can you get that beast out of my husband?" Robert had no answer.

"I need to talk to him," she demanded. "He needs me."

"Not yet," Billy said. "Not after this episode. Let him recover."

Kathy looked back into the regression room. Jamie was still seated there, looking like a vulnerable child. He turned toward the glass window and seemed to stare right into Kathy's eyes. She knew that he couldn't see into the room, but felt that somehow he knew she was there.

"I can't let him fight this thing by himself," she said to Billy.

"He's not alone," Billy explained. "He's got me. And Robert and Dr. Mallach. And frankly, I've got my hands full keeping him safe from himself. I can't be worried about you, too. Just give us another day or two. We must be getting close."

Kathy turned back to see Jamie rising from the floor. The sight of him still disturbed her, but she found herself wanting to put her arms around him nevertheless, to whisper some incantation that might magically exorcise his demons. But she knew no such spell, and feared that she also lacked the virtue of forgiveness, even though she knew it was not Jamie who had traumatized her, but someone who had taken on his appearance.

Right now, she could see no way out—for either of them.

CHAPTER 35

The cab fought traffic all the way back to the hotel. Jamie, squeezed in the back seat between Billy and Robert, felt wilted.

"Robert burned video copies of all the sessions so far, like you asked," Billy said, reaching into a small bag and showing a short stack of CDs.

Jamie numbly nodded his head. "Who uses CDs anymore?"

"You're welcome," Robert said.

"And I ordered a computer sent up to the suite to watch them," Billy added, looking out the window as the cab pulled up to the hotel. "I also made some other arrangements," he said, then stepped out of the cab.

"Like what?" Jamie slid across the seat and exited, stretching.

"To keep track of you. A guard."

Jamie didn't argue, just looked down at his feet.

From inside the cab, Robert's voice called out, "See you guys tomorrow. I'm bushed."

A great hulk of a man approached the cab. He looked like a professional wrestler, and his size dwarfed Billy. "Mr. Smythe?" the hulk said.

Billy turned, surprised at the man's size. "Yes—oh, Gordon. I'd like you to meet Jamie Giles, your new project."

Jamie didn't like the way Billy put it, but he shook the giant paw offered by the giant.

"Okay then, I'm going home now," Robert said, pulling the door closed. Nobody said goodbye as the cab pulled away.

"Let's go inside," Billy suggested.

As Billy and the hulk started for the hotel entrance, Jamie stood his ground. "Not me—I'm going for a walk."

Billy sighed. "How about a little cooperation?"

Jamie's eyes flashed. "Gordie here can keep me under surveillance. Looks like a pro. Been a tough day at the office—just need some fresh air."

Billy gave a nod to Gordon, an obvious *stay with him* order, then walked alone into the hotel.

"Give me a little breathing room, okay?" Jamie pleaded, looking up at Gordon's size. "And try to be inconspicuous, if that's possible."

Jamie headed off in the same direction as Robert's cab. Gordon followed a few paces behind.

As Jamie walked, he noticed Robert's cab turn right, then immediately swerve into the left lane. This caught Jamie's attention because it was not the way to Robert's apartment. The cab drove halfway down a long block, then stopped behind two other cabs in front of another hotel. As Jamie approached unseen, Robert got out of the cab and entered the lobby.

His curiosity piqued, Jamie drew near the hotel entrance and peered inside just as Robert put his arms around a woman, greeting her with a kiss. *So the Kraut has a girlfriend.* Jamie smiled at the thought.

As the couple walked out of the hotel, Jamie was shocked. He recognized this woman.

Maria!

How could this be? What kind of connection could possibly exist between Robert Schmidt and Klassen's concubine?

Jamie backed away from the entrance as the couple entered the cab. As the vehicle pulled away, Jamie jumped into another cab and Gordon stuffed his bulk into the back seat next to him.

"I'll give you an extra twenty if you can stay with that cab up ahead," Jamie said to the driver.

———

Business was great at Philip's Lounge. The crowd made it easy for Jamie to observe Robert and Maria undetected. Robert was clearly under Maria's spell. He looked like a schoolboy about to make out with the most popular girl in his class. The way she held his hand and suggestively nuzzled his neck made Jamie gag.

The waiter brought Jamie a beer. He grabbed the glass and stood up from his table, nodding for Gordon to stay there. Dodging other patrons, he made his way to Robert's table.

"Hi there," he said.

Startled, Maria spilled her drink. Robert sheepishly wiped it up with a paper napkin.

"Sorry if I startled you," Jamie said. "I was told this was a good place. Seems to be popular with people I know."

Robert awkwardly began to introduce his lady friend. "Uhh, Jamie, I'd like you to meet…"

Jamie interrupted. "Isn't it—Maria? We were never officially introduced before. What brings you to New York?"

Robert seemed surprised that Jamie and Maria were acquainted. Jamie took pleasure in Robert's obvious discomfort.

Maria regained her poise. "Here on business, actually. I have interests here."

Jamie nodded. "I'm sure you do. Quite a coincidence that we have a mutual friend." He smiled coyly, noticing that Robert was avoiding his eyes. "Has Robert told you about what we're doing? It's fascinating, really."

"Well, he—"

Jamie leaned forward insistently. "Stop by his office tomorrow and sit in. Robert can work out the details, I'm sure." He turned to Robert, who had reacted with alarm. "She has my permission, Robert. After all, she has a personal interest in what we're working on. Cheers."

Jamie raised his glass to the couple and headed back to his table. Robert suspiciously glanced at Maria.

Gordon sipped his coffee as Jamie reseated himself at the table.

"So I can't getcha drunk, huh, Gordie?" Jamie said, smiling.

"'Fraid not, sir."

"Good. Truth is, I don't want to be alone. You see, I've got this other son-of-a-bitch's soul inside of me. Nasty business."

"Yessir." Gordon's passive expression showed neither belief nor skepticism. He merely listened.

"And I'm being hunted, too, by someone. Don't know who yet. Someone who wants my secret, and once they get it, they'll kill me, probably. Could be Maria, that pretty lady over there…" He stopped and squinted his eyes. "Shit—could be her, true enough. Nehsira was a woman when I was King Darius in Persia."

"Could be," Gordon said, playing along.

"Could also be Robert, the Kraut, who's sitting over there with Maria. After all, von Gudden was a goddam German when I was Mad King Ludwig. That's possible, don't you think, Gordie?"

"Possible, yessir," Gordon replied, taking another sip of coffee. He had no idea what Jamie was talking about, but it didn't matter.

"Didn't know you were with royalty, did you?"

"No, I didn't," Gordon said. "It's a pleasure, sir."

"Of course, it could also be Billy Smythe, the man who hired you. I mean, who's gotten closer to me than Billy? Maybe my 'keeper' is my worst enemy. After all, he killed me once."

At the mention of murder, Gordon instinctively pushed his chair a few inches away from the table, but kept listening to Jamie's odd ramblings.

"Whaddya think there, Gordie. Is it Billy?"

"Uhh, no sir, I don't think so."

"Hmmm." Jamie stared into his beer, then looked up suspiciously at the hulk. "Then maybe it's you, Gordie."

Gordon blinked once, twice, then took another a sip of coffee, setting the cup on the table before standing. "Shouldn't we be getting back to the hotel, sir?"

Jamie nodded and put a ten dollar bill on the table before getting up. "Sure 'nuff. Parole's over, back to jail. Let's go, Gordie. Time to tuck me in."

———

Under Gordon's watchful gaze, Jamie bought a cigar in the hotel gift shop, the kind Klassen favored. As he unwrapped it, he stepped into the lobby and caught a glimpse of a woman who had just turned away. Her back was now toward him, but he was certain he recognized this person. With Gordon in tow, he walked up behind the woman and quietly said, "Maria, we meet again."

The woman turned, and he was stunned.

It was Kathy.

They looked at each other for a moment, speechless.

At last Kathy spoke. "Hi."

"Hi."

In the awkward space that followed, Gordon approached.

"Uhh, this is my new friend, Gordon," Jamie said. "Kind of my bodyguard."

Gordon offered his hand, which dwarfed Kathy's as she shook it. "Nice to meet you, Gordon." The hulk didn't reply, and she couldn't think of anything else to fill the silence, so she said, "My, you're big."

CHAPTER 36

Gordon sat on a sofa in the front room of Jamie's suite as Kathy and Jamie entered the bedroom. Jamie started to close the door, but Kathy stopped him, peeking out at Gordon, her security blanket. "Sorry," she said to Jamie. "I'm just not ready…"

"…to be alone with me." Jamie completed her sentence. "Can't blame you." He sat down on the bed, his back against the headboard.

Kathy sat down next to him, not quite touching.

"I tried calling you," Jamie said.

"I didn't answer. Couldn't. Sorry."

"It's okay."

"Billy helped you out? I'm just guessing here—he'd never tell me."

"He did. He's a good friend—the best. When I needed someone to lean on after… you know… he was there for me. Don't know why he did it, really. I think he saw his own daughter in me. Sorry—under the circumstances, that has a completely different meaning now. What I mean is, he'd been through this before with his own daughter, and lost her. So he kind of adopted me, I think."

"What has he told you about what's going on?"

"He's kept me pretty much up to date. I know about Bernard Klassen and his past lives. I've been here in New York since I left the Bahamas, staying with a girlfriend. And when I wore out my welcome, he put me up here, at the hotel, room 812."

"God, so close…"

"I wanted to be here. I couldn't stay away. I was scared of you, but…"

Jamie took her hand. She let him. "Kathy, I'm so sorry…"

"It wasn't you who molested me, I know that much." Kathy gently pulled her hand away and turned to look him in the eyes. "But it's so confusing. If this other person's soul is taking you over, who am I talking to right now? I mean, how can you be Jamie *now*, but someone else at another time?"

"I don't really understand it either. As Dr. Mallach explained it to me, when I died, my soul left my body. Klassen died at the same time I did. And in that split second, somehow, and for some reason, Bernard Klassen's soul slipped in. A crime of opportunity, I suppose. But my brain, my conscious mind, was still Jamie, so Klassen's soul has had to work hard at taking me over."

"So who are you now?" Kathy asked, looking a bit frightened. "How do I know you're not Klassen pretending to be Jamie?"

"I don't know. I can tell when I'm Jamie, but it's hard to describe to someone else. I don't always remember what I do when Klassen or one of his past lives is in control. But Dr. Mallach says that the soul has memory—that's why I can relive my new soul's past lives. The problem is, my brain has a memory, too. And a personality—Jamie's. And it seems my brain and my soul are slugging it out. At some point, the soul is going to win—that's what Mallach says. If I could just purge this evil soul—get rid of it…"

"…you'd probably die, right? Can you live without a soul? Wouldn't that be, like, the *Walking Dead*?"

"A zombie, yeah. You make it sound hopeless. I guess it is."

"I just need some way to know when it's really you. Otherwise, it's just too damn scary."

Jamie stood up and paced a few steps. "Just a thought here. Somehow, the secret that Klassen is holding onto is locked in his soul's memory. Even Klassen can't discover it, because Klassen—and his past lives—refuse to give it up. What if I had Dr. Mallach, or even Robert, hypnotically implant some kind of information in my brain's memory, and lock it in so my soul doesn't have access to it? But that you could access when you're with me, to be sure you're with Jamie."

"Sounds complicated. You think it would work?"

"If we want to spend any time together—" Jamie leaned to view Gordon in the front room "—even under supervised release, then it's worth a try. It could be, I don't know, a number. Like 123567901345."

"I can't remember that."

"Just count upwards from one, but skip every fourth number until you get to, what?—twelve digits."

"123567901345. Okay, got it. What now?"

"We need someone to program me, to lock that number in a safe place. And you'll need a key to get the number from me. A word…" He paused, trying to come with a suitable word. "Abu."

"Abu? I don't understand."

"Doesn't matter. If you want me to speak the number, you'll have to unlock it by giving me that word."

"Okay."

He leaned over to kiss Kathy, but she pulled away. "I'm sorry—I just… can't." Kathy stood up and tentatively moved toward the open door. She glanced at the hurt on Jamie's face. "God, I want to stay, but…"

Avoiding her eyes, Jamie said, "I wish there was someone other than you I could trust."

"You don't trust Billy?"

"I don't know any more. I don't really trust anyone but you."

Kathy sighed. "Then there's something I need to tell you, Jamie, so you don't stop trusting me. I begged Billy to let me attend your last session."

"Knowing how persuasive you can be, I'll bet he let you."

She nodded. "I had to see for myself what was going on."

Emotions unexpectedly swept over him—anger that Billy would plot behind his back, and humiliation that his darkest secret had become a carnival sideshow. He knew these emotions were unjustified, so he tried to beat them down. In the struggle, all he could give Kathy was a curt "Thanks for telling me."

"Before I go, I should make a quick phone call," Kathy said. "Should have done it earlier, but you interrupted me in the lobby." She held up a pink message slip. "I left my security card in my room, and when I went down for another one, the reception desk gave me a phone message."

Jamie frowned, confused. "Who else knows you're staying at the hotel?"

"That's what's odd. No one except Billy. But this isn't his mobile number. And it's from a name I'd never heard of before your session today. Mr. Nehsira."

Jamie grabbed the message from her. *A call from Nehsira?* He found his cell phone, called the number, and pressed the Speaker button. A male voice answered.

"Good evening, Mortenson Funeral Parlor."

Startled, Jamie said, "Yes—hello… uhh, I'm calling for Mr. Nehsira."

"Oh yes," the male voice said. "Just a minute."

In the pause that followed, Jamie turned back to Kathy and whispered, "I'm surprised he knew the name. What the hell is going on?"

The male voice interrupted. "Here we are, sir, thank you for waiting. Mr. Nehsira isn't here, of course, but there is a message for anyone calling him. The funeral service for Mrs. Kathy Giles will be held tomorrow evening at seven in our chapel. Do you need our address?" Jamie jammed his thumb on the End Call button.

Kathy was trembling. "They said I had died?"

Jamie threw the phone at the mattress. "A cruel way of giving a deadline."

Kathy bolted from the bedroom, scattering words behind: "I've gotta go. Just too weird." She ran past Gordon and into the hallway.

Jamie followed, but stopped as she fiercely pounded the elevator Down button and yelled, "Just leave me alone, Jamie!"

He was afraid for her, but he knew he couldn't make her stay, and he couldn't go with her, so he turned—and bumped into the ever-present Gordon, who followed him back into the suite.

"My wife's scared right now," Jamie muttered. "Her funeral's tomorrow night."

Gordon rolled his eyes as he watched Jamie switch on the computer, then pull a stack of CDs out of a bag.

"Stay tuned, pal," Jamie said as he slid in one of the discs. "Hope you like the History channel."

———

Jamie slid another CD into the computer. Discs were strewn on the floor. Gordon was seated in a chair next to Jamie, staring at the screen, mesmerized by the story unfolding in the videotaped sessions.

"Somewhere in all these recordings is a clue," Jamie explained. "I just don't know what it might be."

"Wish I could be of more help," Gordon replied.

"Well, it's nice not to be alone here. Where the hell is Billy?"

"A night off, sir. He'll be back."

The next movie flickered to life, a continuation of Jamie's remembrance of his past life as King Ludwig. On the monitor, Jamie watched himself cock his head and ask, "Are you from one of my dreams?" Then Mallach replied, "Yes—yes, I am. From one of your good dreams." Jamie watched himself look away, scowling, and say, "I have no good dreams! I pray, to the Holy Mother, that she will take my dreams away."

Jamie paused the movie and turned to Gordon. "I can remember being the child Ludwig, and being afraid of my nightmares, because I had no idea they were memories of my past life experiences breaking through into my consciousness. But eventually, those memories became fully formed and I learned what the secret was. Which meant that I also must have learned the symbol that was used to lock up that information."

"Like a key of some kind," Gordon said.

"Exactly. And once I retrieved that key, I would never give it up to *anyone*, because *everyone* could be Nehsira, and Nehsira has been hunting me down for hundreds—hell, probably for thousands of years, to steal my secret. But he, or she, will never get it without first getting the symbol."

"That secret's gotta be worth a lot," Gordon said. "What do you think it is?"

"No idea. All I know is I have one day left to figure it out before my wife's funeral. And tomorrow I'll be in a fucking trance."

Jamie felt a rush of excitement. He looked at the computer monitor, surprised at his own reflected image. He clicked the Play button and the movie started up again. "Be right back," he said. "Gotta go to the bathroom."

But he only made it to an end table, where he picked up a large ashtray and then slowly walked up behind Gordon, raised the ashtray high…

CHAPTER 37

Billy slid his security card into the slot and heard the satisfying click. Pushing the door open, he entered the suite's front room and immediately shook his head in dismay. Gordon was unconscious on the floor, a glass ashtray lying beside him.

Billy rushed over to the hulk and shook him. Gordon groaned, reaching for the back of his head. Billy helped him sit up.

"How long ago did this happen?" Billy asked.

"Don't know. What time is it now?"

Billy ignored the question, turning instead to the computer. Someone, probably Jamie, had been looking at New York City on Google Maps. The map was zoomed in on a street near the bus station.

———

The Hispanic whore had been scared by the strange man who had roughed her up a couple nights ago, but not enough to give up her trade. She had whined relentlessly about needing some security, and finally her pimp had relented, mainly to shut her up. This evening, he had accompanied her on the street, but she was sure her body guard pimp wouldn't last for more than one night. The bastard was too lazy to work the streets. It was easier to sit at his table and just collect the money.

She resented the way that her pimp kept "coaching" her how to strut her stuff. She'd been doing it for close to a year now. What did he know about it?

She sauntered up to a passing man, giving her most seductive moves, but he walked past.

Her pimp laughed. "See? That's what I'm talkin' about. Ya gotta bring it on more'n that, bitch."

She marched over to the pimp, who was standing near an alley, and stomped a stiletto heel on his toe. He winced.

"Then you try it," she growled.

A man in the alley, partially hidden by shadow, called out—almost a whisper. "Hey, over here!"

The pimp laughed as he dragged the girl toward the alley. "Whatsa matter? Ashamed to be seen with us?" He stopped about ten feet away.

"How much?" the man asked.

"Ya gotta tell us whatcha want first."

The man's hand pushed a wad of bills into a shaft of light. "About three hundred dollars' worth."

The pimp's face brightened. He stepped forward to take the money. "Whatever you want, you got."

The girl stepped back, fearing what she might have to do to earn that much. She watched her pimp take the money and count it, grinning broadly. And then she watched the shadowy figure's other hand appear. It was holding a pipe, which suddenly crashed into the pimp's head.

The pimp collapsed. The girl turned to run, but the man caught her arm, flinging her brutally against the brick wall.

And then she saw the twisted face of the man whose wallet she had stolen.

"About three hundred dollars' worth, paid in advance," Klassen said, his voice raspy with rage.

Klassen grasped the girl by the throat. With his other hand he raised the pipe over his head again.

The girl closed her eyes, preparing for a fierce blow to the head.

But she felt the hand suddenly release her neck. She opened her eyes. Saw the man spinning around. Saw a fist smash into his cheekbone. Watched him crumple to the ground.

A large, dark-skinned man picked up the scattered money lying by pimp. He walked over and handed the money to the Hispanic girl, who was too frightened to run. She flinched when he approached, but he simply put the money into her hand.

"Is your father alive?" Billy asked.

She nodded.

"Buy a bus ticket and go visit him."

She looked at the bodies of the pimp, who was just starting to stir, and Klassen. Slowly, shakily, she walked down the street.

———

Jamie woke up in his bed with a tremendous bruise on his face. He lay there motionless for a minute, then grimaced when he tried to move. His hand moved to the bruise, and he could feel the painful swelling. He sat up stiffly, noticing that he was fully clothed. A mirror revealed another unsightly bruise, and he painfully touched it.

A motion in the room caught his eye and he wheeled, finding Billy sitting in a chair, his hand bandaged. The two of them stared at each other for a moment, and then Jamie touched his bruise again.

"You did this, huh?"

Billy nodded.

Jamie gave a tense smile that made his whole face hurt. "First good night's sleep I've had in a while." The smile vanished. "I don't think I want to hear about it."

"I wanted to kill you last night."

Billy's bluntness startled Jamie. "I think you came close."

"I could have done it, and just left you in the alley next to that pimp."

"What pimp?"

"Jesus!"

"What did I do to Gordie? Something to get away, right? Is he okay?"

"He's fine—thick skull. But you really pissed him off."

"Just when we were becoming friends." Jamie didn't mean to be flippant. His dismissive tone was just masking his fear of losing control.

"I'm going down for breakfast. Gordon's in the front room. I wouldn't cross him again, if I were you."

———

Since the phone call from Nehsira, Jamie had been worried sick about Kathy, and needed to make sure she was safe. She didn't answer his phone call, so he dragged a hostile Gordon down to room 812 and was surprised to find the door open. Inside, a maid was making up the bed. Jamie knocked on the door to catch the maid's attention. "Excuse me," he said, "is this Kathy Giles' room?"

"If it was, she's gone," the maid replied.

"You mean checked out?"

"I mean no longer in this room. Checked out I don't know about."

Rushing to the lobby, Jamie nervously approached the cashier. "This is very important. Can you tell me if Kathy Giles has checked out of the hotel? She was in room 812."

The cashier tapped a keyboard, glancing quickly at the hulk next to Jamie, then announced, "Yes sir. Checked out last night."

Jamie slammed the counter with his hand and pushed away. Walking next to Gordon, he said, "I know you're not crazy about me right now, but I'm worried about my wife. I just know that Nehsira's got her. Damn—I shouldn't have left her alone after that warning. You should've been outside *her* door."

Gordon silently continued to walk, refusing to look at Jamie.

"Yeah," Jamie said, "I'd be pissed off too. I'm a goddam menace to society."

CHAPTER 38

Jamie walked several steps ahead of Gordon to a cab. Billy and Robert were already seated inside. His guard closed the rear door and climbed into the front seat. The cab departed for the Mallach Research Institute.

As usual, the traffic was impossible, which gave Jamie ample time to vent about Kathy. "So I found out Kathy was staying at our hotel. Thanks for telling me, Billy. Last night she disappeared. Checked out. Did you know about that? No way she would've just left without telling me. No fucking way after I invited her to the session today."

Billy turned to Jamie. "Maybe you spooked her."

"No—huh-uh. I know he's got her, dammit."

Robert was confused. "Who's got her?"

"Nehsira! She got a warning last night—actually, it was for me—that if I didn't have a breakthrough today and discover the symbol, it would be her funeral. Literally. I shouldn't have left her alone after that. Gordon should've been protecting her, not guarding me."

"I wouldn't jump to conclusions," Robert said.

"Right. Without certified proof, you goddam scientists don't know anything, do you? Well, you'll have proof when her body turns up in the river." Exasperated, he turned to stare out the window. "What am I going to do now?"

Billy seemed remarkably calm. "You're too close to stop. What you're going to do is go through with today's session like we planned, and come up with some answers. That's what we all want... you, me, Robert, Dr. Mallach..."

"...and Nehsira," Jamie added. "And if the secret comes out today?"

"Then I'm sure it'll flush out Nehsira and we'll have a shootout."

"Yeah, but he's holding a hostage, remember?"

"Maybe I'm just a foolish old man, but I've got to believe that sometimes good triumphs over evil."

———

As they entered the Institute, the receptionist informed Robert that Dr. Mallach was stuck in traffic and would be about fifteen minutes late.

"Maybe I should just take over for her and get started," Robert joked.

The casual remark jogged Jamie's recollection of an idea from the previous evening. As they marched into the control room, he said, "Let's do that."

"Let's do what?" Robert asked.

Jamie filled in Robert on his concept of locking a twelve-digit number in his mind, one that only he and Kathy would know—and no one else could retrieve. "That way, Kathy will have a foolproof way of knowing when Jamie's brain is in control of my body, and not Klassen's soul."

"Clever," Robert replied, closing the door and motioning for Jamie to sit down on the sofa. "And I'm glad you're thinking positive about you and Kathy being together again. This should only take a few minutes. I'd rather Dr. Mallach doesn't know about this. She doesn't like me tampering with her patients. But in this case—let's do it."

Within two minutes, Jamie was under hypnosis.

"I want you to go even deeper and deeper relaxed," Robert said. "I must speak now to Jamie, and no one else. Bernard Klassen, King Ludwig, Darius, and all the past lives who have made yourselves known to us, you are forbidden to recall any conversations between Jamie and his wife, Kathy. Your memory of those past conversations are now wiped away completely, never to be remembered. I want all of you who can hear me now to speak your names."

Jamie opens his eyes. "Jamie Giles."

Summoning the other past lives, Robert said, "Who else can hear what I'm saying?"

Silence.

Satisfied that all past lives had been blocked from detecting Jamie's secret number, Robert continued. "Jamie, tell me if you can recall the twelve-digit number that you and Kathy agreed upon last night."

Jamie nodded.

"I want you to picture that number right now. It is hovering like a neon sign in the space right before your eyes."

The number 123567901345 appeared as a tangible, illuminated group of numbers in Jamie's mind.

"Do you see it now?"

Jamie nodded.

"You will not reveal this number to anyone but your wife, Kathy. It is locked up tight, and must not be given to anyone else. You will reveal it to no one but your wife, and only then if she gives you a secret word that only the two of you know. Can you recall that word?"

Jamie nodded.

"Now, as I count backwards from five to one, I want you to come fully awake." He slowly counted backward until reaching *one*. "How do you feel?"

"Fine. Did we do it?"

"It's done. I need some coffee. None for you, Jamie—but how about you, Billy?"

Before Billy could answer, the receptionist opened the door and Maria walked in.

Billy was stunned. "What the hell are you doing here?" he demanded.

"I invited her," Jamie explained. "This is like one of those cozy little drawing room mysteries, where you get all the suspects into one room and the detective announces the killer. Are we missing anyone?"

"I just wanted you to know, Jamie, that I uninvited her when I found out she had been less than forthcoming with me." Robert glowered at Maria, but she casually glanced away.

Robert jerked his head toward the window as Dr. Mallach entered the regression room.

"Sorry I'm late, everyone." Mallach's words sounded brittle in the control room speakers. "Let's get started, shall we?"

———

Dr. Mallach stepped toward Jamie, who was wired up and under hypnosis. "Very good, five cycles per second," she said. "Now I want you to go back in time to a life you lived before Klassen… before Ludwig… even before Darius the Great. I want you to remember a life you lived before Darius and…"

Though seated, Jamie began to slide onto the floor.

Mallach watched, at first curiously, then with alarm, as he curled into a fetal position. She knelt over him, horrified by the prospect that he had entered this past lifetime before birth. "Listen to me!" she demanded. "You will do only as I say! You will not do as you wish. I want you to find a time in your *thirtieth year*. Now go to it and tell me who you are."

Jamie's body straightened and he sat up, then stood. He took a step toward Mallach, pulling the web of attached wires with him, and uttered a string of gibberish.

"In English!" Dr. Mallach commanded. "I want to understand you."

Jamie frowned, as if trying to understand this command, then started to circle Mallach with a sneer. "I am Pharaoh Thutmosis III. You will address me only when permission is given."

"I am in command…"

"You are nothing!" Jamie roared, causing Mallach to take a step backward. "I know what you want—my *secret*. All right, you'll have it." His sneer became a wide grin. "The secret means nothing without the symbol."

Regaining her composure, Mallach stepped forward. "I insist that you…!"

Jamie slapped her. Hard. "You will obey me!" he screamed. "Only then will I tell you what you want to hear about Nehsira."

CHAPTER 39

In Jamie's trance-state, the images swirl around, finally settling into the focused picture of an attractive man in priestly garments. Seeing this man provokes intense anger. Jamie, understanding that in this long-past drama he was Thutmosis, wants to rush over and strangle the man. But he finds himself sitting down on a throne, still seething, but too curious to vent his anger. Looking around, he sees a dim chamber adorned with mystical Egyptian symbols and cluttered with mystifying paraphernalia.

Words echo in his mind: *Tell me what you are seeing.*

"Nehsira, my High Priest," he explains. "Nehsira summoned me to his chambers, and I was very angry. No one summons the Pharaoh! But the story he told me calmed my anger, because Nehsira had discovered a secret. The secret of the soul."

Thutmosis watches Nehsira begin to chant. He feels the ebb and flow of the baritone voice. The soothing words invoke in him a state of pure relaxation, and then it happens.

"Thutmosis showed me the lives I had lived before… and taught me the secret of remembering them again. And as I remembered them, I saw murder and lust, power and riches. My soul was evil, and so was Nehsira's. We had the power of evil in us. An *enormous* power, beyond that of most souls."

The images blur and dance. Thutmosis understands that he is now back in his High Priest's chamber. Six guards have bound the hands and arms of Nehsira and are leading him away. He follows them down a long tunnel and into another chamber that makes Nehsira scream in terror when he sees the upright coffin-like box. One of the guards opens the box, exposing on the underside of the hinged lid numerous sharp spikes meant to spear a human body. Nehsira, writhing in fear, is strapped into the box.

"I saw the possibilities," Thutmosis explains, obeying the unseen voice. "I decided to hide most of my wealth in a secret location that only I would know. And then, by sheer dominance of my soul, I would choose my next high-born incarnation, and force the knowledge of my plan into his mind. Each time I would live again, I would add to that wealth, until I became the richest, most powerful man in the world. Unfortunately, I had shared this plan with Nehsira."

Three guards force the lid shut. The delirious cries of Nehsira are muffled, then all is silent.

"I could not allow Nehsira to know my hiding place. He was far too clever and vengeful. He would track me, somehow, through the ages."

―――

Dr. Mallach watched Jamie sit down on the floor, cross-legged, and continue to speak the words of Thutmosis.

"And so, after hiding my treasure, and killing all who knew its location, I meditated for days, locking the location of the hiding place into my mind with a symbol. Without the symbol, even Nehsira cannot unlock that location."

Mallach leaned in close to Jamie's ear. "I want you to tell me the symbol."

Jamie laughed. "I had it carved on a special item my weapons maker built for me."

Through the eyes of Thutmosis, Jamie watches the elderly weapons-maker show off an ornate, golden throne. He is impressed with the design and excellent workmanship—*fit for a pharaoh*, he decides. The back of this throne rises well above the height of a seated man wearing the pharaoh's double crown, and features a sharp horn of ivory that evokes the Egyptian word for both its substance and the animal that was sacrificed to obtain it.

Abu.

The weapons-maker proudly sits down on the throne's seat, looks up at the gleaming ivory horn, and smiles. He is the only man, by nature of his vocation, who Thutmosis would ever allow to touch this hallowed seat and live.

Gesturing for the pharaoh to watch closely, the armorer stands and finds a small golden knob, engraved with a hieroglyph of an odd bird-man, beneath the left arm rest. He turns the knob until the symbol is upside down, then summons a slave to approach. Grinning now, the weapons-maker invites the slave to be seated on the royal throne. Glancing nervously at Thutmosis, who nods graciously, the slave sits.

Thutmosis watches expectantly, but nothing happens. He turns to his weapons-maker, who begs patience.

The slave, prompted by the armorer to look more imperial, straightens his back and begins to reposition his arms. As his left arm lowers regally onto the arm rest, the hinged top of the throne abruptly snaps downward. The ivory horn arcs into the slave's torso, pinning it to the throne's back. Blood runs from the gaping wound and pools on the floor.

Thutmosis feels a satisfying rush of excitement and applauds the weapons-maker's dark craft.

Tired of Jamie's silence, Mallach impatiently demanded, "What are you seeing? Tell me!"

"Secrets!" Jamie said.

"I want you to envision this item now. Concentrate on it. I want you to see the carving of the symbol. Describe the symbol to me now."

"Never!"

Mallach bristled at Jamie's defiance. "You will tell me the symbol now."

"I forbid you to ask me!"

Clearly frustrated, Dr. Mallach retrieved a felt tip marker and a tablet of paper, then placed them on the floor next to Jamie.

"If you won't describe it to me, then show me. Draw the symbol now."

Jamie insolently stared up at her, then slowly stood, keeping his eyes on her. She could almost feel the gaze of his eyes as he took a step toward her. She backed away, feeling threatened, then realized that he was only moving to his chair.

As Jamie approached the chair, the digital readouts began to fluctuate wildly. Mallach became alarmed as his pulse and blood pressure began to rise, and his brain waves became erratic. She remembered the episode when Jamie, reliving King Ludwig's drowning, nearly died. As she started to speak, to bring him out of his trance, he violently tore off all the wires and slumped onto the floor, apparently unconscious.

Was he dead?

With her fingers, Mallach checked his pulse. Still alive.

Mallach lifted Jamie into a sitting position and he took a deep breath. Letting go of his body, she found that he could sit upright, though his eyes remained closed.

"Thutmosis," Mallach said. "You will show me now. I know your tricks. Show me the symbol."

She moved the tablet and the marker close to Jamie.

Slowly, Jamie's arm moved. He grasped the tablet, then the pen. With his eyes still sealed shut, he began to sketch an image of a strange creature with the head of an Egyptian man and the body and legs of a bird.

Dr. Mallach took the tablet from him, then said, "All right now, I want you to come awake—fully awake—as I count backwards from five. I want you to come back to the present, to Jamie Giles. You will remember everything that has happened. Five. Four. Three. Two. One."

Jamie awakened slowly as Mallach counted. At last, fully conscious, he stared at the hieroglyph in Mallach's hands, then looked up at her questioningly.

"You didn't use it," he said. "You could have gotten the secret with that symbol. Why didn't you?"

Dr. Mallach's gaze shot through him. "Think about it, hard, before you ask me to use it."

Taking a deep breath, Mallach handed him the symbol and left the room. Exhausted and frustrated, Jamie watched her. He knew there could be unknown dangers of uncovering the secret. After all, no one knew what it was, or what might happen once the secret was identified. Or which of the observers was Nehsira. But he was almost out of time.

———

The observers were stunned by the drama that had played out. All were still standing speechless by the window as Dr. Mallach left the regression room.

At last, Robert broke the silence. "It must be true, all of it," he declared, as if he had been withholding his professional judgment all this time. "The stuff about Ludwig was just how it happened. Ludwig ran out of money—was virtually bankrupt. Or else he managed to hide a whole lot of it someplace."

"It all makes a kind of perverse sense," Billy added.

Robert continued. "When Alexander the Great conquered Persia, he was surprised and disappointed at how little wealth Darius the Great and his son had stored in the treasury. Most of it was gone. Poof! Disappeared—or hidden away."

Maria spoke up. "What about Bernard?"

"Seems like he was still trying to discover the secret himself," Billy suggested. "But he felt he was close to getting it, and he was an impatient bastard. Probably thought it was time to cash in. But then he died."

"You *killed* him, you mean." Maria sounded angry. "And screwed everything up."

Billy ignored her. "Imagine his frustration at being so close to uncovering the secret. Maybe that's what caused his soul to find an adult to take over rather than start from scratch with a newborn."

"What this all means," Robert interjected, "is that somewhere in the world is the combined wealth of Thutmosis, Darius, Ludwig, and possibly others who didn't come forward during these sessions. The location of that treasure is the secret!"

"Even so, we've got a big threat facing us right now," Billy said, "According to Jamie, one of us is Nehsira. I'm not so sure he's wrong."

Billy's eyes turned to Maria. Robert's harsh stare followed.

"Hey, it's not me!" Maria insisted.

Robert sighed. "You were using me. That night in the bar—you picked *me* up, didn't you? I was your mark."

Maria dismissed Robert with a silent turn of the head toward Billy. "When I saw Jamie in the nursing home, you told me he was Bernard's relative. I thought maybe he could get Bernard unplugged from that horrible machine."

"So you could get his property," Billy added.

"It's mine!" Maria was indignant. "But I couldn't ever get to Jamie alone. So I followed you to New York and found out Jamie was no relative. I thought you two were plotting against me, so I did some snooping…"

"Snooping?" It is Robert's turn to be indignant.

Billy sat down on the sofa. "I can imagine how you enlisted Robert."

Maria ignored the dig. "When I found out that Jamie was really—" She hesitated. "That he was really Bernard, I thought, 'What if I could prove it? Then they'd have to admit Bernard was dead.' That's all. If you think I'm Nehsira…"

"Well, one of us is," Robert said. "And that one has kidnapped Kathy."

"My God!" Maria said, looking shocked.

Billy seemed to dismiss her reaction.

"And no doubt will kill Jamie when the secret is out."

Maria plopped down on the leather chair in front of the console. "Have either of you considered the possibility that Kathy wasn't kidnapped? Maybe *she's* Nehsira, and she's off somewhere plotting right now against all of us."

CHAPTER 40

Alone in his bedroom, Jamie paced. He wouldn't admit it to Billy, who had decided to knock back a couple of rums in the downstairs lounge, but Jamie was glad that Gordon was posted in the corridor outside the door. He didn't blame the injured guard for wanting to be separated from him. But he also wanted to be prevented from escaping again.

He looked out the window at the city. How many people on those streets had lived previous lives but were completely unaware? Jamie's brief glimpses into ancient times and the evil forces at work made him shudder. He closed the drape and looked at a photograph of Kathy on his dresser. She was in jeopardy, and he was helpless.

Would Nehsira contact him—perhaps bargain for her safe return?

Restless and frustrated, he marched into the sitting room and stared at the computer. Next to it was his crude drawing of the hieroglyphic symbol and the stack of discs. Maybe he should go over the session videos again. Could he have missed a clue?

He scrunched up in a chair and booted the laptop. Just as the Windows screen flashed on, his cell phone chirped, startling him. He didn't recognize the incoming phone number, which made him nervous, but answered anyway.

Recognizing the voice, he silently leaned back in his chair, relaxing.

But quickly his eyes glazed and he picked up the sketch of the symbol. He struggled to speak, but at last he did.

Then the line went dead. His heart started to drum faster. A terrible pain seized him, and he stood up as if trying to escape a fierce grip on his chest. He couldn't catch his breath. Slumping to the floor, he tried to call out, but couldn't. His eyes opened wide but his vision faded.

He knew he was dying.

———

In the lobby, Robert put his cell phone back into his shirt pocket and pushed the elevator button for Jamie's floor. The elevator took its time coming, and then stopped at almost every floor on the way up. At last, the door opened on Jamie's floor and he stepped out. Five doors down the hall, Gordon sat in a chair outside Jamie's suite.

Robert motioned to the guard, who waved back as Robert approached.

"Is he inside?" Robert asked

"Jamie? Yeah."

"I need to talk to him. Can you let me in?"

Gordon opened the door with a security card. As the door swung open, he was the first to see Jamie on the floor. "Shit. Stand back, could be just a ruse. The guy's a clever one."

Gordon rushed over and tentatively nudged the limp body, expecting Jamie to lunge at him with a knife or an ashtray. But Jamie was unresponsive.

"Move it!" Robert shouted, pushing the hulk away from the body. He leaned over and felt Jamie's neck. "Thready pulse—we're losing him. When did this happen?"

"No idea. Didn't hear anything."

Robert looked down at Jamie's cell phone lying near his hand. "He was on the phone with someone."

"Okay, I did hear his cell phone ring. Maybe some bad news—a shock of some kind?"

Robert tinkered with Jamie's phone but couldn't figure it out. "Damn Android phones. How do you find the call history on this thing?"

Gordon took the phone, thumbed open the history screen, and handed it back to Robert.

Staring at the last number to call in, Robert shook his head and turned to Gordon. "I talked to Billy on the way up here. He's downstairs in the lounge hiding out. Get him up here now!"

Gordon plucked his phone from a pocket and punched in Billy's number.

———

Billy was lifting a rum and Coke when his phone rang. Halfway through a *Hello,* Gordon interrupted. Billy slammed a twenty on the table, caught the next elevator up, bounded into the suite, and found Jamie on the floor. Inexplicably, Robert was searching through the session CDs. Billy couldn't see Jamie's chest moving.

"Is he dead?" Billy asked.

"Will be in a minute." Robert answered. "Unless I can find… ahh! Here it is." He slid a disc into the laptop's CD drive and impatiently tapped his fingers on the table as the disc spun and clattered.

"What are you doing?" Billy was frantic. "Have you called a doctor?"

Robert ignored the questions. The monitor suddenly displayed the Windows Media Player.

"Are you crazy? He's dying!" Billy pulled out his phone but dropped it on the carpet.

"A doctor won't be able to help," Robert finally said. The screen brightened with the video of Jamie in the regression room.

"And you can do better?" Billy picked up his phone and called 911.

"I said a doctor couldn't help him. He's in a trance."

Billy turned to the Robert as the 911 operator greeted him and asked for the nature of the emergency. Confused, Billy hung up. "What the hell are you talking about, a trance?" He stared at Robert for a moment. "*You* did this, didn't you? I knew it was you."

"Don't be an ass! I found him like this, with his phone on the floor and this in his hand."

Robert handed over the wrinkled sheet of paper containing the symbol. "I tried to bring him out of the trance, but I couldn't. Only the person who induced it can bring him back."

As Billy tried to make sense of this, Robert fast forwarded the video, suddenly clicking the Play button.

Gordon leaned over the body, his fingers pressing on Jamie's neck. "I can't get a pulse!" he said.

"My God, we've lost him." Billy was becoming hysterical.

Mallach's voice on the video distracted Billy. He turned his attention from Jamie's body to the video as Mallach was trying to bring Jamie back from King Ludwig's death experience.

"No, no—not yet." she muttered. "Jamie! Jamie, listen to me. You will obey me now and leave this time—LEAVE THIS TIME!" Mallach seemed desperate. "Jamie! You are going to another time—a time far in the future. Listen to me!" In the video, Jamie gagged and sputtered as if drowning. "Please, Jamie—you are going to another time," Mallach implored. "There is no need to die here again. You are going deeper and deeper relaxed. Your pulse is returning to normal."

As he heard Dr. Mallach say, "He's coming back to me," Billy peripheral vision caught Jamie's body jerk and gasp.

"I'll be damned," Billy said. "So it was Mallach who tried to kill him. And Mallach who brought him back."

Robert switched off the video and dropped to his knees next to Jamie, feeling his pulse and smiling as the young man opened his eyes.

"Not exactly the way she drew it up," Robert said.

———

Jamie sat on the sofa, ashen and perspiring. "And all along I thought it was you," he said to Robert.

"Why did everybody think *I* was Nehsira?"

"I can see now how her plan worked," Billy said. "Her books and publicity were the bait."

Jamie looked confused.

Robert explained. "Her fame in past life research made her famous, so whoever was currently inhabited by the pharaoh's soul eventually would find out about her and look her up, like you did."

Jamie nodded his understanding. "So she just waited for me to come to her for help. She was a *soul doctor*, just like von Gudden."

Robert shifted in his chair. "You were conditioned to go into a trance immediately whenever she said the word *mindspan*. So she called you on the phone, then spoke the word…"

Jamie sat up straight, alarmed. "I don't remember what happened, but after I went into a trance, she must have instructed me to look at the symbol. My God! Then she got the location out of me!"

"That was the point of the call," Robert agreed. "She didn't ask you for the location in the regression room because then all of us would have learned it. When she got the location, she asked you to relive Ludwig's death all over again, knowing it would kill you. Death by *natural causes*. Who would ever know otherwise?"

Jamie bolted to his feet. "I've got to do something!" he yelled, but then looked at Robert and Billy, his shoulders drooping. "But even if I could stop her from finding the treasure, I've still got that son-of-a-bitch inside me."

Robert stood and walked over to Jamie, standing close. "I've been thinking about something ever since your last session with Dr. Mallach. That's what I was coming here to tell you."

"I'm glad you came. It saved my life."

"I want you to think back," Robert said, touching Jamie's shoulder.

"That's all I've been doing."

"Think back to the day that Jamie Giles died," Robert urged. "I've been over and over the videos we made, and I've been thinking—what if Jamie didn't really die?"

"What?"

"Dr. Mallach wrote about many cases where a dying person's soul left the body for a short time…"

Jamie interrupted, remembering these stories from Mallach's books. "…and came back. The person could remember what the soul had experienced."

"The *Death Experience*, she called it."

"But I never remembered anything. No light at the end of the tunnel, no ghostly apparitions reaching out to me. I had no death experience at all."

Billy has caught the drift of Robert's idea. "Because—maybe—your soul didn't return, so you couldn't remember anything."

Robert nodded. "Exactly."

Now Billy was standing. "Do you think—? My God… do you think that his soul might still be waiting to come back?"

"It would make sense," Robert replied. "But the way I see it, if he takes you over again—that's it. He's gotten too strong. As long as Jamie stays on top, that soul is trapped."

Jamie slumped onto the sofa deflated. "So it's hopeless."

For a moment, there was absolute silence. Finally, Robert spoke. "I don't know how long you can hold that soul at bay, Jamie. But no matter what, you can't let Mallach get her hands on that treasure. God knows what she might do with that kind of wealth."

Jamie sighed deeply. "I'm sure Mallach is on her way to the hiding place. Trouble is, I don't know remember where it is. Mallach must have instructed me to forget what I told her."

"Allow me," Robert said.

———

With the curtains pulled and the lights off, the sitting room was dark. Only the glow of the laptop screen illuminated Jamie's face as he sat in a wooden chair, wondering if Robert's plan would work.

Robert was placing Jamie under hypnosis. "…Three. Four. Five. You are deeply relaxed. Now I want you to open your eyes and look at this symbol."

Jamie's eyes slowly opened.

Robert handed Jamie the wrinkled paper containing the hieroglyph. "Once before, this symbol raised the memory of a hiding place within your soul, your mind. The symbol will do it again. I want you to remember the location of it again."

Jamie nodded, then said, "I remember."

Images flew through his mind, disorienting him. He was remembering what the pharaoh's soul, once cut off from Thutmosis' dead body, had witnessed as it soared through space and time, unconnected to the physical world, but drawn to the hiding place chosen by the pharaoh. The soul had seen the desert sands and the river, and how the land had been transformed by time into a new, lush world. Jamie watched as a mat of thick jungle swept beneath him. And then, suddenly, in the midst of that thick, verdant foliage, was a glistening spot of light. As his vision drew closer to the light, it became a jewel-like lake. And with a kind of mystical knowledge that transcended longitude and latitude, and GPS coordinates, and all human capacity, he knew exactly the location of this body of water.

CHAPTER 41

Gordon and Jamie, carrying suitcases, entered the hotel lobby. They greeted Robert, who rose from a chair, hands outstretched. He and Jamie hugged.

Looking weary and depressed, Jamie said, "Well—I guess we're off."

"You'll do it, Jamie. Somehow you will. And I know you'll find Kathy and she'll be okay."

"Have you heard from Maria?"

Robert laughed. "I was an idiot, wasn't I? She headed back home. Too much weirdness, I guess. That, plus she couldn't figure out how to get any money from it. So isn't Billy going with you? Where is he?"

"Right here." Billy said, entering the lobby through the main entrance. Next to him was Kathy. Both of them had flight bags slung over their shoulders.

Jamie stared for a moment, wondering if this was an illusion, then ran to his wife. They embraced, smothering each other in kisses.

"Hey!" Billy said. "We're in public."

"God, I was so scared," Jamie said to Kathy.

"I'm so sorry," Kathy said. "But Billy knew I was in danger when I told him about the call from Nehsira. He hid me in a little hotel down the street."

"Well, if he hadn't done that, you might not be here today."

"He's a good friend, Jamie."

Jamie turned to Billy with an appreciative smile.

"I didn't know where we were going," Billy said. "Hope we packed the right things."

CHAPTER 42

Inside the helicopter, Billy sat next to Gordon, who was packing a 9mm Glock in a shoulder holster. Kathy sat next to Jamie. Below them was a thick carpet of foliage. Everyone was studying the terrain, looking for the small lake that Jamie had described.

Suddenly, a clear pool of water appeared on Jamie's side. He pointed at it excitedly. The pool was a sinkhole, a high spot in a subterranean system of caverns filled with fresh, clear water from the rising water table. The thin crust of surface at this spot had finally caved in, exposing the cave system. The pool was quite large, the size of a small Michigan fishing lake.

The helicopter swerved and flew over the sinkhole again, lower this time. The water glistened in the sunlight. As Jamie got a more downward view, he saw marks on the sinkhole floor, probably handmade by the careful laying of stones. Jamie studied the marks, which slowly resolved into a familiar image—the shape of the hieroglyph. The pharaoh's secret symbol.

The pilot found a small clearing about a hundred yards away and set down the helicopter. Jamie stepped off first, then helped Kathy onto the ground. They watched Gordon and Billy lower a few heavy bags onto the ground as the rotors slowly came to a halt. Finally, the pilot joined them.

"Take your time, gentlemen," the pilot said, smiling. "I'll be right here."

Suddenly, Jamie stepped behind Kathy, pulled a small knife out of his pocket, and placed it at her neck. Billy stared at him, horrified.

Gordon's hand moved toward his Glock, but Jamie said "Huh-uh!" and made a threatening move with the knife.

"You're a sick bastard, Bernard." Billy said.

"The tables have turned, Billy. Jamie's gone—for good."

"Jamie, please!" Kathy pleaded. "Don't let him do this to you!"

The pressure of the blade on her neck silenced her.

With cold eyes, Klassen turned to Gordon. "Take out your gun slowly and drop it on the ground."

Gordon did as he was instructed.

To the pilot, Klassen said, "Throw me the key to the chopper. Now!"

"The pilot fished in his pocket for the key and tossed it to Klassen, who caught it in his left hand.

"Now find some rope or something and tie up the pilot," Klassen instructed Gordon. "I'll check your work, so don't be cute about it."

Gordon firmly tied up the pilot and turned back to Klassen.

"Billy, I want you to bind Gordon. He's a big guy, so do a good job. Kathy's life depends on it."

With the pilot and Gordon bound, Klassen maneuvered Kathy over to the dropped gun and picked it up, allowing him to put the knife back into his pocket. He checked the bindings on the pilot and Gordon. Then he waved the Glock, gesturing for Billy to pick up the two heaviest bags, and for Kathy to hoist the smaller one. With the pointed gun, he directed them toward the sinkhole.

"Why don't you just kill me now?" Billy said.

Klassen laughed. "If you make me, I will. But I need you to be my mule right now. And I'd rather watch you slowly drown... the way I did in that hotel room."

They reached the pool. The jungle literally hung over the edge of it. Billy set down the heavy bags.

The sound of several unseen people chattering and walking through the bush caused Jamie to push the gun into Billy's back, a reminder to be quiet.

When the noise stopped, Klassen said, "Go ahead, set 'em down."

Billy lowered one of the bags. The other one, slung over his shoulder, contained a filled oxygen tank for diving. It was heavy and hard. As he began to remove the strap from his shoulder, he pivoted quickly. The bag swung out, slamming into Klassen's chest, knocking him to the ground.

For just a minute, Billy thought about going for Klassen's gun, but thought better of it. With a quick nod, he motioned for Kathy to follow him, and the two dashed into the thick bush.

Klassen, stunned by the blow but still holding his Glock, sat up and fired three rapid shots in the direction of his captive's escape route. "There's no fuckin' place to go, Billy!" he shouted. I've got the key to the chopper!"

As expected, there was no reply.

"Son-of-a-bitch!"

He would have to deal with this problem later. Right now, he hoped to surprise Dr. Mallach.

———

Klassen was almost ready for his dive. He placed the Glock into a Ziploc bag, which he sealed.

"We have some unfinished business, my friend!" he shouted, hoping Billy could hear. "We'll settle up later!"

He pulled down his mask, put in his mouthpiece, and glided into the pool. There was an eerie beauty here. The colors were vivid in the clear water. Klassen swam easily until he reached the west edge of the pool and then dove down about forty feet where a submerged tunnel opened into the pool. Looking at a strange array of tree roots protruding from the edge of the pool, he realized that one of them was a moray eel. It opened its mouth, showing its teeth, but then withdrew.

Klassen switched on a light and swam into the cave system, finding that a guideline had already been strung by someone else, hopefully Mallach.

The dark tunnel was barely large enough for a diver and tank. At one point, it opened into a small chamber, with four branches opening into the opposite wall. One of them was too small for a human. The guideline, glowing in the light, ran into the far right tunnel. He swam into it. This one was larger than the first tunnel for a stretch, but tightened as he moved into it.

It seemed like a long way, but the guideline continued to lead him deeper into the system.

At last he could see a bluish glow ahead. It grew brighter and larger as he swam toward it. He could turn off his light now. He found himself swimming upward into a cavern and could see the surface of the water above.

———

Careful not to be seen, Billy and Kathy had slowly walked along the edge of the pool, watching Klassen swim toward the west side. When Klassen dove, they saw two natives poke their heads out of the foliage, drawn by the splashing sound. The natives started to laugh, which made Billy less nervous. Trying to be as non-threatening as possible, he and Kathy approached the two men—just boys, really—who were sitting against a tree.

The boys wore t-shirts and torn jeans. They looked frightened when the two larger adults appeared suddenly. Next to the boys were two large bags, which could have carried diving equipment.

Billy made a peaceful gesture, which seemed to calm down the boys, and then said, "So you've got someone diving here, too?"

The boys stared at him, obviously not understanding.

Billy mimed putting on a dive mask and mouthpiece.

The boys laughed, understanding him now. They nodded their heads.

Billy looked into the sinkhole, wondering what would happen when Mallach and Klassen met face-to-face.

CHAPTER 43

Klassen broke through the water's surface. He pushed his mask up and pulled out his mouthpiece. Around him was a large cave illuminated by sunlight filtering through various overhead cracks, and several portable lights set up by Mallach. The fact that they were turned on indicated that she was still here. A dry shelf, like a shoreline, extended into the water, and on this shore he could see numerous shapes covered by dusty, moldering cloths.

He climbed out of the pool and took off his diving gear. He found the Glock and removed it from the Ziploc bag, checking it over before racking the breech.

Quietly, he walked over to one of the ghostly shapes and tugged off its covering. Dust flew, and he had to stifle a sneeze. Before him stood a glistening, jewel-encrusted Egyptian statue. He uncovered another boxy shape and discovered a gold chest that contained numerous small Persian treasures. In a flurry of activity, he began pulling off the covers of other shapes, finding treasures from many lifetimes.

As he wandered down the shore, he found another pile of scuba gear. He knew who this gear belonged to, even if he didn't know where she was. He knelt by the gear and with his diving knife cut the air hoses.

"So you did not die!"

The voice was unmistakable. Klassen stood and turned in the direction of Mallach's voice, but she remained hidden.

"Nehsira!" he shouted.

"You decided to die here instead."

"This is where it ends for one of us." Klassen was still trying to find Mallach. He gripped his Glock tightly and began to work toward another grouping of objects.

"You have forgotten one thing." The voice echoed in the chamber. "I can put you to sleep with one word—MINDSPAN!"

Klassen collapsed on the ground.

"You will remain immobile—unable to move," Mallach said as she appeared from behind one of the covered shapes and walked toward him. "But you may see everything. I want you to look upon the one who has mastered you. Open your eyes!"

Klassen did. He saw Mallach dressed as Nehsira, the pharaoh's Egyptian high priest. She walked toward his fallen body carrying a spear, but her path took her past Klassen's diving gear. With a wicked sneer she severed Klassen's air hose, then approached his limp form. She laughed and lifted her spear, preparing to drive it into Klassen.

Suddenly, Klassen's legs kicked up, tripping her. She fell. Klassen quickly sat up, pointing his pistol at her. But Mallach's spear swiftly whacked the gun out of his hand. Another arc of the spear, caught him on the side of the head, knocking him down.

Mallach scrambled for the gun while Klassen was momentarily dazed. She got it, then pointed it at him.

"Clever. A little help from Robert, I imagine. If you won't respond to the mindspan command, I'll just have to kill you."

She stood up and motioned for Klassen to stand. "But first I want you to see me on your throne." She motioned for him to stand and navigate around several covered objects. At last he turned a corner and confronted the incredible throne of Thutmosis built long ago by the pharaoh's weapons-maker.

Mallach seemed positively gleeful. "It's taken me thirty-five hundred years, but it's worth it to see you at my mercy. I think I'll shoot off little pieces of you one at a time. *Kneel!"*

Klassen bitterly kneeled before Mallach. She regally walked up three gilded steps to the throne and sat down, pointing the gun.

He saw that the golden knob bearing the symbol for *soul* was turned upside down. The trigger was set, standard practice whenever the pharaoh left his place on the throne.

"I am your pharaoh," Mallach stated. "Prepare to die!"

Mallach steadied the gun with both hands, slouching slightly as she readied to fire.

Klassen needed to buy some time.

"You don't look very stately," he said. "A pharaoh sits proudly on his throne, not slumped down. He represents the sovereignty and dignity of his entire nation. Frankly, you look like you're watching TV."

Mallach bristled at his insolence. She shifted her body, stiffened her back, lifted her chin. "Better?" she asked.

"Still not very majestic. You don't look like you own that throne."

He knew that there was only one move left for her to make. And she made it. Her left hand released the pistol. She moved both arms to the side, holding them above the bejeweled armrests. Smiling broadly, she drew in a deep breath and lowered her arms.

Suddenly, the top of the throne hinged downward, thrusting the ivory horn through her chest. The gun fell. Blood gushed from the wound and her mouth. But she was still alive, a look of horror and disbelief on her face.

Klassen stepped forward, briefly catching her eyes before they faded. "Nehsira, you'll soon be free again."

Her face contorted in pain, She emitted a high-pitched, other-worldly scream, and then her head drooped.

Klassen looked around. Everywhere there were priceless treasures. The age-old plan had worked! With great effort, he lifted up the hinged top of the throne, latching it in place again. He turned the golden knob so that the symbol was right-side up. Then he rudely pulled Mallach's body from the seat, flinging it onto the cavern floor. From a secret drawer in the base of the throne, he removed a pharaoh's garment. At last, after thirty-five hundred years, he again took his throne at the site of his great secret.

———

Billy and Kathy sat on the edge of the pool with Gordon, whom they had untied, and the two native boys. Once released, the pilot had stayed with the chopper to guard it. Billy checked his watch, then looked back at the water.

"Jamie can't be trusted," Kathy said, still shaken by the knife at her throat. "And he's got the gun. If he comes out, what'll we do?"

"Subdue him somehow," Billy said meekly. "Gordon's bigger."

"But Jamie's got the gun!"

"He's not Jamie anymore, you have to understand that. Jamie never would have threatened you. He's now Klassen. Ludwig. Darius. Thutmosis. But not Jamie."

"I want Jamie back," Kathy said. "That can't happen, can it?"

Billy just stared at the water. He also worried about what they would do if Mallach came out of the water.

———

For a time, the pharaoh in Jamie's body sat on the throne without moving, relishing his joint victory over time and Nehsira. Finally he stood up, shed his pharaoh's garment, and walked toward his diving gear. Time to go and take care of the people he'd left at the chopper.

Staring down at the gear, he experienced a stab of fear. The air hose had been severed.

He raced over to Mallach's equipment, then remembered that he had cut her air hose. All the diving equipment was useless.

He was trapped here with his treasures. Panic swept through him. After all these years, was he going to die here?

There was only one choice. He bagged the Glock, put on his mask and flippers, switched on the headlamp, and jumped into the water.

He would swim out.

He wished he had measured the trip in. Or the time it took. He couldn't be sure it was even possible to make it out without supplemental oxygen. But he had to try. He was glad he had Jamie's young body to assist.

He kicked away from the cavern's shelf, took a deep breath, and then dove down. Following the guideline, he propelled through the tunnel. He had not yet arrived at the first chamber when he grew panicky, fearing that it was taking longer to swim out than to swim in. But at last he entered the chamber and saw the guideline led into the single exit tunnel.

His lungs were burning. His legs felt dead, and his arms were numb. He pushed onward, his face contorted with the exertion of holding his breath and using up so much energy.

But then he saw it. Literally. A light at the end of the tunnel. Was he already dead? Was this his own death experience? Or was this a hallucination created by his oxygen-starved brain?

Like an infant leaving the womb, he erupted from the tunnel and looked up at the bright, sun-spattered surface above. Only forty feet to go. He had just enough air left to make it.

A shooting pain shot through his leg. He looked down and saw the moray eel, no longer timid, fastened to his thigh. He tried to shake it loose, but it stuck to him. He reached down and grabbed it, trying to pull it off, but it stubbornly refused to let go.

Finally, he tore it free, but the battle had almost finished him off. He instinctively gulped for air, but his lungs filled with water. His eyes glazed over.

In a dead man's posture, he slowly began rising to the surface.

———

Billy was the first to see the body break the water's surface, and the first to notice that it was not moving. "It's Jamie!" he yelled. He gestured frantically for the two boys to help. He dove in, reached the body, and awkwardly pulled it toward shore. The boys assisted both of them onto the bank.

Panicked, Billy vigorously shook Jamie, who was unresponsive. Kathy held her hand over her mouth as he started mouth-to-mouth resuscitation, then changed to CPR, pushing down rhythmically on Jamie's chest. The boys watched in amazement.

For almost ten minutes, Billy performed CPR. He finally gave up, but Kathy refused to admit defeat. She took over, her willowy arms pistoning his chest, willing him to survive.

Finally, Billy grabbed her arm and shook his head. He felt for a pulse, found none.

"He's gone," Billy explained, pulling Kathy away.

Sitting next to Jamie's lifeless body, Kathy started to sob.

Suddenly, Jamie's hand moved. By itself. Billy saw it first, but convinced himself it was an illusion.

The hand grabbed Kathy's arm. She jumped at first, thinking it was a jungle creature touching her. She tried to brush it off her arm, but felt Jamie's hand there, looked down at him. He was moving his head.

Billy rushed over and helped Jamie sit up. Jamie coughed up a river of water, and gagged, then inhaled a lungful of air and coughed again.

"Jamie?" Billy asked.

Jamie stared up at him, confused. "Yeah—what?"

"What about Mallach?"

"Dead."

Kathy recoiled, fearing that this was not Jamie, but Klassen, or Ludwig, or... She stood up and backed away.

"Maybe when he died just now—" Billy said hesitatingly, "—like when he drowned in that accident back in Detroit, Klassen's soul departed. And maybe Jamie's soul was hanging around, looking for an opportunity to come back, like Robert said."

Kathy didn't care about the mechanics. She just needed to know who this person was.

"If you're really Jamie," she said, staring at the man, "you can tell me what number we agreed on back in New York. Go ahead—give me the number."

Jamie stared at her dumbly and coughed again.

"That's what I thought," Kathy said. Turning to Billy, she said, "Go ahead, put the bastard back in the water."

"Sorry," Jamie said. "I had some junk in my throat. First you have to give me the password."

Hopeful, Kathy leaned over and whispered into his ear.

Jamie smiled and whispered something back.

Kathy threw her arms around him.

———

Jamie rejoiced in the moment. After all, he was now free of that malignant soul. He had discovered riches beyond his wildest imagination. And best of all, he was reunited with Kathy.

Still, as they marched back to the chopper, he couldn't help reflect on how he had been forever changed by his ordeal... and how he would pursue the challenging task ahead.

Somehow, he must move the treasure.

CHAPTER 44

Jennifer Thomas was lucky. As she woke up in her hospital bed follow-ing surgery, the twenty-three-year-old devout Christian thanked God for saving her life. It seemed obvious that He had planned a life for her that was still unfulfilled.

She sensed a warm hand hold hers. Her dad's. She must have gone to sleep again.

"You're such a lucky girl, Jenny."

"Hi Dad. How long have you been here?"

"They just let me in to see you for a few minutes. Do you remember what happened?"

"Kinda fuzzy. I was doing my run through the park and... I didn't feel so good..."

"You collapsed, honey. A heart problem—they called it some kind of septal defect. Congenital hole in the heart. Undiagnosed until now."

"I heard someone say I died. But here I am, with you."

"And fully alive—an answer to my prayers. You were clinically dead when they got to you, that's what they meant, but you came back to us. They were able to repair your heart, so you don't have to worry about it. You're our miracle!"

"I wish Mom could've had a miracle like that."

"Me too, sweetheart. They want me to let you get some rest now. Glad to have you back."

She watched her father turn toward the door, but something was on her mind.

"Dad…"

He stopped and turned, smiling at her.

"Dad, while I was dead, something happened to me."

Her father came closer again. "What happened, Jenny?"

"I was… I was someplace else. And I saw a throne. I think maybe I was in heaven."

"Some people say they had experiences like that."

"And I was allowed to sit on the throne. It made me very happy."

"You should get some rest now, honey."

"But that's not all. I saw another person there, a man. I think it was Jesus. And he was looking at me, helping me sit the correct way. He wanted me to do it right, to be proud. I can see his face so clearly, Dad."

Tears formed in her father's eyes. "Hang onto that vision, Jenny. Not many of us have the good fortune to have such an experience. Maybe it'll draw you even closer to him."

She smiled at the thought, but wondered—short of dying again—how that would work.